BELLE AMI

ESCAPE

TIP OF THE SPEAR
THRILLER SERIES

BELLE AMI

ESCAPE

TIP OF THE SPEAR
THRILLER SERIES

www.belleamiauthor.com

Published Internationally by Tema N. Merback
Newbury Park, CA USA
belleamiauthor.com

Originally published by The Hartwood Publishing Group, LLC, Hartwood
Publishing © 2017

Revised, re-edited, and re-released by Tema N. Merback Copyright © 2020

Exclusive cover © 2020 Fiona Jayde Media
Inside artwork © 2020 Tamara Cribley, The Deliberate Page

PRINT ISBN: 978-1-7322071-5-8
EBOOK ISBN 978-1-7322071-4-1

This is a work of fiction. Names, characters, places, and incidents are either the
product of the author's imagination or are used fictitiously, and any resemblance to
any person or persons, living or dead, events or locales is entirely coincidental.

This book is dedicated to those who seek peaceful resolutions, and to those who remind us of what is at stake if we don't.

And do not suppose that this is the end. This is only the beginning of the reckoning. This is only the first sip, the first foretaste of a bitter cup which will be proffered to us year by year unless by a supreme recovery of moral health and martial vigor, we arise again.

~ Winston Churchill

PROLOGUE

Tehran, Iran
Spring
Fourteen years ago

Cyrus Hassani ran up the winding path to his home in the Pasdaran district of Tehran.

The villa sat on a hill overlooking the Mediterranean surrounded by flourishing gardens of red and white roses, red hibiscus, tangerine firecracker crossandra, and ancient gnarled olive trees. The long driveway was bordered by fruit trees—pomegranate, lemon, apple, plum, and date. Cyrus often plucked a ripe apple on his way to school.

The neighborhood in the hills had at one time been one of the wealthiest in the city but much had changed since the revolution of 1979 when the Shah had been deposed. As Cyrus bounded up the front steps, he couldn't help but be reminded that the once beautiful red-tiled roof was now chipped, and the walls were crumbling. Despite the disrepair, Cyrus adored the family home designed and built by his father, but more than anything he adored his father a man of deep and moral integrity.

A successful architect in the boom years of the Pahlavi reign, prior to the revolution, Aram Hassani's health had suffered since the corrupt government's confiscation of the Hassani family's wealth. With the rise of the supreme leader, the Ayatollah, came the rise of supreme oppression and the end of prosperity.

With the scent of ripening fruit and flowery perfume swimming in his head, Cyrus waved a letter written on official letterhead. It was his acceptance to the National Institute for Nuclear Science and Technology in Paris.

Recently the totalitarian government of Iran had relaxed some of their stringent policies. It would take a great deal of effort and money to cut

1

through the bureaucratic red tape to be allowed to study abroad, but Cyrus was hopeful. His aptitude for math and science and his desire to study nuclear physics would factor in his favor. Since the war with Iraq the Islamic Republic of Iran was looking to boost its nuclear program, and if all went well, the government would give him permission to go.

He shouted in glee, throwing open the door. "Papa, Mama, it's here!" He ran through the marble foyer toward the kitchen where he expected to find his mother preparing the noon meal. The kitchen table was set for lunch, but there was no sign of his mother. He scratched his head perplexed. His sister Ester and his mother must have gone shopping.

So much for everyone being present to hear my big announcement.

Undeterred, he raced up the stairs shouting with excitement. His father spent most of his days in his study reading. Over the years, Aram had become a quiet, contemplative man, prone to bouts of melancholy and weeks spent in bed. The new regime had crushed most of the old families and intelligentsia, sending many fleeing the country. Aram Hassani had remained, believing the Islamic regime wouldn't survive. He was wrong.

Their villa on the Caspian Sea was gone but somehow Aram had held on to their home in the hills overlooking Tehran. Life had dealt a series of blows to the Hassani family, the worst being the heart attack that had left his father physically frail. Lately, there was very little that made his father smile. Cyrus hoped his news would cheer him up.

Cyrus stopped short of the closed door to his father's inner sanctum. He took a deep breath, smoothing back his unruly black hair, and tucked his shirt in his pants making himself presentable. His father was still a disciplined man and expected no less from his son. "Papa?" Cyrus rapped gently on the door and waited. There was no reply—only silence. He knocked again, "Papa, may I come in I have some news." *Maybe he's napping.* Cyrus looked at his watch and frowned. The table was set for lunch and Aram usually took his naps later in the afternoon.

He turned the knob and opened the door. Aram Hassani sat at his desk with his head slumped to one side in an unnatural position. At first it didn't register that something wasn't right. "Papa?" he whispered. As he inched closer, he spied his father's pistol on the floor.

Everything stopped.

The wind stopped rustling through the trees.

The birds stopped chirping from the open window.

The clock stopped ticking on the mantel.

Cyrus's breath stopped in his chest.

Frozen in place. Immobile. Cyrus stood for what seemed like hours but was only minutes as he stared at his father.

His beloved father who was no more.

A rush of air suddenly burst from his lungs as an agonizing scream filled his ears. He realized it was his own voice…

"No, dear God, no!" he sobbed, tears streaming from his eyes.

A thin trickle of blood ran from the bullet hole in his father's temple down his neck. The Persian carpet on the floor was stained dark with a small pool of blood.

He stared at the spot.

The reality hit him like a sucker punch to the chest. "Why, why Papa? What will become of us without you?" He hugged his father, rocking the lifeless body in his arms, his voice growing hoarse with his keening. He didn't care about the blood that smeared his white shirt, nothing mattered but the stabbing pain of his grief. He'd lost his best friend and his tower of strength. He was too young to fill his father's shoes. How would he tell his mother and sister? They must not see him like this.

In shock, very little registered in Cyrus's mind as he rocked. He was numb. His arms grew weary from holding the dead weight of his father's body. Cyrus released his father, his gaze falling to the desk. The sheet of thick, cream stationery was engraved with his father's name, *Aram Hassani*. Beside it was his father's gold fountain pen. A few specks of blood marred the flowing script of his father's handwriting. With trembling hands Cyrus picked up the paper, mindful that what he was about to read were the last words of his father.

My dears,

I beg your forgiveness. To my son, my daughter, my beautiful wife, know that this was a very difficult decision for me to make. To leave you breaks my heart, but I could not bear another day of this life. It is selfish of me I know to even ask for your forgiveness.

Everything that made me a man is now gone. My health, the architectural projects that were my passion, all gone. The wealth, the properties, all gone. Nothing but a slow, torturous death remained for me.

Even my great love for you could not fill the emptiness and for this too I am sorry.

Cyrus, my son, you are the source of my greatest pride. This is a great burden to leave on your young shoulders, but I know the man you will one day be, and I have confidence you will do what's best and care for your mother and sister.

Ester, azziz-am, my precious daughter. You were and are an unexpected gift. In my darkest of days only you could make me smile. You should have had the dowry of a princess, forgive me for having failed you.

To my beloved wife, you are and have always been the sugar in my tea. You sacrificed everything to make a life with me. I'm sorry for the pain you suffered, pain that I could not erase. I'm sorry I cannot follow our journey to its end. I'm sorry for the tears that will fill your beautiful eyes when you read this.

Forgive me for not taking care of all of you as I should have. Forgive me for being so selfish, in choosing to stay in Iran when I should have guided us to a new home as others did. My misguided belief that our world would right itself was arrogant and selfish.

My loving family, I beg your forgiveness.

Until we meet again,
Aram Hassani

The letter slipped from Cyrus's fingers and drifted like a feather to the carpet.

Downstairs the front door opened and closed, and his mother's voice broke through the desolation that filled his soul. "Ester, run upstairs and get your father and Cyrus. I'll set our lunch on the table."

Panicked, Cyrus's gaze swept the room. He ran to the door and locked it. With great care he lifted his father and laid him on the carpet. The expediency of knowing what he must do brought action. He grabbed a sheet from the bathroom cupboard and covered the body.

Ester knocked at the door. "Papa, Mama and I brought lunch home. It's your favorite *fesenjan*, the one with pomegranate and walnuts from the restaurant on Shariati Avenue." She knocked again. "Papa, may I come in?"

Cyrus unlocked the door, blocking Ester's ability to see inside the room. "Cyrus where's Papa?"

"Ester...I..." he couldn't get the words past the lump in his throat. Her gaze swept his face and landed on the red stain on his shirt.

"What…is that blood?" She pressed her fingers to his shirt. Cyrus was an open book to his beloved sister; she always had been able to read his thoughts and now was no exception. One look at his face told her everything. Her screams reverberated throughout the house. "Papa!"

He hugged Ester to him, her sobs buried in his chest.

"What is going on?" Their mother walked up the stairs, clutching the handrail. Her eyes wide and stricken. "Cyrus, my son, what has happened to your father?"

"M-mama, please do not go in there."

She shook her head and pushed passed them.

For as long as he lived, Cyrus would never forget the sound of his mother's wails of agony…

And there was something else he would never forget, the reason for his father's death. A corrupt government that had taken everything away from him.

The joy he'd felt a short while ago was gone, replaced by a cold emptiness.

He would never forget. Never.

CHAPTER 1

You shall not stand by while your fellow's blood is shed.

~ Leviticus 19:16

Caspian Sea, Iran
Russian Warship Uglich
One year ago

Cyrus Hassani could kill an adversary twenty-five different ways with his bare hands. It was as second nature to him as whipping up a gourmet meal or making love to a woman.

Delivering a death blow, cooking, and lovemaking was a triumvirate of artistic accomplishment. He was a master of all three. Yes, to Cyrus, killing was an artform. He was the best of the best.

His whole life centered on his work. Cyrus had lived in the shadows for so long that everything revolved around the mission.

It had been a long time since he'd felt anything deeply emotional. He had only one focus—to kill or be killed. God and country existed in a foggy dream. Any emotional connection he'd had to his family had faded away. And love? That was for men who were soft in the head and thought only with their hearts. Cyrus was methodical, meticulous, and merciless. Women were good for one thing—sex.

A Russian Spetsnaz commando completing his patrol of the deck grunted an acknowledgement to him, which he ignored. *Fuck him*. Cyrus had far more pressing issues to consider, like the fact that Russia and Iran were forming a new alliance.

Salty spray dampened his face. He gripped a cigarette between his thumb and index finger and leaned against the railing. The Russian warship *Uglich* knifed through the inky, black swells of the Caspian Sea toward

7

the Port of Bandar-e Anzali, Iran. The moonless night provided the perfect cover for the secret shipment in its hold, a prototype for laser technology known as Silex, an innovation in processing uranium.

Laser excitation miniaturized nuclear-fuel-cycle facilities, reducing cost, space, and time involved to manufacture highly enriched uranium. Iran's mullahs were prepared to back their threatening rhetoric by building a nuclear arsenal.

The cargo represented a new relationship between Russia and Iran, a partnership that furthered Iran's race to become a nuclear power. His task as an assistant to the deputy director of Oghab2—Eagle2—the Islamic Republic's nuclear watchdog and most secretive department within the Ministry of Justice, was to deliver that precious cargo to the Fordow Nuclear Enrichment Plant.

The bow of the ship forged ahead through heavy seas, bearing technology that would further destabilize and shift the balance of world power. His eyes were locked on the twinkling lights of the port that lay in the distance. Shivering, he pulled his collar up against the chill. He could only imagine what lay ahead, which only made his mission more crucial.

A caravan of trucks crawled from the Port of Bandar-e Anzali toward Fordow. Accompanying the midnight shipment was a special forces team of revolutionary guardsmen. It was a grueling seven hours' drive to the Fordow enrichment facility built into the side of a mountain just outside of the holy city of Qom.

Cyrus rode in an armored jeep at the head of a caravan of vehicles. Although fatigue burrowed into his skin, he remained alert, his eyes focused on the road. Following them, a semi loaded down with Russian rockets and two sixteen-micron lasers moved slowly over a pass through the Alborz Mountains.

He squinted. Up ahead, something solid was blocking the road.

"Stop now!" he ordered. The sound of brakes squealing and gears grinding down brought the caravan to a halt. Wearing night vision goggles, he discerned something blocking the road. He radioed for three guardsmen and two handlers with their dogs to join him. Grabbing his AK-101 assault rifle, he leapt out of the cab. Three commandos joined him. Pulling their balaclavas over their heads, they adjusted their masks.

"There's a vehicle blocking the road ahead that needs to be cleared. We'll use extreme caution in our approach—two of us on each side of the road with a handler and his dog. If there's even a hint of trouble, I've ordered our team to bring the Aras tactical vehicle forward to annihilate the threat, so be prepared to take cover."

"Sir, if it's Mujadeen-e-Khalq—MEK—resistance, they're pretty worn down. It's doubtful they could mount much of an assault."

Cyrus glared at the young recruit, he was tall but lanky, his dark brown eyes reflected both fear and excitement.

He's just a fucking kid.

Cyrus had seen that look too many times. One or either was dangerous. Both could be deadly. "We'll take no chances." He nodded at his team. "Let's move out. You stay with me," he ordered the young man.

The commandos moved stealthily toward the vehicle, their assault rifles raised and aimed to fire. Something wasn't right. A prickle shot up his spine as they neared the truck. They got within thirty yards of the rear door of the truck when it flew open and machine gun fire blasted out from inside.

Cyrus and his men hit the dirt, rolling and returning fire. He grabbed his walkie-talkie and yelled, "Take the mother out, now!" One of the dogs growled as the unmistakable grinding of the armored vehicle alerted its forward movement. Bullets rained around him, kicking up dirt and rocks, peppering them with sharp projectiles. The young recruit wasn't moving.

"Shit!" *We've been ambushed.*

Furious, Cyrus rolled over, blocking the young man's body from further gunfire. He squinted through the dust. Enemy fighters ran toward him, shooting. He raised his rifle and returned fire. An RPG whistled overhead followed by an explosion. He covered his head and the recruit's body, burying his face in the dirt as fire and metal showered over them.

When he raised his head, his ears were ringing from the blast. The truck that had blocked the road was now a smoldering heap of metal. Just as he glanced over his shoulder, the Aras multipurpose vehicle he'd been riding in exploded in a ball of fire. The enemy had mined the road.

He radioed. "Report."

"Dog and his handler down, sir."

"Alive?"

"The dog is."

Fuck. He hated losing men. He hated losing dogs even more. They'd have to get the dog to a medic.

"Any survivors in the Aras?" He squinted through the still smoldering smoke from the gunfire and explosions and observed his Iranian Revolutionary Guard Corps—IRGC—troops swarming around the Aras.

A panicky voice reported, "Two wounded and two dead, sir."

He placed his fingers on the neck of the young man. "Get a medic to me. I've got an injured young man. As for the rest of the injured, we'll take them with us. The medics can triage and stabilize en route. I'll call command to send a helicopter to pick up the wounded. I want this road cleared immediately. We move in ten minutes."

"Shouldn't we assess who did this, sir?"

"Let headquarters worry about that. We have one priority, and that is to get the shipment to Fordow. No more delays."

The MEK had supposedly denounced its terrorist mission against Iran. However, there were always strongholds of resistance that might not comply. He knew Israel was bound to support any element that continued to fight the mullahs and their regime. He also knew this was a dying gasp of those in opposition. Poorly manned and poorly devised, this attack was a suicide mission.

He checked the fallen soldier again. "Hold on, son. Help is on the way."

Only when the medics arrived with a gurney did he stand and walk toward the grisly mess.

CHAPTER 2

Tehran, Iran
Ministry of Intelligence and Security—MOIS
December 1st
Present Day

Cyrus exited MOIS headquarters and lit a cigarette. The arms of a cold winter's day embraced him, sending a chill down his spine. Today was the kind of day when his duties as an assistant to the deputy director of Oghab2 made him wish he'd gone to medical school instead of working for MOIS.

He had been ordered to Evin Prison to evaluate the condition of a prisoner, an American arrested while hiking near the Turkmenistan border. He took a drag on his cigarette, plumes of smoke rising like tendrils of steam into the colorless sky. He looked up and down the street, annoyed. It wasn't like his driver to keep him waiting.

The screeching of tires losing traction filled the air. A black Range Rover came to an abrupt halt in front of the building. He took a last puff and flicked the cigarette away as he ran down the steps and jumped into the backseat of the SUV. He slammed the door shut, and the car took off, burning rubber as it sped away. Saeed always drove as if they were being chased by a pack of wolves.

"You're late."

"Sorry, sir. I needed to fill the tank, and there was a line ahead of me." Saeed's eyes met Cyrus's in the rear-view mirror.

Cyrus's lips quirked in cynical humor. "Lines for gas in an oil-rich country—what a joke. I wish someone could explain to me why we haven't built adequate refineries and why an oil-producing nation is importing sixty thousand barrels of gasoline per day?" He voiced his frustrations aloud, not expecting his driver to answer. "Just get us to Evin Prison in one piece."

"Is there a problem, sir?"

"There's always a problem at Evin. They think the American is a spy of the Great Satan. More tomfoolery, I'm sure."

"Are you going to question him?"

"No. Mohammad's been interrogating the man, but as usual, he may have stepped over the line. Mohammad isn't the kind of man you put in charge of prisoners." He shook his head with disgust. "The deputy director is concerned that the idiot will permanently damage the American or, worse, accidently kill him. We don't need the UN Human Rights Council not to mention the American government and world press breathing down our throats any more than they already are. I'm going there to put an end to the torture."

"At least the man is still alive."

"He'd better be. By the way, I leave this afternoon for Qom."

"Will I be driving you, sir?"

"No." Regretting his abruptness toward his devoted driver, he added, "It will be no problem to manage on my own, Saeed. You take the day off and spend some time with your family. It's going to get busy soon enough. You may not get any time off for a while."

"Thank you, sir. Is this a routine visit, or is there something brewing at Fordow?"

Cyrus trusted Saeed. However, this was Iran, and no one could be fully trusted—not even his long-time driver. Fordow was top secret. All information sharing was on a need-to-know basis. "Routine."

"Yes, sir."

Saeed drove deftly through the crowded Tehran traffic without further comment. Cyrus took advantage of the silence. After his visit to the prison, he had a few other bits of business and then an interlude of relaxation. On the other hand, relaxing was the last thing on his mind when it came to Zahra. His lover was his only escape from the daily rigors of his work. Anticipating their time together, he shifted in his seat, adjusting his trousers. There would be time enough for indulgence later.

Instead, he focused on the upscale neighborhood beyond the black-tinted window. High-end shops and restaurants lined the streets of the Sa'adat Abad neighborhood, which catered to the wealthy Iranians who lived in villas in the surrounding hills. Above the fray of the city, the air tended to be sweet and clean, making Sa'adat Abad a sanctuary from the smog of Tehran.

It never failed to amaze him that a prison—feared for its reputation of rape, forced confessions from torture, and executions by hanging—was situated in an elite neighborhood. Lying at the foot of the Alborz Mountains, the neighborhood afforded views of panoramic, snow-capped peaks, betraying nothing of the fearful conditions that existed within Evin Prison.

The former home of Ziaeddin Tabatabaee, a prime minister in the 1920s, Evin had been converted to a prison by the Shah's brutal security and intelligence service, SAVAK. After the revolution, the prison expanded to accommodate a growing number of political inmates. The present facility housed fifteen thousand prisoners, who certainly experienced an additional torture knowing their living hell stood next door to a charming park filled with children and adjacent to a popular teahouse and restaurant.

The Range Rover stopped at the armed guardhouse and gate before being waved through. With maximum security clearance, Saeed parked in front of a red brick building, and Cyrus made a quick exit. "Wait for me here. I don't plan on spending a minute more than necessary." He strode away, not waiting for Saeed's reply, and entered the building containing Ward 350.

The infamous section fell under the direction of the Ministry of Intelligence and Security—MOIS—and primarily housed political prisoners. He scowled, reflecting the vile conditions that existed within. Briefly acknowledging personnel, he passed through several layers of security as he made his way to an interrogation room.

When he opened the door, Mohammad's sizeable girth blocked him from seeing the detainee. Before he could intervene, Mohammad's fist punched the man, eliciting a cry of pain.

"Mohammad, cease!"

The sadistic interrogator turned to greet him; his grin dominated by a set of yellowed teeth.

It took conscious effort to conceal his disdain for the brute. "Step aside, Mohammad."

"Sir." The bully nodded and moved to the side.

Cyrus turned his attention to the detainee, swallowing his revulsion. The man had been in custody for only forty-eight hours, yet he already bore the signs of sleep deprivation: hand tremors, rapid eye movement, and bags beneath the eyes. His face was a swollen mass of black and blue bruises. The last punch, clearly one of many, caused the man to grimace with each wheezing breath. *Broken ribs, possible kidney damage.* Cyrus's blood boiled as he imagined the diplomatic nightmare he'd have to resolve.

The prisoner raised his head, daring a glance at him. Their eyes met. Cyrus betrayed nothing and the man quickly averted his gaze.

Though fury raced through his veins, he projected an icy calm as he continued to assess the man's condition.

You're no saint—you're a trained killer.

Cyrus had no difficulty or distaste for taking down or killing an adversary, but this kind of sadistic torture he couldn't condone. A specialist in hand-to-hand combat with a penchant for knives, Cyrus was a master of Kung Fu To'a, the Persian martial art favored by the Revolutionary Guard. But there was no evidence this detainee was a threat to the Islamic Revolution or its Republic.

Unfortunately, the guards at Iran's prisons and the judges of Iran's kangaroo courts were stacked with imbeciles who abused their power. It made his skin crawl when he heard about female prisoners being systematically raped by guards. He'd nearly beaten one guard to death for sexually assaulting a teenage girl. The abuse of power and the hypocrisy within the system were out of control.

In Evin the IRGC had the authority to not only imprison but also to try, sentence, and hang. Hangings were a daily ritual. Cyrus had seen enough of them to last a lifetime.

On numerous occasions, he had tried and failed to bring some change to Evin. There were those in the government who privately voiced their disapproval, but few dared to do anything about the problem. Complaints against the IRGC—the Guardians of the Islamic Revolution and darlings of Supreme Leader Ayatollah Khamenei—for the most part fell on deaf ears.

He commanded, "Outside, Mohammad."

Mohammad stiffened, following him through the door.

Controlling his anger, he addressed his subordinate. "Mohammad, what we don't need right now are human rights advocates breathing down our throats. Ease up on the torture. The American can't take much more. Besides, it's likely he's exactly what he appears to be—a hiker with no affiliation to any government."

Mohammad hissed, "I'm certain he's a spy for the CIA. He will confess…I promise."

"Certain?" Cyrus's hands trembled with suppressed anger. "Bullshit! Your so-called confessions are worthless. Do as I tell you, Mohammad. The deputy director has had enough. Clean up the American and lay off him."

Mohammad's eyes shot bullets at him, but he shrugged in assent. "As you wish, *Agha*."

"See to it, Mohammad."

CHAPTER 3

Cyrus arrived in Qom in time for the afternoon *Asr* prayers. Before checking into his hotel, he stopped at the Holy Shrine of Fatima-al-Masumeh, considered one of the holiest sites of Shi'a Islam. Removing his shoes, he performed the ablution of *wudu*, the ritual washing of face, hands, and feet. He entered the shrine carrying a small *namazlik*, his personal prayer rug, and blending with his fellow Muslims, faced toward the *Ka'ba* shrine in Mecca. Participating in the *Namaz*—the Muslim prayers glorifying God—he joined with fellow worshipers in reciting the passages of the Qur'an that proclaimed blessings on the Prophet.

Following the prescribed ritual, the worshipers began their prayers in a standing position, and then, as a sea of one, transitioned to *ruku*, bending forward and placing their hands on their knees. In the final position of *sajdeh*, each man placed his forehead on the carpet and prayed with the imam, who led them through the *rak'as*, the prescribed postures and recitations. The prayers concluded with *taslima*, the greeting of "*Salaam alaikum*," meaning "Peace be unto you."

Cyrus was careful in his adherence to the five pillars of Islam in which every true believer partakes: *Shahada*, the profession of faith; *Salat*, the five prescribed daily prayer rituals; *Zakat*, the giving of charity; and *Saum*, fasting during Ramadan. The fifth tenet, *Hajj*, making pilgrimage to Mecca, a once-in-a-lifetime requirement, was left to every man's conscience. Every other ritual—without exception—he, like every member of the IRGC, upheld with devotion. Deeply religious clerics ruled the Islamic Republic, and the Ayatollah himself expected no less of his guardians. This was an Islamic country, and no separation between politics, religion, and state existed.

His prayer obligations fulfilled, he drove to the Parsia Grand Hotel on Artesh Square and parked in the underground parking lot, taking the elevator to the marble lobby. The man at the front desk handed him his key.

"I hope you don't mind, but your cousin arrived to see you, and I had someone from our staff let her into your room. She said you were running late, and she would prefer not to wait in the lobby. She asked for tea and I had it sent to the room."

Cyrus's heart pounded in his chest. "No, you did the right thing. A woman should not be hanging about in public places unescorted. Thank you for your thoughtfulness." He shook hands with the man, inconspicuously passing him a generous tip of Iranian *rials*.

Wanting no interaction with other guests, he avoided the elevator and took the stairs to the fifth floor. Letting himself into the room, he found a woman sitting on the bed, her head bent, her face hidden. She wore a *chadar*, a semicircle of black cloth worn like a shawl by devout Iranian Muslim women that covers from head to toe but allows the face to be seen.

He stood motionless and silently observed her. When she raised her eyes to him, a wordless communication passed between them. Zahra was a classic Iranian beauty. The black eyeliner artfully painted around her cat-like eyes enhanced their upward slant. Her coppery brown orbs eyed him appreciatively, sending a surge of lust through his body. Everything about her was delicate and sensual, like a rare, exotic flower. She stood, and he caught a glimpse of her bare feet. *So sexy*.

She walked into his open arms. He drew her to his chest. Lifting her chin, he kissed her. It had been a month since they'd had sex, and he ached to release. He slid his hands over her curves, taking possession of what he knew was a dangerous obsession. Through the fabric, he felt her body, hot as a brazier, burning with an unquenchable need as great as his own.

"I've missed you, Cyrus." Her hands caressed his broad chest, her touch whispering, 'my body is yours'. "I only have an hour before I must be home for the boys. Bend me to your will, my lover, until I cry out your name in rapture."

He released her and sat on the bed and removed his shoes. He leaned back against the headboard—his gaze locked on her.

Zahra slowly turned in a circle—her hips undulating—dancing. The *chadar* floated around her body like a cloud. Then, as if the music had suddenly ceased, she stopped dancing and dropped the veil. It fell in a pool of fabric at her feet.

Cyrus smiled, amused by her audacity. She stood before him completely nude. Confident in her allure, she pulled the pins from her hair and rich, dark waves cascaded down her back. His cock hardened at the prospect of ravaging her voluptuous body.

Enjoying the freedom from the *chadar*, she resumed turning in sinuous circles. It was a dance meant to arouse him. Her full breasts rose with each breath, tilting upward with the lifting of her arms. Her nipples peaked and flushed deep pink with excitement. His heart raced as she made her way to the bed. When he opened his arms to her, she joined him and snuggled against him, pressing her flesh against his. Taking her face within his hands, his tongue filled her mouth with a hungry kiss. She answered him with a firm grip on his manhood, attuning him to her desire as if she were a maestro conducting an orchestra. He buried his lips in her neck and inhaled the perfume of her skin. A rush of dizziness clouded his reason as the scent of musk, amber, frankincense, and roses engulfed his senses, swelling his cock into a rod of steel. He took her swiftly, unable to delay what was purely a physical need.

As always, their lovemaking was satisfactory but left him questioning the wisdom of their liaison. He collapsed beside her, his chest heaving from his exertion.

Finding her breath, she crawled to him, lying prostrate across his chest. "You have brought me great pleasure."

Her kisses, sweet with gratitude, rained upon him as they lay together in physical exhaustion.

She sighed. "Who could have dreamed that my husband's death would lead me to you?"

Cyrus stroked Zahra's hair. "Poor Darioush…" The young man had just begun a promising career as a nuclear physicist and deputy director of the Fordow Nuclear Enrichment Plant when he was assassinated. "Our country lost a true hero."

"One day the Israelis will pay," she said vehemently.

Cyrus recalled the quote Zahra had given to every newspaper in Iran. *Darioush was dedicated to his goal of eradicating Israel. He died a true believer in the service of his country.* "Yes, it's a shame they got away with murder," he said. "I remember when I saw you at the funeral, how sad, yet beautiful, you were. I knew I had to have you."

"Yes. We have the perfect arrangement, Cyrus. None of the complications of each other's lives. Just the purity of our desire deliciously fulfilled by the other." Her teeth bit his nipple.

"Ow." He grabbed her face. "Perhaps, I wasn't rough enough with you, Zahra."

"Perhaps you weren't. I think you need to redeem yourself."

He growled and shoved her back onto the bed.

He remained in the hotel room, relaxing in bed after Zahra had left. Tomorrow would come soon enough, stealing the minutes of his life. The infrequency of time without purpose was a precious distraction.

As always after their lovemaking, a profound emptiness enveloped him like a shroud. Zahra fulfilled his needs sexually, but beyond that basic satisfaction, he felt nothing for her. In fact, if the truth were known, he disliked her. She was calculating and selfish. He was not fooled by her seeming devotion. He was her tool of pleasure as much as she was his.

Following the murder of Zahra's husband, Cyrus's boss, Jalal Rahimi, assigned him to head up an investigation into this most recent assassination. Jalal answered directly to the minister of Oghab2, MOIS's counterintelligence directorate. Oghab2 had the reputation of being one of the most successful espionage organizations in the world, yet they had not been able to stop the assassination of scientists involved in Iran's race to acquire a nuclear bomb.

Jalal, ordered by the Supreme Council to beef up security at Fordow and for all of its employees, put Cyrus and his team on the case. When Cyrus presented his findings and suggestions, Jalal was so impressed, he kept Cyrus on in an advisory capacity at the nuclear facility. He now spent a couple of days a month in Qom, assessing and tightening security at the Fordow uranium enrichment facility. During these visits, he fell into the habit of paying a call on Zahra.

At her husband's funeral, he'd been attracted to the doe eyes of the young widow. Against his better judgment, he found himself unable to forget her. Zahra was exotic, beautiful, and brilliant. Perhaps he'd imagined not just a physical partner but a lover that would fill the loneliness that pervaded his days. However, with time he'd come to realize that although she fulfilled a fantasy, she would never be more to him than a distraction. Their clandestine relationship served them both well. He had no room in his life for marriage or family, and Zahra, with no desire to remarry, seemed content with the status quo of their love affair. They found a fair trade in each other's arms.

At least, we're equally at risk. Neither of us can afford for this arrangement to be discovered. The consequences would destroy us.

An illicit affair for an ordinary woman might be punished by flogging or imprisonment, but in Zahra's case, because of her national prominence and stature as a national treasure, the punishment would be more brutal and the humiliation unbearable. In Cyrus's case it would mean his expulsion from government and the end of his career.

Cyrus rose early the next morning and drove the less than thirty miles across the desert, through the tiny town of Fordow, to the nuclear enrichment facility built at the base of the Fordow Mountains. He cleared security and entered the two-mile defense perimeter around the mountain. The antiaircraft batteries loomed large, pointing at the sky, protecting the top-secret facility of Fordow situated at the Revolutionary Guard Corps military base.

He parked his car and entered one of the tunnels leading into the mountain. Dressed in green military garb, he wore gradient aviator sunglasses that he frequently adjusted. A man wearing a white lab coat, Sharif Kashani, the director of the facility, greeted him.

"*Salam*, Sharif."

"*Kheili khosh amadid*, Cyrus." The men shook hands and walked to an oversized elevator. Behind them, the huge tunnel, large enough for trucks carrying massive equipment, descended into the mountain.

Although the two men knew each other well, this official visit demanded they follow protocol. However, Sharif's voice could not conceal his excitement. "I have much to show you, Cyrus. We have made great progress since you were last here."

"This is good, Sharif. I'm anxious to see the new secured level."

The high-speed elevator descended underground and stopped on a floor coded red. Sharif placed his hand on a black panel, and a beam of light scanned it. The elevator doors opened, revealing a cavernous tunnel blasted out of the mountain. The walls were solid rock. They walked toward reinforced steel doors that loomed in the distance.

"As you know, for the sake of the Geneva Interim Agreement between Iran and the P5+1, we have agreed to limit uranium enrichment to no more than five percent and to leave seventy-five percent of our centrifuges inoperable."

Cyrus nodded, well aware that the five members of the permanent UN Security Council: China, France, Russia, the United Kingdom, and the United States, plus Germany, known as P5+1, had entered into a temporary agreement that would hand over more than a hundred billion dollars to Iran.

Sharif continued. "The International Atomic Energy Agency—IAEA—will have access to the main Fordow facility for inspections, so long as we are given twenty-four days' notification." Again, Sharif placed his hand on a black panel embedded in the rock, and the steel-plated doors swung open. They entered a space with endless rows of cylindrical centrifuges spinning uranium-hexafluoride gas and separating the U-238 and U-235 isotopes, necessary to fuel a nuclear power plant and for creating a bomb. The centrifuges, chained together in cascades, spun at 100,000 rpms. At the end of the line of thousands of centrifuges, the enriched hexafluoride gas, containing high concentrations of U-235 atoms, reached its desired state for processing.

Fordow had over three thousand cascading centrifuges. However, most of them were inactive. Even if they were operating at full capacity, they would not produce enough low-enriched uranium to power a nuclear power plant. However, they would produce enough to make one nuclear bomb per year.

Scientists moved about the room, monitoring the centrifuges. Cyrus adjusted his glasses as he looked about. "I presume, Sharif, this is what the IAEA inspectors will have access to on their inspections?"

"Precisely. Now"—he pointed to a door—"let us proceed to the new facility." They entered a series of adjoining offices. Cyrus followed Sharif to one office separated from the others. Sharif held his palm in front of what looked to be a security camera in the corner of the ceiling. The office wall rose from the ground and, as if by magic, disappeared into the ceiling. About four feet in front of them stood a solid wall of rock. Cyrus followed Sharif into the narrow space between the rock barricade and the office.

He adjusted his sunglasses, looking back into the office as the wall descended from the ceiling, sealing them between the wall of rock and the office wall behind them. His stomach tightened. He was claustrophobic, both in small spaces and in large crowds. He took a deep breath to quiet his nerves and watched Sharif place both his hands on the rock, somewhat like Jews praying on the Temple Mount. This time the wall separated in two, the rock slowly parting, allowing them access to the secret tunnel within.

"Now we have to walk about a quarter of a mile. The new facility is underneath the missile base." He grinned. "Of course, missile bases will not be accessible for inspection."

"Who else besides you has access?"

"Only a handful of people that have the highest level of clearance—you, me, and the most trusted members of my team."

Cyrus nodded. "I would like dossiers on everyone who has clearance to this level."

"Of course, *Agha.*"

They continued to walk through the cavernous space until they arrived at another set of steel doors, and Sharif once more placed his palm on a black glass scanner, gaining entry to a complex that was a quarter of the size of the main Fordow centrifuge facility. At either end of a gray-metal, industrial-sized chamber were two sixteen-micron lasers, producing a loud hum that caused the rock walls to vibrate.

Sharif looked at Cyrus expectantly.

He let out a breath and again readjusted his glasses. "It's working? You've begun separating isotopes by laser excitation? When did you go active?"

"About a week ago. This process is a godsend. Silex only requires seven stages to produce perfect, weapons-grade, enriched uranium. It's remarkable. The cost of operation, the size of facility needed, and the power required for operation and production is about one-fifth that of our existing centrifuge enrichment plants. The best part is, because of its size, it's virtually undetectable and will not be discernible by the IAEC. If required, it can be quickly disassembled and moved. We have already requested the go-ahead to build seven more secret Silex processing plants."

"I didn't expect you to have made this much progress, Sharif. The ministry will be pleased."

Sharif smiled, posturing like a peacock, his chest swelling with pride. "I thought you would be pleased, my friend."

"Of course, I am, but it's the Supreme Leader who will be most pleased." He clapped Sharif on the back. He took a last look around. "Sharif, I need to go over all security measures that have been implemented. If word of this got out, the reaction from the international community would be immediate, and Israel's leaders would be forced to respond."

"Then we would destroy them."

"We're not ready yet, Sharif. In good time we will be, but not yet."

"You're right, *Agha*. Of course, the time will come, and we must be ready. Perhaps some tea would be welcome while I prepare the information you require?"

"Yes, before the drive back to Tehran, it would be much appreciated."

CHAPTER 4

Cambridge, Massachusetts
Harvard Yard
December 6th

The snowstorm had hit with a vengeance the night before, but that didn't deter Layla Rose Wallace's excitement as she shouldered her backpack and trudged through the knee-deep snow drifts. She'd just finished her final in History of Art and Architecture: Manet to Man Ray.

One more week, and I'm outta here. Hasta-la-bye-bye, Cambridge.

Layla would be spending winter break in Dubai, sunbathing on a sandy beach and swimming in the warm waters of the Persian Gulf.

A chilly wind sent flurries of white crystals flying from the leafless branches of the trees. Layla brushed away the glittery dust landing on her lashes with her mitten. Bundled in layers of wool, her red scarf trailing behind her, she made her way toward the neo-classical brick building and its colonnade of twelve Corinthian columns, spanning the portico of the Widener Library. Behind her, Memorial Church and its white steeple rose above the campus, silhouetted against the gunmetal gray sky.

The sound of ice crunching beneath her snow boots was amplified in the quiet of the yard. The students she passed, all focused on getting to wherever they had to be, ignored each other. She hunched forward, anxious to reach the warmth of the library.

Her cell phone rang, stopping her forward momentum. She dropped her backpack in the snow and retrieved her cell, grumbling to herself, "You always pick the worst times to call, Dad." Pulling her mitten off with her teeth, she tucked it under her arm, trading in her complaining grumpiness for an enthusiastic, "Hi, Dad."

"Hi, honey, sorry I'm such an absent-minded professor. I should have gotten back to you sooner. You know how it is. I've been flat out mentoring doctoral candidates and working in the lab."

"It's okay Dad," she said, shoving her mitten into her pocket, hauling her heavy backpack to her shoulder, and resuming her plodding pace to the library. Her brilliant father was nothing if not dedicated to his work.

"I got your message that you're not coming home for the holidays. What's this all about? You said you were going to Dubai? Dubai, Layla? Are you crazy?"

She nervously adjusted the folds of her scarf as she prepared herself for an argument. "Whoa, Dad, one question at a time. You do remember I mentioned to you that I'm seeing someone. He's invited me to Dubai to meet his parents."

Silence met Layla's announcement.

"Dad, it's only for a week, and I'll be home afterward to spend the rest of the holidays with you."

"Layla, this is not a good time to be traipsing around the Middle East. Besides, I thought you were this big advocate on campus, dedicated to stopping the Boycott, Divest, and Sanction—BDS—movement. This boy, he's an Arab. I wouldn't think he'd be too keen on your efforts to stop the boycotting of Israeli products, and certainly he wouldn't be in favor of investment in Israel."

"You're wrong, Dad. He's a Saudi, but he's different, more accepting. We've argued about the BDS movement, and he's well aware of what I think. Zamir is brilliant. He understands that Israel isn't going to disappear. He gets it—that there needs to be a new paradigm in Arab thinking that doesn't focus on endless wars. I told you he's related to the royal family. His dad's one of the financial advisers to the House of Saud."

"Does he know you're Jewish?"

"Of course, he knows. Nobody cares about religious stuff at Harvard. Besides, I'm only half Jewish."

"Wrong, Layla. I've told you before that college campuses are like living in an idealistic bubble with no basis in reality. You're a Jew, Layla. Your mother, may she rest in peace, was a Jew, which makes you a Jew. I can assure you the Nazis would have labeled you a Jew and dealt with you accordingly."

"Papa, Mama passed away eleven years ago," she said in a gentle tone. "The Nazis were defeated more than seventy years ago, and you're a Scottish atheist—a nuclear physicist at MIT. You've never cared about religion."

"Just because I raised you to be accepting of all people, regardless of their religion, color, or beliefs, doesn't mean I want you to go off with someone from a culture that is inharmonious with yours. Besides, Layla, your grandparents…it would kill them if they knew you were involved with an Arab. I really have to put my foot down on this ill-advised trip to the Middle East."

"My grandparents live in Israel. I've only seen them a few times. I hardly know them. You can't expect me to live my life according to their old-fashioned beliefs. Besides, Zamir and I are more good friends than anything else. He's considerate and respectful of my opinions. I mean, we care for each other, but we're not intimate."

Geez, admitting something like that to your father! What a douche you are.

Her discomfort only grew as she remembered the promise she'd made to her mother on her deathbed. To remain a virgin until she was sure she'd found the one man she truly loved. That promise had stood between her and every man she'd ever dated. Layla shivered, her teeth rattling from the pressing cold. "I'm going, Dad."

"What's that sound? Where are you?"

"I'm outside, on my way to the library. In case you haven't left your laboratory lately, Dad, we had a huge snowstorm. It's freezing. I only stopped to answer the phone because I knew it would be you."

"I appreciate that, honey, but we're not done discussing Dubai. Call me when you're back in your apartment, or somewhere warm."

Not wanting to hang up on a down note, Layla added, "By the way, I've submitted my proposal for my doctoral thesis. My advisor was very enthusiastic about the premise." She couldn't help the slight boastful quality to her voice. She'd worked her butt off on that proposal. "I think I have a good chance it will be approved."

"You know how proud I am of you, honey. You're so much like your mother—If only Rebecca were here today to see what a wonderful young woman you've grown up to be…" his voice trailed off on a husky note. Whenever her father spoke of her mother he usually ended up in tears. She knew her father still suffered the pain of losing the love of his life.

Layla never tired of hearing her father recount the story of how he and her mother had met at Harvard. She'd heard it so many times she had it memorized. Her father had been a foreign student from Scotland and her mother, a foreign student from Israel. Her father had clumsily spilled coffee all over her mother's research paper in the library. The beautiful, red-haired Israeli woman berated him, and he'd gotten down on his knees begging for her forgiveness. The fury of the redhead had quickly turned to forgiveness and in the months that followed to love. Layla had always wondered if her father had purposely spilled the coffee in order to gain her mother's attention. She'd also wondered how her mother knew so soon that Aleck Wallace was the love of her life. Layla wasn't sure about her own affections for her boyfriend Zamir but maybe she would after this trip to meet his parents in Dubai. She missed her mom every day, but it was times like these that she wished her mother was alive so she could ask her about love and all the other messy emotional stuff that mothers always seemed to know the answers to.

Her father interrupted her musings. "Now get inside, before you catch pneumonia."

"I'll call you later, Dad. I love you."

"I love you too, sweetheart."

Layla made her way through the barrel-vaulted rotunda of the reading center to a desk situated in the far corner of the room.

Zamir looked up from his book. "Hi," he whispered. He stood and helped her remove her backpack. "How'd you do?"

His English boarding-school accent never failed to make her smile. "Great! How about you?"

"Difficult. The professor is a real *arse*, a frigging master of bait and switch. Threw in a bunch of false clues and made us formulate backward. I'll be lucky to get out of there alive."

"I know better, Zamir. You'll probably get the highest grade in the class. By the way, my dad called me back."

Zamir raised his black brows quizzically. "What did he say?"

"He's not thrilled. He wanted to know why a rich Saudi Arab would want to have anything to do with a spoiled, opinionated, adversarial, Jewish American princess." A smile teased the corners of Layla's lips as she watched his puzzled expression. Sometimes American slang confounded him.

"Ah, I get it." Zamir flashed a gleaming white-toothed smile. "Did you tell him the young man in question has the hots for you?" Zamir took her hand, and the warmth of his touch spread throughout her body.

His smiled deepened to a grin as heat flushed her cheeks.

She pulled her hand away. "I certainly did not."

Zamir burst out with unrestrained laughter, causing a chorus of "shushes" from the students studying nearby. Layla's hand covered his mouth. "Zamir, you're going to get us thrown out of the library," she whispered. "Keep your voice down."

He nodded. His eyes, the color of hot chocolate, glowed with merriment.

She shook her head at him as if he were an errant child. "You're such a jerk, so irreverent."

"You're such a tease."

"We can argue about who's what later. Right now, I need to study for my last final tomorrow." She unzipped her backpack, taking out several books and setting them on the table.

"Are you still coming? To Dubai, I mean." His eyebrows rose with amusement. The double entendre was not lost on her.

"Yes." She unwound her scarf and draped it over a chair to dry. "Why wouldn't I enjoy a free, no-strings-attached vacation in one of the swankiest spots in the world? Especially since my only obligation is to make nice to your parents."

"You certainly know how to make a chap feel wanted, Layla."

"I have no idea why I put up with you at all. You're such a pompous, arrogant twit."

He bent close to her and whispered in her ear, sending a thrill down her spine. "That's exactly why you like me—I don't suck up to you like every other male around here just because you're the prettiest girl on campus."

Layla rolled her eyes at his antics and unbuttoned her coat. Zamir helped her off with the coat and draped it on the back of the chair next to her scarf.

She rewarded him with a kiss. For all his superiority and chauvinism, she loved his gentlemanly ways.

She removed her red knit hat and hooked it over the chair arm. Shaking her wavy auburn hair, it fell free past her shoulders. She gave him a flirty smile, knowing the effect her tousled red mane had on him.

His eyes gleamed as he watched her.

"Later," she whispered, settling into her chair. "We both have to study."

He sighed and returned to his chair on the opposite side of the table. She smiled to herself as she opened her textbook to study. There would be time enough for fun and flirting over the break.

A few hours later, they called it a night and packed up their books. Zamir suggested they grab a bite to eat. Walking shoulder to shoulder over to Brattle Street to one of Zamir's favorite restaurants, Algiers, they shared a feta salad, falafels, and shish kabob, drank a beer, and talked about their upcoming trip to Dubai.

Layla finally found the nerve to ask him about what had been bothering her since her conversation with her father. "Zamir, I want you to tell me the truth. Have you told your parents I'm Jewish?"

Zamir looked uncomfortably at his beer, avoiding her eyes.

"You haven't, have you? Zamir, they're going to freak out on you. It isn't fair to put them in that position without forewarning them."

"It's not true, Layla. My parents are sophisticated people. We live in London, Paris, New York, Geneva. We have all kinds of friends, from all over the world, including Jews."

"It's different when their only son, their prized stud, suddenly presents them with his Jewish girlfriend. Zamir, they aren't going to be happy. You have to tell them, or I'm not going."

He took her hand in both of his and kissed it. "I promise you, I'll tell them before we leave." He held her gaze. "I'm prepared to tell them that they're going to have to learn to live with my decision and to love you the way I do."

Layla stared into Zamir's eyes, for once speechless. *Did he just say he loved me?* She wasn't sure how she should react.

He cleared his throat. "Earth calling Layla. You do love me just a little, don't you?"

"I...I...of course I do." She took a sip of beer. "I mean...I love you as much as anyone could, who hasn't actually made love with someone." Her cheeks flushed and it wasn't because of the alcohol.

"We both agreed to wait, Layla, until we finish graduate school, which is only a year away. Which means I'm only a year away from ravishing you." His eyebrows raised suggestively.

Layla's heartbeat kicked into double time. Sometimes the things he said took her breath away. Always unafraid and willing to romance her with words, he never wavered from his dedication to winning her. Although their relationship fulfilled so many of her dreams, something inside of her remained unsure and unwilling to commit herself completely to him. "I think I need an espresso."

"Of course, *habibati.*" He looked around the room for the waiter. "I'll order one on my way to the loo. Be right back."

Layla watched the way women's eyes followed him. Who would have thought she'd end up with the hottest boy at Harvard? Certainly not her.

When they'd first met at a frat party, they'd fought like cats and dogs over the BDS movement against Israel. She was adamant that the whole notion of boycott, divestment, and sanctions was really just a new name for anti-Semitism, while Zamir dared to counter that it was a just and valid response to Israel's apartheid policies.

She had called him an entitled ass and stormed out of the Kappa Sigma frat house hoping never to cross paths with him again. But like a bad penny, wherever she went, he turned up. Even when surrounded by other girls vying for his attention, he ignored them. He focused on her like a laser beam, teasing her with embarrassing compliments, doing everything he could to get under her skin.

One day she'd finally had enough. "You're a stalker!"

He couldn't quite control the laughter threatening to engulf him. "I suppose I am."

"You don't find that disturbing?"

"Not really."

"Well I do, and I'd appreciate it if you'd stop."

"Have coffee with me. I'll stop if you still want me to afterward."

"Fine! Where? When? I want to get this over with. You're driving me crazy."

"Crazy is good. Why not now? Let's go to Algiers coffee shop. It's only a few minutes from here. You can try to persuade me that you're not worthy of my attention."

"Fine."

Layla sipped her latte, remembering that first, unremarkable date.

Funny how everything can change in an instant, she mused. *His apology, a meeting of gazes, the touch of his hand, a quiet conversation, and a sharing of hopes and dreams is all it took for us to become inseparable.*

His words to her that night had changed everything. "Layla, you and I are the solution to the problem. When two people from opposing sides— opposing worlds—can find common ground, find love, only then is peace possible. We are the solution to the problem in the Middle East. Give me a chance to prove to you that my intentions are honorable. I want nothing from you, other than getting to know you."

More than a year later and she was still unsure whether they could sustain a successful relationship, although he'd proven himself to be devoted and she'd grown to care deeply for him. He was respectful of her promise to her mother to wait for sex until she was sure she was in love. They somehow managed, even without intercourse, to have an active if less than complete sex life.

Now Zamir was pressing for them to meet each other's parents. She knew this would force the issue. She felt certain the differences of their religious beliefs and their cultural backgrounds could not be ignored by their parents. Although she was not religious, she would never convert to Islam, and she could not possibly ask him to convert to Judaism.

There it stands. If either of our parents are opposed, we are an impossibility.

She sighed, staring into her cup as if it might contain tea leaves with a solution to her dilemma.

"What's wrong, Layla? You look like the world's coming to an end." His brow furrowed as if he was trying to read her thoughts.

"Oh…nothing, nothing at all. You ready?"

They walked back to Zamir's BMW. He drove her to the apartment she shared with two other girls. She gave him a quick kiss. "I'll see you tomorrow after finals. We should celebrate." She turned to get out of the car.

"Layla." His hand on her shoulder held her in place. "You're not going to change your mind about Dubai, are you?"

She took his face in her hands. "No, Zamir, it's time we met each other's parents. First yours and then my father when we return. We need to settle this once and for all."

She kissed him and was about to pull away, but his hand behind her head lengthened the kiss until the heat between them built into an unbearable desire. Then they broke apart. Zamir buried his lips in her neck, breathing in her scent. "Sometimes it's so hard to leave you, Layla, so hard not to touch all of you, or taste all of you."

Her eyes closed as she savored the warmth of his mouth on her skin and the implicit desire in his words. "I know," she said. "It gets harder all the time." She pulled away and was out of the car in an instant, needing some space to muddle through her conflicting thoughts.

CHAPTER 5

Emirates Airlines Flight
Flight A380
First Class Cabin
December 13th

"Are you two on your honeymoon? The tall leggy blonde asked as she set her empty glass down on the bar in the first-class lounge, where Layla and Zamir were sitting. The United Arab Emirates flight to Dubai was their first chance to relax since they finished finals.

Layla and Zamir had toasted each other with champagne and fed each other hors d'oeuvres. Giggling, their heads close together, they made up stories about their fellow passengers. At one point, Layla gave Zamir a nudge and drew his attention to an older couple seated nearby. "That Texan over there is getting so drunk," she whispered. "I'm beginning to feel sorry for his wife."

"She's used to it, look at her face," he whispered back. "In about a minute she's going to grab that bottle from him and either give it to the flight attendant, or she's going to empty it over his head."

Layla giggled. "Yeah, you're probably right. She looks like she can handle him. Wow, do you see the rock on her finger? It's humongous."

"Wait until you see my mother's…"

The blonde waved at the bartender for a refill. "You're so cute together," she said. "I thought you were newlyweds."

"We are most definitely not married," Layla replied.

The blonde chuckled. "Not for long, I bet. Cheers!" She lifted her glass in a toast before returning to her seat.

Zamir scowled and whispered to her, "We're getting a lot of disapproving looks. Confound it. It's none of their blasted business. Let them think we're on our honeymoon."

"But I'm not wearing a ring," she giggled.

"If you want a ring, I'll buy you one."

Laughing, she tossed her head. "Make it a big one."

"Are you sure you're talking about rings?"

The ambiguity of her response had opened a window for his teasing once again. The big gorilla in the room was the fact that they'd never had sex. Embarrassed, she clasped her hand over her mouth, realizing the grinning man sitting next to Zamir had been listening to their conversation. Her cheeks burning, she grabbed Zamir's hand and pulled him away from the bar and back to the first-class cabin.

Layla had never flown first class before, and she'd squealed when she saw her seat become a bed. She'd opened and closed it several times, delighting in the extravagance.

She pulled Zamir into her space, screened off her compartment for privacy, and gave him a big kiss. She poured them each a glass of wine from her personal mini bar, and they watched a movie.

They landed at four in the afternoon Dubai time, Layla actually felt rested after the flight, something she'd never experienced flying coach. The first-class seat and sleeping pod had been like a deluxe hotel room in the sky. After passing through customs, they exited the arrival's terminal. The eighty-degree temperature and high humidity brought a flush to her face and made her skin glisten with beads of moisture.

"Oh, Zamir, after all that snow, this heat feels like heaven."

"And this, baby, is the coolest month, I promise you. A couple of hours in the desert sun is going to brown you like a pat of butter in a skillet."

"Don't you worry, I brought lots of block."

"Forget the block. I'll spend the week laying on top of you protecting you from the wicked sun."

"Yeah, then who's going to protect me from you?" Their flirty banter was a game they both enjoyed. Somehow it eased the sexual tension that existed between them. For two young, healthy people, abstinence was a constant struggle.

He took her hand, waggling his brows teasingly. "In this country, no one's protecting you from me. Come on, I see the hotel's VIP guest car."

Layla stared in disbelief. "Zamir, that is no car, that's a white Rolls Royce." He laughed. "It's still a car."

She shook her head, wondering if this was all a dream. The airport had been her first surprise. It was the most modern and efficient airport she'd ever been to, architecturally stunning in its use of space and light. A welcoming oasis in the desert Gulf State.

As the Rolls sped to the hotel, Zamir held her hand tightly. She shook with excitement and nervous energy.

"Lay, we aren't meeting my parents until nine for dinner. What do you say we check into our rooms, unpack, and go for a swim and a walk on the beach? After being cooped up on a plane for over twelve hours, you're rattling the bars like a caged tiger. Besides, I've been dreaming of you in a bikini, and I'm ready for my dream to come true."

"Count me in. I feel like a rocket about to blast off. I could use a dunk in the sea—and making your bikini dreams come true is the least I can do in return for this dream vacation." She laid her head on his shoulder and sighed contentedly.

Their arrival at the hotel prompted another burst of excitement in Layla. "Wow! I've seen pictures, but it's much more imposing in person," she said, her eyes wide.

Zamir grinned. "Fifty-six stories of decadence."

The Burj Al Arab Hotel gave the illusion of rising organically out of the pale, aqua waters of the Persian Gulf. Built on an artificial private island and commissioned by Dubai's ruler, Shiekh Mohammad, the Burj embodied a new vision of the Gulf state. Spectacularly constructed and engineered, designed to resemble the mast and sail of a *dhow*, an Arabian sailboat, the hotel stood poised to symbolically sail into the future.

The Rolls crossed the private bridge leading to the front entrance, and once out of the luxurious car, they were greeted by friendly doormen wearing bright red and gold striped vests over their traditional white linen *dishdasha*. Layla's head swiveled left and right trying to see everything in the soaring lobby. The elevators whisked them to their rooms, overlooking the Persian Gulf with a picture postcard view of Dubai City and its towering skyscrapers.

The bellman, with great ceremony, instructed Layla on all of the benefits of her suite. She was so taken aback by the luxury, all she could do was smile and nod. The suite was ostentatiously over-the-top. The sitting room alone was larger than her entire apartment in Boston and richly adorned with jewel-toned fabrics and furnishings of turquoise, gold and red.

Have I been transported to another time? The Arabian Nights?

She texted Zamir—*come see my room. It looks like a harem. You're right. Totally decadent.*

His room was just across the hall from hers, and it took less than a minute for him to knock at her door.

"Zamir, honestly, I can't believe this. It's crazy."

"I wish I could get as excited about it as you, but having grown up with this shit, I guess I'm pretty blasé about the whole thing. But I'm happy if you're happy."

She loved that about him. That he felt so comfortable in his own skin and nothing, not even his wealth, meant more to him than being with her. "Zamir, you haven't given me my welcome to Dubai good luck kiss."

Her come-here-boy smile was intended to make his head spin.

"How could I be so remiss? Welcome to Dubai, baby." He took her in his arms and pulled her close. The passionate kiss made her ache inside. She'd been struggling to fight her body's desire for so long. The promise she'd made to her mother had become tougher to keep, but Zamir had supported her. Family was everything to him, and he admired her determination to be respectful of her mother's last request. He did his best to refrain from pushing her beyond her limits.

As she leaned into him, his arousal pressed against her. The force of his desire made her gasp a hot breath into his ear. "Do you think we're the only sexually unfulfilled people in Dubai?"

"I live my whole life with a perpetual hard-on for you," he chuckled. "There's only so much a man can take. Let's not forget this is the sin city of the Middle East. I think there are plenty of people getting lucky. My guess is we're the anomaly." His sudden intake of breath told her that he too was struggling to maintain control.

Her fingers twisted in his hair. "Oh, Zamir, you know I want you…I just can't…" Her frustration was getting the better of her.

"It won't be much longer, *habibti*. Soon," he growled. "You'll be mine, and there won't be any more of this bullshit. I'm going to fuck you every day until your voice goes hoarse from your screams of pleasure." He pulled her hips hard against his so she could feel what she did to him. He kissed the tip of her nose. "We're going to live in a chic apartment in London, and I'm going to spoil you like a princess."

She furrowed her brows. "Oh, Zamir, I'm not a princess. Please don't talk like that. It makes me uncomfortable. I don't want to live in London, it's too far away from my dad."

"Fine." He pulled away and ran his fingers through his hair, annoyance filling his face. "Layla, I've told you that I must take my place in the family business. London is the center of that world—my world. You'll have a private jet at your disposal and can visit the renowned Doctor Wallace anytime you choose. You'll see, it's manageable if we both compromise."

It seemed unfair to argue with him, but the thought of living in a foreign country without her dad was unnerving. Since her mother's death, he'd been her rock. "We'll figure this out, Zamir. I'll try to keep what's best for both of us in mind."

His face lit with a smile. He cupped her cheeks in his hands and kissed her. "*Enta habibi*, you are my love. I know you'll do what's best for both of us. We have a lifetime to get this right."

She met his smile with her own. "Yes, a lifetime. I really do want to make you happy, Zamir. I think we'd better get out of this room before we get into trouble."

"Let's go for a swim. I think a bit of cooling off is in order."

Layla and Zamir swam in the pristine waters of the Gulf and then strolled on the sun-bleached white sand. On their way back to their rooms, they passed a beauty salon named Posh. Zamir squeezed her hand and gave her a devilish smile. "Wait a minute. I'll be right back."

"What are you doing?"

"You'll see." He disappeared into the shop.

He returned, took her hand, and they continued walking.

"What was that about?"

"I have a surprise for you. You're going upstairs to take a one-hour nap, and then you're going to shower and be downstairs at this salon at seven thirty p.m., at which time your hair and makeup will be seen to. Bring your clothes, and you can change at the salon. When you're finished, you will meet me and my parents at the Al Mahara restaurant. You'll have to take a special elevator to the lower level—the desk clerk will direct you."

"But—"

"No buts. I need you to do this for me, Layla. It's my only request. I want my parents to see the woman who has conquered my heart looking her best. Believe me, you'll get it when you see my mother."

She hugged his arm, leaning her head on his shoulder. "If it pleases you, my lord and master," she teased.

The grin that spread across his face was a reward of its own. She had to admit that pleasing him thrilled her.

CHAPTER 6

Emirate of Dubai
Al Mahara Restaurant, The Burj Al Arab Hotel
December 13th
8:00 p.m.

Layla's knees shook as the host led her to the table where Zamir and his parents were waiting.

Please don't let me stumble in these heels.

She was having trouble focusing on anything other than the vision before her eyes, the ginormous, 700,000-gallon, floor-to-ceiling aquarium with over 280 species of fish.

Oh, dear lord, we're dining in a fish tank! It's surreal.

Al Mahara was so elegant, she felt like Cinderella on her way to the ball. At least, that was what she hoped. She tried not to think of her worst fear, that she was Marie Antoinette being led to the guillotine.

For this first meeting with Zamir's parents, she'd chosen a turquoise silk dress that matched the hue of her eyes. She'd left the rest up to the experts that Zamir had hired. The hairdresser had swept her thick, auburn hair into a French roll, which gave her an elegance and sophistication she knew she didn't possess. The makeup artist had gone on and on about her flawless skin and created a vision of her face she'd never seen before. The aestheticians gushed about her beauty, but all she could see when she looked in the mirror was a stranger. Her confidence soared when she noticed every male in the restaurant turned to admire her.

Zamir and his father stood to greet her.

"*Amy w 'abi*, I'd like you to meet Layla Wallace. Layla, my parents, Omar and Myriam Kamel."

Zamir's father, dressed in a Saville Row suit, was a dashing, silver-haired version of his son. He took her hand. "My pleasure to meet you, Layla."

Layla shook hands and extended her hand to Zamir's mother, elegantly attired in Chanel. A blinding array of diamonds encircled her neck and glittered in her ears.

Myriam hesitated before extending her fingertips to her. Smiling, she briefly brushed them against Layla's, the coolness of her greeting disconcerting.

"Please sit, my dear." Omar's polished, British-modulated accent sounded much like his son's; a reflection of his years spent in boarding schools in England. "Welcome to Dubai, my dear. Zamir has sung your praises to the heavens. We are very pleased to meet you."

The waiter arrived to take her drink order, suggesting a glass of rosé champagne. While his parents were discussing an acquaintance they had run into in the lobby, Zamir leaned in and whispered, "You are the most beautiful woman in this room. You take my breath away. Even my mother can't deny your beauty. You outshine even her, and that's not easy to do."

Zamir's compliment sent a blush to her cheeks. When she reluctantly drew her gaze from him, she found Myriam coldly appraising her. The moment of exquisite joy vanished in an instant.

"My son tells me your mother died when you were a teenager and your father never remarried."

Layla sat straight, her shackles rising at the impolite question, which sounded like an interrogation. Determined to win Myriam over, she regained her composure as best she could. "My father is a renowned nuclear physicist at MIT. He's devoted his life to me and his work. Of course, I would love for him to remarry, but my mother was the love of his life."

"How romantic," his mother said expressionlessly. "It must have been very difficult for him to raise a daughter without a mother's love."

"Yes, I'm sure it must have been, but I tried my best not to make it harder for him than need be. I'm very devoted to him, as he is to me."

Zamir addressed his mother. "*Umi*, Layla, like me, is an honors graduate student at Harvard. She's pursuing her advanced degrees in art history."

Myriam caressed her son's hand. "My son, in our culture, a woman's place is in the home, caring for her husband and children. We place no value on self-aggrandizement or ambition in a woman. We live in a man's world that requires the support of a woman who knows her place and can uplift her husband and help him achieve his ambitions." Myriam's stare was locked on Layla. Her eyes glittered with animosity, projecting daggers across the table, challenging her.

"My mother taught me otherwise," Layla replied in a soft voice. She sat up straighter in her chair as memories of her mother's strength and love wrapped around her like a warm blanket. "My mother taught me that while marriage and children are a joy, a woman is not solely defined by her role in the home. Women have been proving that for centuries, including Arab women. Take Shaikha Lubna, a cabinet minister in the UAE." Layla ran down a list of Arab women who were making waves in government and industry. She'd spent hours online before their flight, hoping to impress Zamir's mother.

A smile iced Myriam's lips as she addressed Layla. "Ah, my dear girl, you are a product of academia. The world of the university creates such idealism in youth, but the real world is much different."

Layla's breath caught in her throat. Myriam's words almost echoed her father's. *So much for making a good impression.* She glanced at Zamir imploring him with her eyes to support her. *Please, Zamir, show them you're strong and independent and fight for me—for us.*

Zamir's gaze skittered away from hers as he took a sip of champagne.

"Why don't we order," Omar interjected in a smooth tone, nodding at Zamir.

"Yes, you both must be hungry," Myriam added reaching out and patting Zamir's hand.

"Whatever you say, *Umi.* I'm starving." Zamir handed Layla a menu. "How about caviar and oysters, Layla? It's a specialty of the restaurant."

The color drained from her face. Zamir had failed to defend her. Her spine grew rigid. She clasped the ridiculously tall champagne flute and took a generous sip. "You order for me, Zamir…you always know how to please me."

Myriam's gasp and Zamir's and Omar's raised eyebrows made Layla wish she was back at Harvard, trudging through knee-deep snow. She was sorry for her comment immediately and downed the rest of her champagne.

Myriam's censorious stares and thinly veiled barbs continued throughout dinner. Layla was miserable and barely touched her food. Coffee and desert had just been served when Layla excused herself, feigning exhaustion. She needed to get away from Zamir's parents. His father was nice enough, but simply oblivious to anything other than pleasing his wife. It was Zamir's mother who represented a serious problem.

41

Zamir escorted her back to her room, telling his parents he'd be right back. As soon as the elevator doors closed, Zamir attempted to take her into his arms. When she pushed him away, he shot her a glare.

"Zamir, I'm very tired, please let's just call it a night."

"That's bullshit, Layla. What the hell were you thinking acting all Susan B. Anthony?"

"What about your mother? The Queen of Sheba. She was baiting me all night, and all you did was ignore it."

"What did you expect me to do, have a shouting match in the restaurant?"

"Yes. If that's what it took for you to stand up for me, then that is exactly what I expected. Not a whimpering little boy."

Zamir's eyes burned with a fury she'd never seen before. "I think we've said enough about this for tonight," he said.

"Agreed." She trained her eyes on the doors. When they opened on their floor, she dashed out ahead of him to her suite. She fiddled with the key-card but was unable to unlock the door. Frustrated tears flooded her eyes.

"Let me." Zamir took the card from her hand and opened the door.

She blinked back the water works and faced him. "Zamir, I'm sorry that the night was ruined. Let's just sleep on it, and maybe tomorrow will be better."

"Of course, *habibti*, a good night's sleep is what you need. I'll explain to my parents that your behavior was accountable to a little too much champagne and jetlag."

Layla shut her door, furious. *How dare he make excuses for my behavior when it's his mother who acted like a bitch?*

She swallowed a couple of aspirin and changed into sweats. She stormed about the room, switching lights on and off, staring out the window, flicking the TV on and then off. The more Layla thought about Zamir's failure to stand up to his mother, the angrier she became.

Why didn't he stand up for me? How can we even think of moving forward, let alone get married, when we can't even get through a dinner with his parents?

Layla seethed and paced for the next hour, refusing to put up with a future-mother-in-law-from-Hell. Unable to bear another minute, she picked up her phone and texted, *I need to talk to you now!* She threw her cell on the sofa, her foot tapping on the carpet impatiently. A few minutes later she picked up her phone and texted him again. *You have five minutes to answer me. We need to resolve this now, Zamir. If you don't answer, I swear I'll march straight over to your room and give you a piece of my mind.* She kept checking her phone in exasperation. *Nothing, nothing, nothing!* "Grrr!" *Enough is enough. I'm going to wring your neck!* She grabbed her phone and left the room.

The hallway was empty, quiet as a church, when she raised her fist to knock on Zamir's door. She heard no sound from within—she knocked again, this time harder. Still nothing.

"I'm not leaving, Zamir, until we resolve this once and for all. Answer the door before I scream." Her raised voice brought the sound of footsteps. *Finally*, she thought.

The door opened wide enough for her to slip inside. Caught up in her anger, she strode in, ready to do battle. She gasped. Zamir lay slumped in a chair, as if sleeping. She took a step forward. Something was wrong, very wrong. Only then did she register the upturned table and lamp next to the sofa. Before she could put everything into perspective, a hand grabbed her from behind and pressed a damp cloth over her mouth and nose.

Adrenaline raced through her veins as self-preservation kicked in. She tried ineffectually to kick her assailant, only to feel more pressure on her nose and mouth. A sickly sweet smell and taste overwhelmed her, hitting her with a wave of nausea, and a strange numbing sensation turned her legs to Jell-O.

Oh, my God, what's happening? The world began to spin, and her legs collapsed beneath her. She whimpered, "Zamir," before sinking to the floor.

CHAPTER 7

Somewhere over the Persian Gulf
Private Jet
December 14th
12:00 a.m.

What kind of nightmare is this? Am I awake? Asleep? Is this a dream? I hear voices. She listened. *What the hell language are they speaking? It sounds like… Could it be Arabic?* No, she knew enough to know that it wasn't Arabic. She shifted. *My hands, my feet, I can't move them. Oh shit, my head is splitting. Where's Zamir? Something happened to Zamir! Try to remember. Is he dead? Oh please, don't be dead. I'm sorry Zamir, I'm sorry I got so mad. Please God, don't let Zamir be dead.*

Layla tried to pry her eyes open, but she had little control over her muscles or limbs. She concentrated on her eyelids. A tiny fraction of light filtered in. She looked around, trying to focus, but everything was fuzzy.

Breathe. It will help your blood circulate. Try to remember what happened. You and Zamir fought. No, that's not what happened. She groaned. *You didn't fight with him. He didn't fight for you. His mother and father, we had dinner— fish tank—a disaster. We walked back to our rooms, and what happened next? I stormed around mad, furious. I went to his room…and…?*

It all returned to her in a rush, and her eyelids blinked open. She looked around, trying to get her bearings. She jolted upright, her eyes growing wide with disbelief.

Where am I? Her head swung left and right. She was confused. *This is a jet. We're flying.* She shook her head to clear it. All the window shades were pulled down. *No passengers. There are no passengers. It must be a private jet. Who kidnaps people with a private jet?*

45

Her bound hands restricted her movement. Swiveling in her seat, she let out a low cry. Behind her sat a bound Zamir, slumped over, unconscious. His chest rose and fell. Tears blurred her vision. *He's breathing. Thank heaven we're both alive. Who did this, and why?*

She whispered, "Zamir, Zamir, wake up. Please wake up. We need to talk, to make a plan."

The clump of heavy footsteps made her swivel her head back around. A scowling man with a beard approached her. He spoke to her in a harsh voice, but she didn't understand a word he said. He repeated himself. She could tell he was questioning her, but she hadn't a clue to what he wanted from her.

"I don't know what you're saying. Do you speak English? Who are you? Where are you taking us? Why are you doing this? I'm sure you've made a mistake." Her head nodded up and down, trying to make him understand. "A mistake, yes? Surely you can see you've made a mistake. We're college students on vacation. I'm an American citizen! You can't just kidnap people from their hotel rooms."

Her tormentor's glare served only to exacerbate her further. She became agitated, pulling at the bonds ineffectually. She tried to stand, but her bound feet tripped her, and she fell out of the seat to the floor. She screamed, "Help me! Somebody, help me!"

The man yelled, and another man came running. Together they picked her up off the floor and threw her back in her seat. She began to cry, and then she screamed. The other man pulled a syringe from his pocket. When she saw the needle, she went crazy, screaming and thrashing, "No! Please, no! Zamir, wake up. Don't let them do this." Her screams filled the air until the prick of the needle. A second later, everything faded—the world went black.

CHAPTER 8

Tehran, Iran
December 14th
3:00 a.m.

Layla woke, swimming in a sea of grogginess. Her temples throbbed, her lips were cracked, and her mouth was as dry as the Sahara Desert. She was in the backseat of an SUV. From the corner of her eye, she could see Zamir next to her, his head bent forward, bobbing with every bump in the road. On either side of them two bulky figures, large, muscled bookends, braced them in an upright posture.

It was the middle of the night, and they were speeding through a city. Snow blanketed the ground and, in the distance, mountains. Peaks of white shone in the light of the full moon. She caught sight of a billboard, a reproduction of a Picasso painting. The lettering beneath it was squiggly and indecipherable like Arabic.

Where am I?

Then it crystallized when she saw a massive architectural structure of white marble rising in the night sky.

I've seen that before. The Shah something. No, they don't call it that anymore— it's the Azadi freedom monument. They changed the name after the revolution. We're in Tehran.

She glanced at the rearview mirror. The driver's look was fixed on her. His voice aggressively addressed the man who sat next to her. Before she could protest, a cloth bag descended over her head, and she could no longer see anything.

"No, please don't cover my head," she begged.

"Layla, are you all right?" Zamir's fingers reached for her hand.

47

"Zamir, you're awake. What happened? Do you know these people? Do you know what this is about?"

"We've been kidnapped and taken to Tehran. I'm sure this is about money. Don't worry. My father will get us out. Do as they say. Don't fight them. I promise my father will do everything he can to free us."

Layla heard a loud slap, simultaneous with Zamir's cry of pain. A man's voice growled in heavily accented English, "Shut up. No talking!"

For the rest of the drive, Layla and Zamir sat in a forced silence. After about thirty minutes, the vehicle stopped, and she heard an exchange of voices. Then the sound of a gate squeaking open. The vehicle started again, drove forward, and then jerked to a stop. The doors flew open. Hands dragged her out of the car and up steps into a building. A steady barrage of angry orders assailed her ears. Pulled and pushed forward, she felt like an animal on its way to slaughter.

"Zamir, are you there?" When he didn't answer, fear filled her. She screamed, "Zamir, answer me!"

Somewhere in the distance, Zamir's voice echoed back to her. "Stay strong, *habibti!*" Steel doors slammed.

A woman's voice broke the silence that followed. She dragged Layla down meandering hallways, continually barking orders. The woman must have known she couldn't understand a word, yet she continued to hurl a harsh verbal diatribe at her.

Finally, they came to a stop. Layla's ears perked at a metallic scraping sound and the deep groan of a heavy door. She was shoved into a room. Her hands were untied and the sack of cloth covering her head ripped away. Blinded by the flood of fluorescent light, she squinted, trying to make out the figure standing before her. A woman dressed in a uniform scowled at her. Layla looked about the bare room with its concrete floors, narrow bed pushed against the wall, and walls so grimy they were more gray than white. If she were to spread her arms across the width of the room, they would touch the walls on either side. The cell was maybe twelve feet long at most. She tried to suppress the desire to cry, but a large tear escaped, rolling down her cheek.

"Please, can you help me? I need to go to the bathroom, and I'm desperately thirsty."

"You are an enemy of the Islamic Republic of Iran and will be treated accordingly."

"You speak English?" Layla couldn't contain her joy. "I'm a student. I'm no one's enemy. I have no idea why I'm here."

"Ha, you are a liar. Soon you will be properly interrogated, and we'll know everything there is to know about you. Then you will pay for your crimes."

"What crimes? I was drugged and kidnapped from Dubai." Fearfully she looked around her. "Where am I?"

"You are at Evin University…a place prisoners know as hell on earth." Layla looked around, confused. "University?"

"Prison, you fool. You're at Evin Prison."

The guard handed her a light blue prison uniform and a *chador*—an Islamic female robe that covers from head to toe. She tossed a pair of rubber slippers at her. "Put these on, and I will take you to the toilet. Make sure none of your hair shows. In your country you may dress like a whore, but in our country, women dress to a strict code of decency."

"How long am I going to be here?"

A cruel laugh burst from her. "You could be here for years. In the morning, they are going to question you. Now, ask me nothing more, or you will be holding your pee for the rest of the night. Everything you need is on the bed."

She left, locking the metal door behind her. Layla quickly changed and inspected the items on the bed. Three folded blankets lay on the thin, bare mattress. Under them she found a cup, a toothbrush, and a bar of soap. The door behind her opened, and the guard returned. Layla followed her out.

The bathroom was filthy, with only one toilet. Layla had to wait in line with other women prisoners for nearly thirty minutes. The women were all staring at the floor, not once looking up. The guard pushed Layla's head down to do the same.

There must be hundreds of women in here.

By the time the woman guard returned her to her cell, the reality had hit home. Evin Prison was worse than Hell.

How will I ever get out of this place? Where did they take Zamir?

Tears poured down her cheeks as she huddled on the thin mattress in her cell.

Will I ever see my father again?

Her heart squeezed into an aching knot of despair.

CHAPTER 9

Tehran, Iran
December 14th
7:00 a.m.

Cyrus sat in his kitchen, sipping a cup of black Turkish coffee, staring out the window. The flowerless garden and the achromatic sky seemed a mirror of his own life. Barren. Devoid of any color or warmth.

Since his trip to Fordow he hadn't been able to sleep. Deep shadows darkened his eyes. At night he tossed and turned unable to get the images of spinning centrifuges out of his head. The increasing production of enriched U-235 meant the world was hurtling toward a point of no return—a nuclear Iran. The arms race in the Middle East could only lead to death and destruction.

He finished his coffee, got up, strode to the sink, and washed his cup. Setting it on the rack to dry he shook his head. The banality of every-day life never failed to remind him of the weight he carried on his shoulders. A heavy weight indeed. Shrugging off the traces of self-doubt, he grabbed his sunglasses case and stuffed it in his pocket. He'd devoted his life to one thing, and that one thing, he must accomplish. He was capable of making a difference—he might be the only person who could prevent a nuclear apocalypse.

His breath steamed from his brisk pace down the hill. Most of the stores in the business district were not open yet. A few early risers passed him on the sidewalk, which suited him just fine. Wrapped in an overcoat, ever watchful of his surroundings, Cyrus attuned his senses to anything that might appear outside the ordinary. In thirty minutes, Saeed would pick him up at a local coffee shop. If he wanted to keep to his schedule, he would have to hurry.

The sign on the optical shop door said it was closed, but when Cyrus knocked, an elderly man, his thinning gray hair and beard neatly groomed, appeared and unlocked the door. Taking a brief look about the street, he greeted Cyrus. "*Sobh be kheyr, Aghaye* Hassani! Good morning. Please, come in." With another glance at the street, he closed the door and locked it. Cyrus followed him to the counter, took the sunglasses case from his pocket, and handed it to the optometrist.

"Thank you for opening early, Mr. Banai. It seems my sunglasses have become loose again and are slipping off my nose. If you could tighten them, I'd appreciate it. I have a very busy day, and I will need them."

"Not a problem. Perhaps you'd like to watch me fix them. It will only take a few minutes." The man disappeared through a curtain leading to a workshop in back. Cyrus followed him, stationing himself at the curtained entry where he could monitor the street while watching Mr. Banai.

Mr. Banai filled a small tub with a solution. Dipping the sunglasses in the liquid, he waited a minute before removing them from the solution, careful not to touch the lenses, he laid them on a towel. Using a tiny pair of tweezers, he lifted the edge of a clear, protective film of plastic covering one of the lenses and slipped it into a square pocket made of felt that fit it like a glove. Sitting on the counter, another case with a pair of glasses awaited his attention. Taking out the glasses, he removed the inside liner of the case and replaced it with the felt pocket holding the clear lens he'd removed and returned both the liner and eyeglasses to the case. Under the table lay a small safe. "Now, we'll just put these safely away, and that should do it." He unlocked the safe, placed the glasses on a shelf, and closed it, spinning the dial.

"They'll be picked up today?" Cyrus, asked.

"Yes. This afternoon."

"Good. I would hate to think …" he paused, "of you being inconvenienced."

"You must not worry about me."

A slight smile framed his lips. "Of course not, Mr. Banai." It bothered him that the elderly man had been placed in such a dangerous position. He pulled aside the curtain and surveyed the street beyond.

"Now, let's get your sunglasses back into working order."

Mr. Banai turned his attention to Cyrus's sunglasses. With another piece of felt cloth, he dried the lenses, and using the tweezers, he peeled a new protective plastic lens from a sheet that held several more identical clear lenses and carefully adhered it to Cyrus's sunglasses. Once attached, the clear plastic film became invisible. With a small optical screwdriver, he tightened the screws on the end pieces of the frames. "There we go, good as new." He handed the glasses to Cyrus. "Try them now, *Agha*, and see if they're not better."

Cyrus slipped them on. "Perfect, Mr. Banai. As always, you provide a most excellent service. Thank you."

Mr. Banai inclined his head with a smile. Walking past Cyrus to the front of the shop, he unlocked the door, and the tinkle of chimes rang out. "Blessed are the peacemakers."

Cyrus nodded at the elderly man and walked out without a word.

It only took a few minutes to walk to the coffee shop where he found Saeed waiting in the Range Rover. As soon as he shut the door, Cyrus's phone pinged, and he studied the text coming in. "Saeed, there's been a change of plans. Take me to the Ministry."

"On our way, sir." Saeed whipped the Range Rover around, made a hasty U-turn, and sped away.

The turbaned, bearded, Jalal Rahimi rose to greet Cyrus. He extended his elegant, manicured hand, inviting Cyrus to sit. "Ah, Cyrus, *Salaam alaikum.*"

Cyrus shook the proffered hand. *"Assalamu alaikum."*

Cyrus observed his boss. The deputy director of Oghab2 had the responsibility for protecting Iran's nuclear program. A man of moderate stature with a benign smile, Jalal Rahimi possessed an indomitable nature. Ironically, Jalal was the son of a mullah, whom the Shah's brutal secret police, SAVAK, arrested for preaching sedition. When Jalal was a child, the SAVAK dragged his father from the mosque, while he was leading prayers. The government denied the mullah a trial and imprisoned him in Monkerat Prison. After a year of being tortured, Jalal's father was released a broken man, no longer capable of challenging the oppressive regime. Jalal never forgot his father's weakness or forgave the regime that had caused it.

As a youth at the religious Haghani School in Qom, the clerics singled Jalal out as a devout follower and sent him to university in Tehran. Like many from the provinces, he had grasped the opportunities made possible by the revolution. The power in Iran had shifted, and Jalal seized the moment, becoming a key player. A ruthless hardliner, he rose through the ranks of MOIS, leaving a trail littered with the bodies of those that dared to oppose him. Where other men's fortunes fell, Jalal's cunning kept him above the fray, aiding his rise through the cutthroat politics and petty jealousies of men grasping for power.

Beneath his slight exterior dwelled a man of great physical strength and intellect, capable of single-handedly disarming his opponents, whether it be in the combat arena or in a match of wits. Married but childless, he had brought the orphaned Cyrus under his wing, seeing in him a reflection of himself and a trusted conduit to expanding his power within the ministry. Jalal's hand and guidance had helped precipitate Cyrus's meteoric rise within Iran's secretive intelligence service.

Jalal's office was Spartan, save for a fish-design, yellow silk Persian carpet from Tabriz. It was a rare indulgence for a man who scorned luxury. The carpet, a family heirloom confiscated from a wealthy landowner, was the only public display of its new owner's stature. Jalal told Cyrus that it symbolized the righting of wrongs, the balancing of the scales. The powerful who had ruled for so long now kneeled, and Jalal, a man of humble beginnings, now topped the new order.

"I trust your trip to Fordow proved beneficial. Qom is such a beautiful city, a perfect break from the chaos of Tehran, even if your visit bore a far more serious purpose. I myself have fond memories of my school years there."

"Yes, *Agha*, attending prayers at the Holy Shrine of Fatima-al-Masumeh, blessed be her memory, is an inspiration for all." He handed Jalal a folder containing the report he'd prepared. "Our scientists have made remarkable progress."

Jalal's eyes lit with satisfaction. "Excellent! As to be expected. Sharif is a capable director."

Cyrus nodded and waited, knowing Jalal had not insisted upon his presence at headquarters only to converse about his trip to Qom.

"Cyrus, there is something I need you to attend to personally. We have a small problem at Evin Prison. It seems some overly enthusiastic members of our Quds Force have kidnapped the son of a wealthy Saudi financier. The desperate need for additional funds in our blessed nation due to the evil sanctions imposed by the sanctimonious western powers and their devil's kin, the Israelis, have driven our people to make a troublesome error. In their earnestness to provide for us against our enemies, our comrades may have overstepped the line."

"How so?"

"When they kidnapped the Saudi, an unforeseen mishap occurred. Complications arose, and they found themselves forced to kidnap a young American woman. Normally, this would not be a problem, and we would find a diplomatic solution. However, further investigation has revealed she is a Jew and has traveled numerous times to Israel. Word has crept through the chain of command, and the powerful are not inclined to release her. I believe they sense she is of value to us."

"She's an American, sir. There are bound to be political repercussions."

"Yes, yes, I agree. The most expeditious solution is to return the infidel, but this will require some time. In the interim, her safety at Evin is tenuous. Apparently, she is unusually beautiful, very exotic, with red hair and blue eyes like the Tajiks."

Cyrus frowned. Jalal's implication was clear. A beautiful Jewess would be in grave danger at Evin Prison where rape by unscrupulous guards was rampant. Not long ago, a female journalist died in Evin of reported natural causes. Cyrus suspected she'd been raped and brutalized—in all likelihood they murdered her to cover up the crime. The thought of an animal like Mohammad holding dominion over this girl turned his stomach. "What do you want me to do?"

"You will need to get her out of Evin, create a bond, a trust between the two of you. I want you to find out everything about her. She could be a valuable bargaining chip—both American and a Jew she would hold interest to both our hated enemies. Of course, she will be your prisoner, within your control. She will also be your responsibility. I will arrange for her release to you. You will bring her to one of the ministry's safe houses." Jalal licked his lips. "I would have liked to interrogate her personally. However, it would be inappropriate for a man of my station, but for you, my son, it could prove a welcome distraction. Far better for her to experience a love affair with a man such as you than the abomination of forced copulation with, well, someone not of your refinement."

"A love affair? I don't understand." Jalal's encouragement to seduce this woman raised his hackles. It would place him in a dangerous situation, where a young woman's life would be in his hands. The possible complications were already wreaking havoc in his mind. How would he protect her from becoming a pawn in a game where she might lose everything, including her life? And yet, the thought of a hideous monster like Mohammad defiling her filled him with revulsion.

"She needs to trust you, to confide in you, to believe her life depends on you." It was clear that Jalal was intent on his vision that a romantic liaison between Cyrus and the young woman would be of potential benefit with the Americans.

"I am, of course, at your service, *Agha*."

"Good, our meeting is concluded. You have your mission. See you don't fail me."

Cyrus rose from his chair.

"Oh." Jalal's eyes darkened to the color of dull steel as he fixed them on Cyrus. "One thing more. Perhaps it is time you ended your dalliance with Zahra Amiri. I have overlooked the ambiguous nature of your relationship until now. It is time for *Khanome* Amiri to remarry. We do not want our national heroine embroiled in a scandal. Considering your unwise entanglement with Zahra, the American girl should be a pleasurable distraction while your heart mends."

Cyrus's jaw clenched as he pasted a banal smile on his face. Jalal knew of his secret love affair with Zahra. Nodding his assent, he turned and exited the deputy director's office.

With few words, Jalal had communicated his warning. The insinuation was as clear as a bell. Zahra would accept the situation. She was a survivor and would fulfill her duty. As for the American girl, Cyrus understood he had no choice but to take her under his protection. He realized he was in a precarious position—Jalal was going to make him pay for Zahra.

As he exited MOIS, Cyrus contemplated the best way to handle the situation. He would not force himself on the American. He would find another way. The seeds of a plan began to formulate in his mind. It would require his taking this girl into his confidence, which could prove dangerous for both of them. Whether he could trust her to cooperate, or even more worrisome, whether she would trust him and his intentions, could not be determined until she was in his custody. He glanced at his watch—he needed to hurry. Every minute inside Evin Prison put the American woman's life in peril.

CHAPTER 10

Cambridge, Massachusetts
December 14th

Aleck Wallace sat numbly in his living room, his tea had gone cold, the evening news droned in the background.

His daughter. His beautiful Layla had been kidnapped.

He'd gotten the call just after six p.m. The information from the State Department was sketchy. The FBI knew little about what had happened except that a few hours earlier, Layla and Zamir, without any witnesses, were abducted from their hotel rooms in Dubai. Their whereabouts were unknown, the reason for their kidnapping was unknown, and the identity of the abductors were also unknown. There had, as of yet, been no contact from the kidnappers. The State Department had turned the case over to the FBI, whose office in Dubai would be handling the investigation. FBI agents would be working closely with the authorities from Dubai to assess the situation. As soon as they had any information, they would contact him.

As the hours passed with no word from the authorities, a lifetime spent in the utilization of scientific reasoning kicked in. Aleck put his problem-solving skills to work. He searched his memory for everything Layla had told him about Zamir, weighing the possibilities that could play out. It seemed obvious to him the young man had found himself a target for ransom, and his daughter had the misfortune of being in the wrong place at the wrong time.

Everything now depended on whether or not they figured out that he was Layla's father. If and when they did, they would use her, and he would become a target for blackmail. He could only hope that if the FBI had not yet put two and two together, it stood to reason neither had the Middle Eastern kidnappers.

He didn't have much time to decide what to do. The clock was running, and Layla's life hung in the balance. One thing he knew without question—he would do whatever it took to get his daughter back, even if it meant breaking his promise to Layla's mother.

His wife, Rebecca, had understood Aleck's invention could be misused by any terrorist organization with the will to steal. The haunting vision of a terrorist organization, or a rogue dictator gaining access to the technology and utilizing it for mass murder, the blackmail of nations, or world domination had terrified Rebecca.

The most troublesome aspect of his discovery? It was virtually impossible to detect and would render the International Atomic Energy Agency virtually useless.

When Rebecca fell ill, Aleck had voluntarily shut the entire project down, promising her he would never share his discovery with the world. He severed all ties to the National Nuclear Security Agency, refusing to complete the project, and no amount of persuasion or political pressure could get him to restart it. For a time, both he and Rebecca feared repercussions from the government—possible lawsuits—but no threat ever materialized. After Rebecca passed away, Aleck Wallace accepted a professorship at MIT and moved with his young daughter to Boston, abandoning his ties to the US government.

As he awaited word from the State Department, the irony of the situation did not escape him. He'd silenced his research to make the world safer for his daughter, never imagining events in the future might force him to use his discovery to save her life.

I should have fought harder to convince her not to go to Dubai, damn it.

But the reality was, he'd raised her to be independent.

Independence coupled with stubbornness. Just like her mother.

He wished Rebecca were here to advise him.

He nodded off in darkness, sitting in his recliner, exhausted from trying to determine a definitive course of action that would lead to his daughter's release. The persistent ringing of the phone woke him. Looking at his watch, he'd slept for an hour. He shook his head in an effort to clear away the cobwebs of restless sleep. The nightmare situation returned in a flash.

"Hello, this is Aleck Wallace."

"Hello, Dr. Wallace, this is Curtis Jackson from the Federal Bureau of Investigation in Washington."

Aleck bolted upright. Fear gripped his chest. "Yes, Mr. Jackson, what have you learned? Is Layla all right?"

"Our office in Dubai has notified us that Zamir Kamel's father, Omar, has been contacted. They're asking for a ransom. Of course, Omar was warned by the kidnappers not to discuss anything with law enforcement. Naturally, he is fearful for his son's life. He won't disclose the ransom amount or the kidnappers' identities. Fortunately, Dubai officials have been monitoring and tracking his phone. The ransom call originated from Tehran."

"Tehran? The Iranians? I don't understand. Why? Is this common?" Aleck now knew that his worst fear would become a reality.

"Iran has been under sanctions for a long time. I imagine the Revolutionary Guard has tried to figure out ways to supplement its enormous overhead. It's rare, but it makes sense. A wealthy Saudi would be an easy target. We believe Layla wasn't a target but a coincidental victim."

"Did Omar Kamel make any mention of Layla or whether the Iranian's included her in the ransom discussion?"

"Mr. Kamel has turned completely uncooperative. Our sources have informed us he has already left Dubai for Saudi Arabia."

"But that's crazy. Doesn't he understand my daughter was only in Dubai because of his son? This is outrageous!"

"Yes, Dr. Wallace. We understand your concern. I assure you we will do everything in our power to get Layla back."

"I'm sure you will, Mr. Curtis, but I'm not sure you or our government's best will be good enough. Please keep me posted."

"Certainly, Dr. Wallace."

Aleck stared long after the line went dead. His heart was racing as he pictured Layla's name at the bottom of a memo, a footnote in history, a casualty of US-Iran relations.

He knew what he must do. No turning back. He could not count on the US government to negotiate Layla's release, whatever the FBI agent claimed. The current administration was intent on resuming relations with Iran in their Joint Comprehensive Plan of Action—JCPOA. So intent, they hadn't even included any provisions for the release of American citizens currently being held prisoner or up for trial in Iran. If Americans who'd been held for years had no method for getting released, what hope did Layla have, especially given Aleck's own past relationship with the United States government.

Jerusalem was seven hours ahead…it would be morning in Israel. He pulled a piece of paper from his pocket with a phone number on it. Before he'd fallen asleep, he'd searched the internet for the number. His best option was a phone call away.

The phone rang several times before a woman's voice came on the line. "This is the prime minister's office," she said in Hebrew. "How may I direct your call?"

"I'm sorry, do you speak English?"

"Yes, of course. How can I help you?"

"I need to speak to the prime minister. This is urgent."

"I understand. I can put you through to his assistant. May I say who is calling?"

"Yes, thank you. Tell him it's Aleck Wallace, Dr. Aleck Wallace." He hoped his title would resonate with authority.

"Yes, Dr. Wallace. Hold, please."

Aleck tried to calm his nerves as he prepared to speak to a man he hadn't spoken to in thirty years. Of course, his former roommate would remember him. The question worrying him was not whether the prime minister would remember their four years of college together but whether those years of friendship would compel him to help.

"Hello, this is Sarah Mazar at the prime minister's office. Who am I speaking with?"

"Ms. Mazar, I am Dr. Aleck Wallace, an old friend of the prime minister. In fact, we were roommates at Harvard. I wish I could say this is a friendly call, but in truth, I have an urgent matter to discuss with him. A matter of life and death."

"I see. Dr. Wallace, the prime minister is in a meeting right now, but I am more than willing to slip a note to him making him aware of your call. I'm sure he will get back to you as soon as he can."

Aleck sighed with relief. "I would very much appreciate it, Ms. Mazar. Have you any idea how long he will be in this meeting?"

"I'm not sure, but I know when he sees your request is urgent, he will make every effort to get back to you as soon as possible. Rest assured, Dr. Wallace, I promise you'll hear from him soon."

"Thank you, Ms. Mazar." He gave her his number, willing his voice to a calm he did not feel. "Please tell him I'll be waiting for his call."

Aleck gripped the phone to his chest and leaned back in his chair going over in his mind the plea he would make to the prime minister.

CHAPTER 11

Cyrus wasted no time getting over to Evin Prison. He flashed his top-level security clearance card, scarcely pausing to wait for entry. He made little effort to acknowledge the familiar faces that vied for his recognition.

When he reached the women's section of Ward 350, he brusquely ordered the guard to take him to the American prisoner's cell at once.

The guard, a woman incapable of making a good impression, hemmed and hawed. If he hadn't been so worried about the American woman, he would have addressed the guard's unprofessional behavior. Instead, he glared at her, impatiently waiting for her to obey his command.

"*Agha*, which woman are you asking about?"

"Are you deaf? How many American women do we have in this prison?"

"Only one, sir. However, I'm not sure if she is in her cell at the moment."

"Not in her cell? Where the hell is she?"

"Uh…She may be getting *hava khori*, exercise in the yard."

"Stop with this bullshit and take me to her. Now!"

"Yes, sir, follow me."

Cyrus fumed. *Is everyone in this country incompetent?*

When they reached the cell, he ordered, "Open it!"

The guard unlocked the door. The cell was empty. Cyrus turned to the guard "Where is she?"

"I-I" the guard stuttered, her eyes skittering away.

Another female guard rounded the corner and ran up to them. "Mohammad took her for interrogation," she said out of breath.

"Take me to her. Now!" he bit out.

Fear constricted Layla's throat. Her breath came in shallow gasps as she fought to understand what was happening. A burly guard had dragged her from her cell, his every word a contemptuous snarl. A poker dug into her back as he pushed and shoved her down a maze of hallways. When they reached a remote room, he opened the door and shoved her into the cell. Behind her, the metal door clanged shut with a bang. Adrenaline rushed through her veins. Her body trembled in terror of what was to come.

She frantically scanned the room. There were no windows, only a table and two chairs resting on a concrete floor.

Why is no one else here with us?

She'd been informed that a female guard would be present with her during interrogations. Before she could rationalize what was happening, the brute shouted at her again. "Turn around!"

Layla pulled the *chador* close around her. The black, cloak-like garment worn by Iranian women in public had felt constrictive and confining when Layla had first put it on. The female guard had ordered her to do so before leaving the cell. Now, Layla gripped the heavy folds as though it were a protective shield against the interrogator's leering gaze.

He grabbed a fist full of black fabric in his hands, wrenching it over her head and threw it to the floor. He grabbed a fistful of hair and yanked her toward him.

"Don't touch me," she spat out, jerking her head away.

He grinned. "Take off your clothes."

Layla's jaw dropped open and she gaped at him, her insides clenching in fear. "I…I…No, I won't."

She never saw the open-handed slap coming. Her head flew sideways with the force, her cheek burning. Tears stung her eyes. She tried to blink them back. "This is illegal. It goes against the Geneva Convention and Islamic law, the Qur'an."

The lascivious smirk on the guard's face told her he didn't care about any moral code let alone any international law.

He laughed. "No witness, no crime. In our culture, without a witness, the woman is guilty. Take your clothes off, now!"

When she still did not move, he swung her around toward a metal table in the center of the room and slammed her face down.

He laughed, rubbing himself against her. "This can be enjoyable, or it can be unpleasant. It's up to you."

Pain gripped her, her temple throbbing from the impact of the unforgiving metal desk. Bile rose in her throat as his hands and body mauled her. She tried to resist, squirming to break free, kicking out with all her might, she even managed get him in the groin. It only made him more enraged. He shook her like a rag doll causing her head to hit the table with a heavy thud. She swallowed the bile in her throat as he held her pinned like a bug.

The cold clank of his belt buckle hitting the floor, escalated her fear. She started to scream and kick again, and he flipped her onto her back, punching her in the ribs. The impact left her gasping for air.

"I told you," he hissed, "do not fight! Relax—it will be over soon enough."

Like a beast, he ripped her pants and underwear down around her ankles, restricting her ability to kick.

"Please," she begged in a whisper, "don't do this."

He laughed again, stroking himself in front of her. She gagged as the tepid air in the windowless room magnified his body odor and sweat.

"You will like this, American whore. Relax and enjoy."

Layla scrunched her eyes shut, as tears streaked her face. Her body, where he'd hit and punched her hurt like hell.

She'd saved herself for the man she loved. She thought that man would be Zamir. A wave of hysteria bubbled inside her as the brute grabbed her arms in a tight grip.

Her first time was going to be a brutal rape.

Please, God, help me.

"Where the fuck is she?" Cyrus growled as he followed the female guard down corridor after corridor. Finally, at the end of an isolated hallway, they stopped as a muffled cry reached them from behind a steel door.

Drawing his ZOAF PC-9 pistol, he pushed the female guard out of the way and kicked open the door.

Rage.

Blood red rage flooded his nerve endings. His finger pulsed on the trigger, itching to fire. Cyrus hated Mohammad, but never more than at this moment. Everything he detested in his fellow man—the cruelty, the abuse of power, the ignorance and disrespect for human life—every vile human characteristic lived in this one individual. With pleasure, he would have shot and killed Mohammad, ending the life of an animal who didn't deserve to live.

Had Mohammad actually raped her, Cyrus would have killed him on the spot, but he had arrived just in time. His jaw clenched as he reined in his impulse to exact punishment. His plan of action did not allow for deviation. He needed to stay focused on the goal of getting Layla out of Evin Prison.

In Farsi he ordered, "Put your hands up, Mohammad, and don't move." In English he asked the girl, "Are you all right?"

Mohammad slowly raised his hands. "Don't shoot, *Agha*. I can explain. The girl is a witch. She seduced me." His bulky frame blocked the young woman who was crying behind him.

Still in a shooter's stance with the gun trained on Mohammad, Cyrus ignored the man's ridiculous statement. "Miss Wallace. You're safe now. Please, if you can manage, get dressed and stand behind me."

Rustling sounds and sniffles were his answer. "H-he was going to rape me," she whispered.

"It's going to be all right Miss Wallace," Cyrus said in a calm voice.

When the girl emerged from the behind the swine, Cyrus temporarily lost his focus. Even with bruises and swelling distorting her features, he was awestruck by her beauty—the large, turquoise eyes, the glorious auburn hair. With a mighty effort, he regained his composure and trained his gaze once more on the hulk who was still standing with his pants down around his ankles.

Layla, shaky on her feet, held fast to the table for support. Her heart still pounding a fearful arrhythmic beat, she tried to regain her composure. Tears welled in her eyes from her close call. A miracle had occurred, and someone had saved her. Following the gentle command of the man who'd arrived just in time, she dressed quickly and stepped around the hulking brute putting as much distance between herself and him as she could.

Her rescuer glanced at her waving her behind him. Her breath caught in her throat. His eyes. A striking green framed with thick black lashes. He was tall and broad-shouldered, his imposing presence no doubt caused even that monster to cower in fear. She thought she saw a flicker of kindness in his gaze. But then it was gone.

"You're through, Mohammad," he growled at her attacker. "As much as it would please me to kill you, I'm going to let you live today, which is better than you deserve." Her rescuer glanced back at Layla. "Take the *chadar* and put it on. The fewer people who get a good look at you, the better."

Layla complied without answering, still reeling from the attack.

From the moment they left the room, everything proceeded at a rapid pace. Mohammad was led away in cuffs, by a commanding officer and two guards. The devil's dog delivered a curse on her rescuer and brandished his fists in a threat of vengeance.

A female guard took her arm and led her back to her cell. Her rescuer followed close behind. "Don't worry, Miss Wallace," he said in that calm deep voice, "you'll be out of here very soon."

She turned to her rescuer as she entered her cell. His striking green-eyed gaze was fixed on her. Her cheeks flushed with heat, but she couldn't look away.

"Thank you," she whispered.

He nodded, turned, and left.

CHAPTER 12

Tehran, Iran
Evin Prison
December 14th

To say Layla was exhausted, bewildered, and shaken up, was an understatement. Her rescuer had ordered the female guard to get Layla an ice pack. In the tiny cell, Layla lay on the thread-bare mattress.

What's going to happen to me now?

If she was going through this violence, what was Zamir going through? She closed her eyes at the sting of the ice pack against her swollen cheek.

Zamir.

Their fight seemed ages ago. What would happen to them? The brooding man with the striking green eyes had told her everything would be all right. But would it? Did he mean that she wouldn't have to fear being mauled by Mohammad? Or was Zamir's father working to release them?

Oh, how she wished she'd taken her father's advice.

Papa, will I ever see you again?

Time inched along and her anxiety grew. She dozed off and on, the aches and pains from the attack having drained her of what little energy she had left. Her eyes were growing heavy once more when the scratching of a key in the lock on her cell door made her sit up with a gasp.

On shaky legs, Layla got up and clutched the melted ice pack to her chest. She cowered in the corner of the cell. Despite her rescuer's reassurances, she was terrified of what would happen next.

The cell door flew open and the female guard walked in with an armful of clothes, threw them onto the bed, and ordered her to dress. After she left, Layla slowly made her way to the bed, and her eyes filled with tears. She quickly slipped on the sweatpants and hoodie, the very same clothes she was wearing the night she and Zamir had been kidnapped. She hugged herself, comforted by their familiarity.

A short time later, the guard returned to Layla's cell to inform her she was being released.

Overwhelming relief flooded her senses as she stumbled after the female guard down the hallway.

Zamir's father came through. He must have arranged our release just as Zamir said he would.

Perhaps that was why the man with the green eyes had shown up. She couldn't wait to get home and spend The Holidays with her father.

Her processing out of Evin Prison was expeditious. As she exited the red brick building, two guards handed her into a black Range Rover with tinted windows. Before she could utter a word or ask where they were going, the SUV drove away with a screech of tires. A man she'd never seen before was driving.

Next to him sat the green-eyed Iranian man who'd rescued her. While he was deep in conversation on his cell phone, she waited. It gave her an opportunity to study her rescuer. He had on dark aviator glasses this time and was speaking softly on the phone, the deep timbre of his voice reverberating in the car. His face was all hard angles, with a determined jaw, emphasizing a strength of purpose.

He looks like an old-fashioned movie star. He even has a dimple in his chin like Christopher Reeve.

She shook her head at her foolishness. She'd watched too many classic Hollywood movies with her dad on Saturday nights. She wiped her eyes as they teared up again at the thought of her father.

Just because Superman saved you, doesn't make him an actual hero.

He was doing his job, and was no doubt paid well for it.

She gasped and grabbed onto the leather hand strap as the driver made a sharp turn. The driver drove erratically, swerving around cars, veering into the opposite lane, barely missing colliding with oncoming vehicles, and coming only inches away from sideswiping a delivery truck.

"Hey, he's going to kill us!" she screamed.

Superman turned to her, lifted his dark, aviator sunglasses, and revealed his penetrating gaze. "Miss Wallace, sit back and relax," he said in that deep, smooth voice. "No one's going to hurt you. This is my driver, Saeed. It might not seem like it, but"—a hint of a smile deepened the dimple in his chin—"he's very good at what he does. Please, trust me."

She didn't understand why, but something in his calm reassurance comforted her.

He said something in Farsi to the driver, and to her relief, the man slowed down, adjusting his driving to the flow of traffic.

"Where are we going? Where's my boyfriend, Zamir Kamel?"

"Please relax. Why don't you save your questions until later? I promise you I'll answer all of them. Right now, I have several calls to make, okay?" He gave her a wide, warm smile.

Layla blinked at how his face transformed from intense and brooding to compassionate and charming. She breathed deeply. The events of the day had exacted their toll. She was tired, achy, and hungry. Evening approached, and the light of day had begun to fade. The neighborhoods racing past the windows all began to look the same. Before long, her head bobbed from the repetitive scenery and hum of the engine. She closed her eyes and gave up to her exhaustion.

Cyrus slipped his phone into his shirt pocket. Jalal Rahimi had congratulated him on his last-minute rescue of the girl from Evin Prison and had given him the address of a safe house. Nothing had changed about his assignment. He was to gather information on her and encouraged to develop a relationship with her.

Cyrus was in a catch-22 situation with no way out—an untenable position. To disobey would be taking a risk. Jalal's knowledge of Zahra hung over his head like the blade of a guillotine.

MOIS kept several safe houses in and around Tehran. Some were utilized for the private dalliances of the higher ups, others for the temporary housing of foreign dignitaries clandestinely visiting Tehran when discretion was required. All the safe houses were equipped with cameras and listening devices.

Saeed pulled into the driveway of a townhouse in an upscale neighborhood on the outskirts of the city, a neighborhood unfamiliar to Cyrus. He grabbed the key that had been left for him in the mailbox and handed it to Saeed. Opening the rear passenger door of the Range Rover, he found Layla still sleeping. He imagined she hadn't slept a wink in Evin Prison, but who could? Gently, he lifted her into his arms, carrying her while Saeed ran ahead and opened the door.

"We'll be fine, Saeed. I'll call you when I need you."

"Yes, *Agha*. Will you be staying here with the girl?"

"Yes, those are my orders. Leave the key on the entry table."

He walked up the staircase to the second floor where he assumed the bedrooms were located. Layla's head rested on his chest. The swollen bruises on her cheek only intensified her delicate beauty. His eyes strayed to the sprinkling of freckles peppering her nose.

You're too fucking beautiful for your own good.

He shook his head remembering Jalal's comments regarding how useful it would be for the girl to develop a case of Stockholm syndrome, a documented psychological condition where a captive identifies, defends, and can even fall in love with her captor. Jalal believed she might turn out to be an excellent agent for the regime.

The irony was, Cyrus was already attracted to the young woman, had been from the moment his eyes met hers in that cell.

I can't allow myself to become attached.

It was too dangerous. Even as his mind said no, his heart and, God forbid, his body said yes. It was the first time since meeting Zahra, that a woman had affected him with such intensity. But even though he'd been with Zahra many times, his feelings had never grown beyond the physical. Zahra's aloof sophistication and almost voracious desire to remain unencumbered by a husband had created a virtual emotional firewall around her.

He glanced down at the sleeping young woman in his arms and blew out a breath of frustration. This petite red-head with her American bravado masking a trembling fear in those luminous turquoise eyes had awakened his male instinct to protect. The only other women he'd ever felt such a deep connection to, were his mother and sister and he hadn't seen them in more than ten years.

He found the master bedroom and laid her on the bed. She sighed and rolled over onto her side. A blanket lay at the foot of the bed. He grabbed it and covered her. He fought the urge to wake her so he could look into those eyes again. Regrettably, he had things to do before she woke.

He familiarized himself with the house, noting the pinhole cameras hidden everywhere except in the bathrooms. He closed the drapes and peered outside. He spied two men in a nondescript vehicle sitting kitty-corner across the street from the house. Their unnecessary loitering meant they were part of a hunting team sent to monitor his comings and goings.

Jalal had ordered them watched.

He would sort it all out later—right now, he needed to prepare a meal for the girl. She'd been through a horrific experience. The thought of an animal like Mohammad laying a hand on her made his blood boil. He would have to work hard to win her trust.

CHAPTER 13

Tehran, Iran
December 14th

Layla bolted upright, gasping for air. The nightmare of being drugged and abducted had vividly replayed in her dream. Her face and ribs ached. She looked around the unfamiliar room.

How did I get here?

Her last memory was of sitting in the Range Rover with Superman and his driver. Panic filled her.

Zamir? Where are you?

She swallowed the lump of emotion as she wiped the sleep from her eyes. She glanced around the room. A lamp bathed the spacious bedroom in a soft light. She was clearly in a house somewhere. Was Zamir in another room? Was he okay? Had his father already negotiated for their release and arranged their departure? Or was he in the process of doing so? She needed to talk to Zamir. Was he hurt? Did he need medical attention? Could she ask Superman? What if her taciturn hero had left her here with someone else to guard her? Her mind spun with a million questions.

Determined to get some answers, she rose from the bed. She crept out of the bedroom suite and tiptoed down the stairs. The fragrance of cooking meat and spices teased her nose. Her stomach growled in response. She was starving. She followed the delicious aromas to the kitchen. Superman stood over a stove stirring a pot. He dipped a wooden spoon into whatever delectable dish he was cooking and tasted it. "Hmm…" With a smile of satisfaction, he turned down the heat and placed a lid on the pot.

"It smells yummy. What is it?"

He whirled around, his hand reaching for his holstered gun. Then seeing her standing there, he quirked a smile. "You scared the hell out of me."

"Sorry." She smiled back, thinking how cute he looked with an apron tied around his waist.

Get a grip Layla, you don't even know this guy. Yes, he saved your life, but you're still a captive.

She shrugged. "I woke up and it just smelled so good, I followed the scent to the kitchen." She refrained from saying she also had a gazillion questions.

One thing at a time, Layla.

"It's called *Fesenjan*," He turned back to the pot and gave it another stir. "It's a traditional Persian stew made with pomegranate, chicken, walnuts, onions, saffron, cinnamon, and a pinch of sugar. Are you hungry?"

"Starved. Who taught you to cook?"

"My mother. This should be ready soon. Why don't you sit down?"

"You're lucky. My mother's gone."

"So is mine."

They stared at each other, taken aback by each other's candid answer.

Layla blinked back the sudden tears and took a deep breath. "I-I have some questions. I hardly know where to start."

Cyrus pulled out a chair for her at the kitchen table. "Start with the first one." He sat across from her.

She sat, folding her hands on the table. "What's your name? I can't very well call you Superman."

"Superman?" He raised a dark eyebrow.

"Oh, I've been calling you Superman in my head." Her cheeks must have been beet red. "Um—the way you rescued me from that guard. You kinda swooped in like a superhero."

The dimple in his chin hollowed out with his slow grin.

She dropped her eyes in embarrassment.

He's way too good looking. Every time he smiles, I can't even form a coherent question.

"I like that." The dimple in his chin grew even deeper.

"Really?" she breathed.

"Really." His eyes danced with amusement.

Shite. Her favorite curse word she'd inherited from her Scottish father popped into her head. *A smile like his could bring a woman to her knees. Not good, Layla. He may have rescued you from Mohammed but he's still on "the other side".* She pushed her constant stream of conflicting thoughts away. "Oh, for God's sake, please tell me your name," she blurted.

"Cyrus Hassani at your service." He bowed his head. "What would you like to know about me? Unlike you Americans, I don't have a Social Security card with my entire life's information."

Her back straightened at the smirk that crossed his face. He'd just reminded her of the great divide between them. "Mr. Hassani, I would like to properly thank you for saving me from—from…" She gripped her hands together as a memory of Mohammed's brutality flashed through her mind. "I am beholden to you. Would you tell me a little bit about yourself so that I may understand more about," she looked around, "all of this?"

Cyrus rubbed the shadow of stubble on his face. "I'm 33 years old. I am not married. I was accepted to MIT and the University of Paris. I decided on Paris. I hold a degree in nuclear physics from there. I also have a law degree from the Imam Mohammad Bagher University, here in Tehran. I was conscripted by the Ministry of Intelligence and Security when I graduated, and since then I have risen to the rank of attaché to an important government official.

"My father teaches nuclear physics at MIT," said Layla.

"Does he? What a coincidence." His expression revealed nothing of what he was thinking.

"How or why am I here in this house?"

"You're here for your own protection. My assignment is to keep you safe from harm until your release." A smile settled on his lips. "Shall I continue?"

"Yes, please do." She couldn't help but gaze into his beautiful green eyes.

"My favorite movie is *The Godfather*, although technically it's a tie with *Godfather Two*. My favorite ice cream is chocolate, and I like my coffee black—no sugar. How am I doing?"

She giggled. "Good. You're doing well. That wasn't so hard, was it? Although, I must admit it sounds a bit like a speed-dating intro."

His laughter filled the room. "I suppose the presentation might have seemed a bit canned. You're welcome by the way."

She must have looked at him perplexed because he chuckled again.

"For rescuing you. You're welcome."

"Oh!" She smiled.

"And please call me Cyrus."

"All right—Cyrus." It sounded nice on her tongue. She liked it.

"What is your favorite movie?" he asked.

She grinned. "*Casablanca*, hands down."

"You are a romantic at heart," he said softly.

Her face heated again. "Is there something wrong with that?"

"No, there isn't, but life can be harder for true romantics, like you."

"Can't you be a romantic and tough as well?" she challenged.

"Spoken like a true American." His lips curved up in a smile. "Now tell me, have I passed the first hurdle with you? Have I gained your trust enough for us to be on a first name basis?"

She leaned back in the chair crossing her arms over her chest. "I appreciate your candor and I'm grateful for your rescue. I guess you are a Superman of sorts. I still have a lot more questions. I agree, first names will make this easier for both of us. Nice to meet you, Cyrus. Please, call me Layla."

"*Layla, Layla,*" he said with a grin, repeating her name melodically as if it were the lyric to a song. "A very pretty name."

"It's my name, Cyrus, not a song."

He mirrored her earlier action and leaned back in his chair, crossing his arms over his chest. "Oh, I'm surprised at you Layla. Your name is most definitely a song. By the great Eric Clapton. What you Americans now call, classic rock."

She rolled her eyes, "I know about the song. People have been singing it to me my entire life." He was getting under her skin. Oddly she enjoyed bantering with him. "I'd appreciate it if you stuck to answering my questions."

"My apologies, *Layla.*" He inclined his head. "Please continue."

"My boyfriend, Zamir, and I were abducted from Dubai. His father, Omar Kamel, is a wealthy Saudi businessman. I'm sure he's begun negotiating for our release. I want to know how Zamir is, and can you tell me how much longer we'll have to be here?"

Cyrus glanced at his watch. "Zamir is fine. In fact, he should be getting on a private jet right about now on his way to Saudi Arabia to be with his family."

A heart-wrenching pain tore through her chest. Tears blurred her vision. "I-I d-don't understand," she said around the thickness in her throat. "I'm supposed to be on that jet with him. He would never leave without me..."

Cyrus placed his hand over hers. "I'm sorry, Layla, but he did," he said in a soft voice. "Don't think too poorly of him. His father made no effort to include you in the negotiation. You could not possibly believe an Arab family would open their arms to you. You're an American Jew. Zamir is a boy who does what his parents tell him to do."

Layla stared at Cyrus, trying to process what he'd said. Taking a breath, she wiped her tears away.

Oh God, I've been such a fool!

Her poor father. She should have listened to his wisdom. She was such a stupid, silly girl to think Zamir's family would accept her.

They didn't even have the decency to pay for my release. But then they'd have to get rid of me some other way. This is so much easier.

She stared at her folded hands, trying to catch up with her thoughts. The realization she'd been left to fend for herself hit her like a punch to the gut. She took a deep shuddering breath...

You can get through this. You've come from a long line of fighters. Your grandparents are Holocaust survivors. It's time to become who you really are.

She looked up at Cyrus. His striking green eyes were filled with compassion.

Is he a friend or a foe?

This flipping gorgeous hunk of a man sitting across from her, might be her only chance out of Iran. She looked down at her hands. It was not in her DNA to use people, but under the circumstances, Cyrus might be her only hope. She had to come up with a plan.

One step at time, Layla. You can do this.

She straightened her shoulders. "I guess that's all the questions I have for now. I really am hungry, though."

"Good. Then let's eat." He stood and went to the stove, taking two bowls out of the cupboard.

She found herself unable to resist. "I hope Superman can cook as well as he rescues damsels in distress."

"Be sure to let me know what career I'm better suited to—cooking or taking down bad guys."

"Right now, I'm hoping it's cooking."

He threw his head back and laughed. "Feel free to tell me what you think.

CHAPTER 14

Cambridge, Massachusetts
December 15th
12:30 a.m.

The persistent ring of his cell phone shook Aleck out of his trance. His eyes were bloodshot from fatigue, his thoughts in turmoil as he stared at the unfamiliar number lighting his cell phone's screen. "Hello, this is Aleck Wallace."

"Dr. Wallace, please hold for the prime minister."

He waited, shaking himself awake—tension gripped his shoulders.

"Aleck?"

"Mr. Prime Minister, it's good to hear your voice. Thank you for calling me back. It's been such a long time, and I wasn't sure you'd remember me."

"Time can never dim the memories of youth, and friends do not stand on ceremony. As I recall, you called me Dodi and I called you Aleck. I think it appropriate that we resume that familiarity."

Aleck sighed with relief. "Of course, Dodi."

"Good. Now before we continue our chat, old friend…"

A knock echoed from the kitchen. "Dodi, I'm sorry to interrupt, but someone is knocking at my back door. I can't imagine who it might be, but I need to find out."

"It's okay, Aleck. I was just about to tell you that I've sent someone to you. Go answer the door and call me back. Don't worry. I had a feeling this was important, so I've made arrangements for us to talk. Go now." Aleck heard the click of the line going dead.

Rising from his chair, he went to the kitchen door and asked through the window, "Can I help you?"

"Don't be afraid, Dr. Wallace. The prime minister sent me."

Aleck opened the door and stood back to allow the man entry.

"Thank you, sir." The man was dressed in a white parka and white jeans, his attire seemed a form of camouflage, worn so he would blend in with the snowy landscape outside. "Please don't be afraid, Dr. Wallace. I've brought you a secure phone that will allow you to have a private conversation with the prime minister. My name is Aram, and I belong to an ultra-secret division of Mossad that functions here in the United States. Please allow me to call the prime minister now. He wishes to speak with you about what is planned."

The agent pulled out a cell phone and pressed a button. Dodi answered right away.

Aleck filled him in on the events that had led to his call. It was bizarre, but the prime minister seemed aware of Layla's kidnapping.

"This is a lot to discuss in such a brief call," Dodi said after Aleck finished relating everything he knew. "I want you to know that I would never abandon the daughter of Rebecca Rose, may she rest in peace. I have a proposal to make to you. I'm offering you my help personally, and I'm offering you the help of the state of Israel. But before we discuss our options and devise a plan, we need to get you out of the United States and get you to Israel. We need to make sure you don't become a target for blackmail. We don't have much time and we need to act quickly. The FBI is going to figure out your value sooner than later. You need to pack a bag and leave now with Aram. He will see you safely to a private jet at Logan Airport. Aleck, you need to make a decision, and you need to make it now."

"There is only one decision available to me, and that is to take you up on your offer, Dodi. My daughter's life is the most important thing to me. I will do anything to see her to safety."

"Good, then we're in agreement. Aram will help you in any way he can. I look forward to seeing you in Israel. Pass the phone back to Aram, and I will instruct him." Aleck couldn't hide a sigh of relief. "Thank you, sir."

"My friend, call me Dodi. *Le'heet'ra'ote*, until we meet again."

Leaving Aram and Dodi to their conversation, he headed upstairs to pack. For the first time since he'd learned of Layla's kidnapping, a tiny ember of hope sparked in his heart.

An hour later, a fleet of black SUVs arrived on Huron Avenue, pulling to the curb in front of Aleck's red brick Colonial home. Agent Jackson jumped out of one of the SUVs and strode up the walkway between snow-covered flowerbeds to the front door. The entire house was in darkness. No lights were on inside or out. Strange, considering every other house on the street was decorated with colorful twinkling Christmas lights. He rang the doorbell and waited, then knocked a few times. No one came to the door.

He spoke into the button on his lapel. "Go around the back. We need to get inside."

The two other agents ran to the back. In a few minutes the lights came on in the house, and one of the men opened the front door.

"He's gone, Curtis. It looks like he packed his things and left in a hurry."

"Shit! Show me." Curtis followed his men upstairs to the master bedroom. The room looked as if a tornado had passed through. Discarded clothing lay strewn across the bed and the floor. The open closet revealed even more disarray. It looked as if someone had been carelessly casting aside unnecessary items, trying to decide what was important to pack. He looked about the room and saw faded spots on the wall where pictures had hung.

Curtis pulled out his cell phone and made a call. "Sir, it seems the professor's packed his things and left." He listened. "No, there doesn't seem to be any signs of struggle. It looks methodical, as if he picked and chose what to take. I don't think the Iranians were here." Curtis held the phone away from his ear as his superior's curses rang out. "Yes, sir, I'll see that all passenger lists for all commercial flights are checked. We'll get him. He can't have gotten far."

Onboard the Gulfstream 550, Aleck took the satellite phone Aram handed him.

"Dodi?"

"Aleck, good, I'm pleased we were able to get you out of Boston without incident. My field agents tell me the FBI arrived at your home a few minutes ago to place you into protective custody. The good news is they haven't a clue as to your whereabouts or your destination."

"Any news about my daughter?"

"No, Aleck, not yet, but don't worry. I've set the wheels in motion. We are activating a deep-cover mole, a man whom we know will do everything he can to keep Layla safe and get her out of Iran. Understand, Aleck, this man is one of Israel's greatest assets, and this is a great sacrifice. Once our man in Tehran goes active and his cover is blown, his life will be forfeit. There will be only one way out, one possibility left, for him and your daughter to get out of Iran. They will be hunted, but he is a very resourceful agent."

"But won't this put Layla in extreme peril?"

"Layla is already in extreme peril. Once the Iranians figure out who you are, Layla will become a pawn in a deadly game. They will never let her go."

"Dear God! How are you going to get them out of Iran?"

"We have a plan, Aleck. Once you're safely on Israeli soil, I will explain all of it to you. In the meantime, get some sleep. We have many things to do when you get here. You won't be any use to your daughter if you're not thinking clearly. Rest well, my old friend."

CHAPTER 15

It was laundry day.

Cyrus had gone out that morning to take care of what he told her was personal business. He'd warned her not to do anything that might draw attention to the house. The drapes were to remain closed, and she was to stay away from the windows.

She decided to keep busy or she would go bonkers.

Layla normally hated doing laundry but since she had nothing else to do, she pulled all the linens off her bed. She wore her towel wrapped snuggly around her. With nothing else to wear, she was glad for some private time so she could wash her clothes while Cyrus was away. She'd hoped to wash Cyrus's sheets as well but the door to his bedroom was locked.

She'd already explored the house, aside from the modern furniture, linens, and food in the kitchen there were no books or a TV to pass the time and no computer or phone that she could use to try to reach out to her father.

Her stomach growled and she padded into the kitchen and heated up some of the delicious stew Cyrus had made the night before. Cyrus certainly knew his way around a kitchen. At least she wouldn't starve as his prisoner.

Am I his prisoner?

She wasn't quite sure what she was, nor what he was. He'd saved her life, rescued her from that hell hole prison and brought her here. But she wasn't free to leave the country, or even go outside. Hell, he'd even told her to stay away from the windows and doors. She had no idea what his mission was as far as she was concerned. If Zamir's father had paid Zamir's ransom, why were they keeping her? Was it because she was American? Were they hoping to gain something from the US government in return for her release?

She sighed as she washed her bowl and spoon and set them in the dish drainer. She took her cup of tea into the living room and tucked her feet under her as she pondered her mysterious Superman/Warden.

Cyrus seemed intent on keeping her safe, so for the time being, she would follow his instructions and try to get to know him better. Her mind wandered to their conversation the night before. He had been charming and kind…

And really cute and funny.

Yes, he certainly was good looking. But was he being so nice because of his job or did he actually care about her welfare? She hoped he did care. Then maybe he'd help her get out of here. But if he did help her, what would become of him? Would his superiors punish him or worse if he helped her escape?

She didn't want Cyrus to get hurt…

Oh, God, what a mess I'm in!

All because she'd foolishly followed her heart and Zamir.

Her heart wrenched at Zamir's betrayal. And she was not so naïve to think otherwise. Zamir's parents were rich and had many connections. They could have gotten her out. But they had chosen not to because they didn't think she was good enough for their son. Or rather, that she was Jewish and therefore, unacceptable as a wife for their son.

It was all just a fantasy.

Zamir was wealthy, had traveled all over the world in first-class comfort. Everything had been handed to him on a silver—no golden platter. Yes, he was handsome and super smart, which only added to his appeal. He could have had any woman and yet he'd chosen her. It had gone to her head. Looking back, she realized there had always been signs that he wasn't the one.

His complete disregard over the cost of things had been an ongoing source of tension between them. He didn't think twice about whipping out his credit card and buying something on a whim. He was generous with her as well, but if she refused a trinket, it usually led to an argument.

She wasn't poor by any means, but she certainly didn't come from unbridled wealth. Her mother's death had made her even more determined to make her family proud. She'd worked part time jobs throughout high school and volunteered for so many charities she couldn't fit them all into her college application. Not to mention, she'd worked her butt off to get her scholarship. Her strong work ethic was something her father had instilled in her. And she was damn proud of her accomplishments.

Then there was their intimacy, or lack thereof. They'd certainly kissed and fooled around, but they'd never actually had sex because of her promise to her mother.

Her mom wanted her to save herself for the man she truly loved.

She'd hesitated with Zamir because she hadn't been sure about her feelings for him. He'd been vocal about his feelings for her. But sometimes she'd catch him staring at other girls on campus and she'd heard from a few friends that he flirted a lot when she wasn't around. All reasons why she'd hesitated. She didn't want to have any doubts with the man she made love with. And so, she told Zamir that she wanted to wait. She wanted to see what happened over the Holidays.

A snort of bitter laughter escaped her.

So much for that.

Looking back, she was relieved she hadn't had sex with him. After that disastrous dinner with his parents, it was equally clear to her that his mother and father would never have accepted her. His mother had made her disdain clear. She would have done whatever it took to sabotage her relationship with Zamir. His parents certainly proved that by not paying for Layla's ransom.

Let it go.

She wiped the tears from her eyes. That was Cyrus's advice as well. She had to let it go. Zamir belonged in her past. And her future remained uncertain.

Worry about her father consumed her. Guilt besieged her. He had warned her not to go to Dubai. Why hadn't she listened to him? Maybe she could convince Cyrus to let her call her dad and let him know she was safe. She couldn't bear the thought of her father worrying about her. He'd been through too much tragedy in his life.

She clutched her hands together as she tried to think of what to do. Her only hope was Cyrus, a virtual stranger, a man she knew little about. The more she thought about him, the more she wondered who he really was. He didn't seem like a religious fanatic, although she'd seen him praying first thing in the morning. He also didn't seem to be a blind follower, a cold-hearted killer, or a man of war. He seemed reasonable, thoughtful; a person capable of empathy. At the same time, he seemed to be hiding something, able to turn himself off and on at will. His green eyes were mesmerizing but unreadable. She couldn't put her finger on it.

Not that you're such a great reader of character, considering how you misread Zamir. But to be fair, Zamir was a boy, his future controlled by his parents.

85

Cyrus was a man and her only lifeline. She had no choice. She would have to place her trust in him for the time being. More importantly, she had to work on getting to know him and gaining his trust. That certainly wouldn't be a hardship, considering how gorgeous he was. She yawned, and pulled the woolen throw over her. There was so much to think about, and she didn't know where to start. Her eyes grew heavy as she settled back against the pillows. Her drowsy mind floated once again to Cyrus and how kind he'd been to her. How attentive. She closed her eyes and remembered his smile.

I don't care what you say, Cyrus, you are my Superman...

Cyrus returned to the house with a dark cloud hanging over his head. Pressure was mounting. Jalal wanted information. The man had an agenda, and he clearly thought with Layla he had stumbled upon some kind of rare bargaining chip, someone he could use against the Americans.

He thinks my having sex with her will unlock state secrets like a password on a computer. It's insane.

He unlocked the back door leading to the laundry room and into the kitchen. It was dark, except for the dim light coming from the stove. He set the bags of clothes and necessities he'd purchased on the kitchen table. The hairs on the back of his neck stood on end. Something was wrong. And then he heard it. A scream.

Layla!

He pulled out his gun and ran toward the living room prepared to do battle with her attackers. Rushing in, his eyes flew to Layla thrashing on the couch, her legs tangled up in a blanket. His eyes scanned the room for any threat. No one else was there.

"Stop. Please stop!"

He ran to Layla, tucking his gun back in its holster. Throwing the blanket on the floor, he pulled her into his arms and held tight. "It's all right Layla. It's going to be all right," he soothed, rocking her back and forth. "You're safe now. I promise."

Her luminous eyes opened and gazed at him in cloudy confusion.

"Cyrus, you saved me," she whispered. "Thank you."

"You're welcome." He smiled and caressed her tear-stained cheek.

"He was there—"

"Who was there, my beauty?

M-Mohammad. He was going to—to." She burst into tears again and buried her face in his neck.

"Shh…He can't hurt you ever again. I promise. It was just a bad dream. You're safe now."

"Safe…"

He didn't know how long he'd sat there holding her as she wept. Her tears were raw and broken, as though she didn't have the words to explain her pain. He'd seen the impact of trauma, hell, he'd lived it first-hand. Everyone dealt with it in their own way. But this brave young woman had remained strong through the face of it all, had been kidnapped by association, forced to put up with harsh treatment in prison and had fought off Mohammad with everything she had, and now, in the aftermath, the horrific ordeal she'd gone through shattered the wall of self-protection she'd constructed around herself.

As he continued to hold her tightly against his chest, whispering soothing words into her ear, caressing her hair and back, Cyrus realized that something had shifted inside him. Something he couldn't yet fathom. But this slip of a girl had begun to wind her way around his heart, and he had no idea what he was going to do about it.

CHAPTER 16

Mr. Banai waited until after *Maghrib*, the prayer time that falls after sunset. He locked the door of his optometry shop and left while the last rays of sunlight were beginning to fade. Gathering his wool scarf close around his neck, he walked slowly up the hill from the business district to the neighborhood of homes dotting the hills. The wealthy neighborhood once known as Saltanat Abad, named for the Pahlavi monarchy that had built it, held many mansions. After the revolution, it was renamed the Pasdaran District, an informal name celebrating the Army of the Guardians of the Islamic Revolution, the IRGC. Most of the original owners of the beautiful villas fled after the revolution or became victims of the tribunals that eliminated enemies of the state. The old owners were replaced by collaborators with the IRGC. Through these proxies, the Revolutionary Guard controlled the economy of Iran, lining their pockets with billions of dollars of revenue from all manner of business, whether construction, agriculture, chemicals, or oil.

The elderly man stopped for a moment to catch his breath. It probably would have been wiser to hire a taxi, but he rarely got out of his shop, and his doctor had advised him to get more fresh air and exercise. The cold evening made it a good idea to walk. Fewer people out and about to witness what he did or where he went.

He checked the piece of paper in his coat pocket again, confirming the address. A few blocks later, he arrived at the house. Peering through the gate, he saw a moderate-sized, European-style home with a red-tiled roof. He opened the gate and stepped carefully along a worn, brick pathway to the front door. The yard sported numerous trees now slumbering in winter, their branches bare and leafless. He could easily imagine the garden in summer, filled with flowers, a green sloping lawn, and an abundance of fruit-filled trees, their branches weighted with pomegranates, cherries, figs, apricots and plums. The house had definitely seen better days. He supposed a young man with no wife and children could not be bothered with the upkeep necessary to keep an old home in good repair. A sadness pervaded his thoughts as he envisioned a house that, in all likelihood, had once echoed with the laughter of children and had once been the center of a family's world.

The house was shrouded in darkness. On shaky legs, from nerves, Mr. Banai combed the stoop, wondering where he might leave the small package he carried in his coat pocket. He knocked at the front door, not expecting an answer.

A screech of tires shattered the quiet when a black SUV pulled into the driveway and stopped. The old man's eyes opened wide in alarm. He took a deep breath to calm his racing heart. Absent-mindedly, he clutched the eyeglass case in his pocket.

Cyrus jumped from the backseat of the car and ordered his driver to wait. He ran up the steps to where Mr. Banai stood, his brows raised in question. "Mr. Banai, what are you doing here? Is there something I can do for you?"

"Ah, Mr. Hassani, good evening to you. I am pleased to see you. The new eyeglasses you ordered are ready. I thought you might have forgotten to pick them up. I thought you might need them."

"My new eyeglasses?" The young man's forehead creased in a momentary frown, then cleared. "Oh, those glasses. You're right, I'd forgotten about them."

Mr. Banai smiled, nodding. "The special lenses arrived sooner than I expected, and it occurred to me you might have need of them. I didn't want you to wait. I thought it far too important you should have them." He reached in his pocket, his eyes never leaving Cyrus's face as he pulled out the eyeglass case and handed it to him. He made a slight bow of his head, indicating his task completed.

"Well, I'll be making my way home now. If you have any problems with them, please let me know. I will do my best to fix them."

Cyrus placed his hand on the old man's arm, staying his departure. "Wait, Mr. Banai, I'm extremely grateful for your devotion. I also think it's too cold for you to be walking about. Please, let my driver give you a lift home."

"I could not possibly inconvenience you."

"I will not hear otherwise. You have always made yourself available for me, and I appreciate it. Please?" He took Mr. Banai's arm and led him to the Range Rover. "Saeed, please, give this gentleman a ride home and come back for me in an hour."

He watched the SUV drive away, gripping the glasses case in his hand. Collecting his mail, he hurried into the house, aware he didn't have much time before Saeed's return. In the darkness, he walked in silence down the hallway leading to the interior spaces of the home. He walked past the unused formal reception rooms, where muslin-draped furniture and rolled Persian rugs cluttered the floor. Like the memories he tried to forget, these objects were all that were left of his family and a world long gone.

What was left of his family was no longer in Iran. After his father's suicide, he became the head of the household. He had his mother and sister to take care of. They sold what was left of their mother's jewelry and barely managed to hold onto the villa, the dream home that his architect father had designed and built. He made his way upstairs to his father's study, the memories of that day forever emblazoned in his mind. Crossing the threshold, he walked slowly to his father's desk. He laid his hand on the elegant dark wood, now covered in inches of dust.

Why, Father? Why couldn't you stay for us?

He shook his head, knowing he would never have the answer. His father's suicide letter had only left him with more questions.

At least he'd been able to take care of his beloved mother and sister.

A full scholarship had enabled Cyrus to attend the National Institute for Nuclear Science and Technology in Paris and it was there that his life had taken another turn. A Mossad agent had approached him his first year of university. He'd known everything there was to know about Cyrus and his family. Everything. He'd made him an offer and Cyrus accepted. Thirteen years later, Cyrus had no regrets. When he joined Mossad, he'd insisted on one precondition—to get his mother and sister out of Iran and set them up with a new life in Israel. Considering Cyrus to be a once in a lifetime opportunity, Israel agreed.

The police report read that on a vacation to the Caspian Sea, his mother and sister had taken a small catamaran out for a sail despite warnings of a possible storm. The sudden appearance of the storm must have taken them by surprise. The small catamaran, no match for the gale-force winds or the walls of water that engulfed it, must have capsized. When notified, Cyrus rushed home from Paris. Their bodies were never found.

The truth was Mossad had kept their part of the bargain and staged their deaths. The catamaran was intentionally capsized, and the two women were safely boarded onto a fishing boat and sailed up the coast to Azerbaijan. Two days later they were flown to Israel. Cyrus hadn't seen them since, but he periodically received messages from them and knew they were safe and content in Israel.

Having long ago made peace with the loss of his family, he progressed through the rooms, oblivious to the ghosts that lurked in the shadows, and made his way to the kitchen in the back of the house. Another gift from Israel. Enough money for him to keep the family home. The only connection he had left to his father.

He filled a tea kettle and lit the stove before sitting down at the kitchen table. He removed the glasses case from his pocket and opened it. Inside were a pair of ordinary reading glasses, displaying no outward sign of uniqueness.

From his pocket he took out a leather bound notebook, inside the fold was a pen and a pair of tweezers. He pulled both out and set them on the table. He removed the glasses and set them beside the notebook. With the tweezers, he lifted the protective liner in the case where he found another lens. Carefully, he lifted the delicate protective shield from the lens and affixed the lens to the reading glasses. He put on the glasses and sixty seconds later, an unknown to the world technology revealed itself. A transmission appeared before his eyes. He picked up the pen and began to write. Every sixty seconds a new message appeared, replacing the one before it. The invisible lens cover was both a computer and a video camera, the thinnest in the world. The advanced nanotechnology enabled communication through a satellite at an undetectable frequency exclusive to itself, capable of seeing what the wearer sees in real time and capable of directing events from thousands of miles away.

Ignoring the whistling of the boiling teapot that sent plumes of steam into the air. He remained focused on his task, his forehead damp with sweat despite the chilly temperature in the kitchen. When the last message disappeared from his vision, he removed the glasses and wiped his forehead with his sleeve. He stared straight ahead. What he'd just read didn't make sense—impossible to comprehend. Thirteen years of a carefully constructed career and cover were about to be compromised, and all because of a red-haired American girl who'd upended his life the moment he'd met her.

The continued whistling of the teapot broke his reverie, and he rose and turned it off. He stuffed the pad deep in his coat pocket with the glasses and their case. He would rather have destroyed the glasses, but his directions were clear. All future communications were to be transmitted through the glasses. Once he and the girl were in a secure location, he would receive his next set of instructions.

He gave a bitter laugh. There was no such thing as a "secure" location. At least not while he was still in Iran with Layla. His new orders would plunge him into a world where death would pursue him at every turn. Layla's presence had compromised his life and his mission. He had no idea why she was so important—but suspected her father was a person of interest, an asset that must not fall into Iranian hands. He considered what Layla had told him about her father. "He's a nuclear physicist at MIT."

Ironic considering he'd gotten accepted into MIT as well but had opted for Paris because it was closer to his mother and sister. He'd heard of Aleck Wallace, had read some of his research papers. The Scottish born physicist was known for encouraging bright young students. Cyrus had done some of his own digging and had found out that Wallace had worked for the US government before leaving his post and accepting a position at MIT. Wallace's academic focus was in theory. He taught mostly graduate students. Nothing jaw dropping.

Wallace was married to a Jewish woman, named Rebecca. They had one daughter, Layla. Rebecca died of uterine cancer. Layla was twelve when it happened. Shortly after, Rebecca's death, Aleck made the move to MIT. Was his wife's death the reason why he left his research post for a life in academia?

Cyrus couldn't find anything detailed from his initial search other than Wallace had worked in a highly classified department. Unfortunately, he hadn't had time to do any deep dives. And he knew Jalal was keeping an eye on him. Cyrus had to be careful.

Cyrus's orders from Mossad had been clear. Aleck Wallace must not become a target for blackmail. He had to get Layla out of Iran, which would mean compromising a decade of deep cover. All that work down the tubes. Helping Layla escape from Iran was treason, he would never be able to return to Iran.

An idea had begun to form in his mind, and he needed to talk to Layla without observers, without their conversation being recorded. There was only one way to do that, and he hoped she would agree without fighting him on it.

The ticking of the clock reminded him that time was running out. He needed to pack a few things before Saeed returned.

CHAPTER 17

Tehran, Iran
December 17th

What am I going to do about Superman?

Layla turned on the water in the master bath and poured in liquid soap. No bubble bath foam so it would have to do. Exhausted from crying her heart out in Cyrus's arms last night she'd slept in and had missed his leaving that morning. He'd left her a note beside the coffee pot, saying he had some business to take care of and would be back by evening. It didn't matter in any case. Embarrassed by her weep fest and the fact that he'd carried her up to bed, she needed some time to herself to gather her thoughts.

In addition to holding her most of the night, Cyrus had left a bag of new clothes and underthings and toiletries on the counter next to the note.

He's perfect. He's too damn perfect.

Which only confused matters more. She was developing a serious crush on Superman and it would only lead to trouble. If she fell hard for him then what? Yes, he saved her life but now he was her sort-of captor. She had no idea how long he'd keep her cooped up in this house. The only way she could safely get out of the country was with Cyrus's help. And the only way she could think of to convince him, was the old-fashioned way...

Seduction.

Yeah, like he'd fall for me anyway. He's way older, and sophisticated. He said he wasn't married but he probably has tons of women on the side. Like some sort of Iranian James Bond. Besides, I made a promise to Mom...

But everything had changed. Two weeks ago, she was so excited about her trip to Dubai with Zamir. Now, because of Zamir and his parents, she'd

95

been kidnapped, nearly raped, beaten, scared out of her mind, and stuck in a house in the middle of nowhere in a country with a justice system that could very well shove her back in prison and throw away the key.

Mom, please forgive me. I don't know what else to do to get out of here.

Layla stepped into the steaming tub and sighed as the hot, soapy water welcomed her. She closed her eyes and leaned her head against the cool tile wall.

A virgin seducing an older man!

She snorted with laughter. He'd figure out what she was up to in no time. But what if she made him fall in love with her?

How the hell do I do that?

Even worse, what if she fell in love with Cyrus? She was already suffering from a mega crush on him, thanks to his Mr. Hottie good looks and his Superman ways…Cyrus was the very opposite of Zamir—courageous, tough, and super intense.

No, if this plan were to work, she'd have to make Cyrus fall in love with her, but she could not fall in love with him.

Absolutely not!

Besides, she'd just been screwed over by one man, she refused to let that happen again.

I can't fall for him. I can't fall for him. I can't fall for him…

She began to hum the words out loud like a chant.

"You can't fall for whom?"

Layla's eyes flew open and she let out a yelp of surprise. Crossing her arms over her chest and drawing her knees up close she glared at Cyrus. "How dare you barge in here. You didn't even knock!"

"I did knock but you were humming some silly American pop song." Cyrus grinned. He closed the door, placed his finger over his lips, and handed her a note.

Please don't say anything. The entire house is bugged and rigged with cameras. The only safe place to talk is in the shower. With the water running it will be sound-proof. What I have to tell you is very important. I want you to invite me to take a shower with you. Pretend that you're trying to seduce me. There are cameras and recording devices just outside the bathroom that will pick that up. Will you trust me? Please?

Layla gulped. Here she was trying to figure out how to seduce him and he handed her a note to do just that. In the shower no less!

Don't be a ninny! The note said he only wants to talk to you.

She glanced at him. He was staring at her with that intense look in his eyes. But he hadn't moved an inch. He'd simply handed her the note and stood back, his hands in his pockets. Looking all gorgeous and James Bond-ish.

What if this is my only chance? Maybe he has orders to turn me over to someone else, someone like Mohammed. Or maybe he's supposed to take me back to jail. What would I do then? The fact that he wants to talk to me privately means he must care about me a little bit…

Layla blew out a breath. *Well, I didn't get an A in high school drama for nothing. It's show time.*

She turned to him and gave him a little nod.

Cyrus let go of the breath he'd been holding at Layla's nod of agreement. He slid open the shower door and turned on the water. Three jet sprays began to steam up the shower in a matter of seconds. He turned back to Layla as she unfolded her legs and stood in the tub. And he forgot to breathe again. The filmy soap bubbles clung to her peachy cream skin like glittering diamonds.

She was petite, but everything about her was perfect from her full breasts to her tiny waist to the gentle curve of her hips. She reached up to the top knot of her hair and pulled the elastic, letting the red curls cascade down her back she shook out the luscious waves. She smiled at him, a glorious smile, a smile he'd never seen before and one he would never forget.

"I want you, Cyrus."

Good girl! He winked at her. She'd spoken loudly enough so that the recording devices would pick up her voice.

"I've never wanted a man more than I want you." She grinned. "Please make me yours."

"I've been waiting to hear those words from you since the moment I laid eyes on you, my beautiful Layla. You are the most desirable woman I have ever met."

She gaped at him for a moment. Her eyes were as wide as saucers and her mouth had formed into an O.

He almost hooted with laughter at her expression. Well, he had to put on a show for the bugs, didn't he?

She seemed to get a hold of herself once more and held out her arms. "You're the hottest guy ever, Cyrus. I WANT YOU INSIDE ME NOW!"

Now, it was his turn to be shocked. Layla had practically yelled that last sentence.

It was time to put an end to this outrageous conversation. He cleared his throat and lifted her out of the tub, carrying her into the glass shower. Setting her down, he stepped out and quickly shed his clothes. He stepped in again and closed the shower door.

Layla immediately wrapped her arms around him, pressing her luscious little body against his. Her pouty lips touched his in a sweet kiss, an invitation.

Shit! I can't take advantage of her like this.

He groaned, trying to pull away but she wrapped one leg around him and rubbed herself against him.

"You don't have to do this," he whispered. "I just needed a safe place for us to talk."

She stepped back from him, her eyes wide with hurt. "You don't want me?"

"Of course, I want you. I would be made of stone, if I didn't."

"So, you only want me because I'm convenient. Because, I'm right here naked in the shower with you." She crossed her arms over her chest and began to tap her foot on the tile. "Is it my hair?" She flung her wet hair over her shoulders. "You're used to sultry, dark-haired women not some freckled red-head."

He chuckled. God, she was stubborn. And gorgeous. Too gorgeous for his peace of mind. "No, that's not what I meant?"

"Then what did you mean?"

"I'm trying to be an honorable man here."

Her eyes widened at that. "You mean you do want me?"

"Yes. You're beautiful Layla. Stunning. Brave. Smart. Funny. Of course, I want you."

She blushed but her smile could have lit up the night sky. She stepped closer to him and her arms wrapped around his waist, her pebbled nipples teased the hair on his chest.

"Thank you," she whispered. Her gaze was fathomless.

"You're welcome," he whispered back.

She pulled his head down, her soft lips touching his once more.

This time he didn't stop himself. He kissed her. Deeply. Passionately. Lifting her curvy bottom, he pressed her against the marble tile. Her legs wrapped around him. He wanted to kiss her forever. He wanted to carry her to the bedroom and lay her down and kiss every part of her body. But he couldn't. He had to tell her the truth.

He pulled away and gazed down at the delicate beauty of her face. Her eyes were closed, her lips swollen. She whimpered and tried to pull his face back to hers. He touched her lips with his finger, and she opened her eyes. Those stunning eyes. "I have to tell you something. Please give me a few minutes."

She nodded and holding her hand he led her to the built-in marble bench. Sitting down next to her, he raised her hand to his lips and kissed it.

"Layla, I'm not who you think I am."

With his confession, he would literally be placing both their lives in her hands.

Surprise mixed with curiosity clouded her eyes. "What do you mean?"

"I'm a spy for Israel. I'm a deep-cover agent for Mossad."

"That's impossible. You're a Muslim. I saw you praying. I know you were born in Iran. Your accent is not Israeli, it's Iranian. You're lying."

"That part is true. I was born in Iran." He closed his eyes. "This story is going to take a while to tell." Cyrus studied Layla's face as he spoke. "Fourteen years ago, I was granted a scholarship to study at the National Institute for Nuclear Science and Technology in Paris. Iran's nuclear program began in the 1950s. However, it was abandoned after the revolution. Only after the war with Iraq did the Ayatollah in earnest throw the weight of our resources into developing a nuclear program. Desperate for nuclear scientists, the government allowed me to study in France. In Paris, I befriended another student, a Jew. I shared with him a secret—both my maternal grandparents were Jews. My mother met my father at university in Paris, and they married. My father, a Muslim architect, came from a wealthy family who lost everything after the fall of the Shah. In Islam, if either parent is Muslim, any child born from their union is a Muslim. In Judaism, as you know, the mother is the determining factor. I am considered by both religions to be one of theirs. I have chosen to identify as a Jew." He paused and stole a breath.

"When my mother converted to Islam, her family disinherited her. As far as the world was concerned, she'd left her past behind like a snake shedding its skin. What no one knew, including my father, was that her new skin was no different from her old skin. In her heart, she was still a Jew. That Jewishness, part of my sister's and my DNA, she nurtured and kept alive with her stories about the history of Persian Jews, and particularly her identification with Esther, the Jewish queen who saved her people from genocidal annihilation."

"You have a sister?" Layla whispered. "Where is she?"

"I can't tell you. Or I'd have to kill you."

"You're not serious?" she gasped, pulling away from him.

He reached for her shoulders, pulling her back. "I'm sorry, Layla."

She shivered and he smoothed her hair away from her face.

"You're cold."

"I'm okay."

He turned the heat up on the water. "This is not a game, Layla. I know we had fun back there playing pretend, but this is serious. Life and death stuff. You have to trust me no matter what. You cannot question me, or I won't be able to get us out of this mess alive."

She nodded. "I'm sorry. You're right. I-I was just curious…it's nice that you have a sister. It makes you seem less – James Bond-ish."

He burst out laughing at that. "I thought I was Superman. Now I'm James Bond?"

"It's because you're so intense and all with those green eyes of yours. Like you're in some spy movie—you're the Iranian James Bond."

He ran a finger down her check. "What am I going to do with you?"

Her lips quirked up into a smile. "I hope you're going to get me out of this mess alive, like you promised."

He blew out a breath. "I will or die trying."

She cupped his face in her hands. "Please don't say that. I don't want you to die," she whispered. "Tell me the rest of the story."

"Over time my friend seized on my discontent with the regime, suggesting I might want to defect and get out of Iran, insinuating I might even play an important role in the future of the world. I was young, ambitious. I wanted to live in a free society like I experienced in Paris. I hated the religiously intolerant world of the mullahs. Alain, my friend, had become a *sayanim*, a volunteer helper. *Sayanim* are Jews that live outside Israel. Usually they have friends or relatives in Israel that have brought them to the attention of Mossad. They live in the diaspora—car dealers, secretaries, doctors. You name the career or business and they exist. Mossad knows they are sympathetic to our cause. Most will do whatever is necessary to help Israel survive. Mossad never puts them in danger. In fact, often they don't even know they are helping Israel. They provide a secret army, one that has proven to be useful when needed.

"Alain introduced me to a man, a *katsa* for Mossad. *Katsas* are recruiters, agents who gather spying assets for Israel. I confided in him I might want to seek asylum in Israel. His eyes lit up. I was a dream-come-true, a native willing to betray his country. He promised he would submit my case to his superiors. It didn't take long for the Israelis to decide." He closed his eyes, remembering it all as if it were yesterday.

He continued. "Mossad knew they'd hit the mother lode with me. Never in their wildest dreams did they think they'd ever have a deep-cover agent in Iran, one who would end up as an attaché to the assistant director of Oghab2, which translates to Eagle2. It's almost impossible to imagine the Israelis with a mole with that kind of access. Oghab2 is responsible for the security of Iran's nuclear program, facilities, and the scientists who work in them. I have complete access to those facilities.

"Of course, I didn't start out with that position when I began spying for Israel. In fact, I told my *katsa* I didn't want to stay in Iran. I only wanted to defect. Although they claimed otherwise, Mossad never intended to give me a choice. They knew I was their golden ticket. I fought them tooth and nail, but in the end, they convinced me.

"That first year they found a look-alike to me—a doppelganger—someone who could double for me and attend classes for me at the institute in Paris. While he went to classes in Paris, I was smuggled to Israel, where I began a year of intense study and training. During that year, I learned Hebrew, hand-to-hand combat, weapons training, and intelligence gathering. To put it in simple terms, I became a mole, a spy. Apparently, I was very good and surpassed their expectations."

Layla rolled her eyes. "I have no doubt. You're the Hebrew James Bond."

He laughed. "I thought I was the Iranian James Bond."

"Well, now that I know you're Jewish…" She shrugged and smiled. "Sorry, continue your story."

"All through my university studies, as I shuttled between Paris and Tel Aviv, the thought of putting myself in such a dangerous position seemed insane. Hell, I wasn't any kind of hero. I was a student. I knew how things were in Iran—if compromised, I would hang.

"After I graduated, I returned to Tehran and enrolled at Imam Mohammad Bagher University to study for a law degree. IMBU's connection to MOIS is well known. They do their recruiting there. After receiving my law degree, I went through testing and training at the Intelligence Bureau in Hamedan, a city in western Iran. My qualifications were impossible to ignore. I came to the attention of the deputy to the Minister of Intelligence and Security, who sits on the Supreme Council. He recruited me into MOIS, the highest intelligence authority in the Islamic Republic of Iran. Because of my educational background, I rose to the position of assistant to the second in command of Oghab2, Jalal Rahimi. Jalal is a dangerous man, ruthless, but he took me under his wing. I've become the son he never had.

"For several years now, I've been instrumental in supplying Mossad with intel on everything to do with Iran's nuclear program. Personally, my mission from the start has been to prevent Iran from becoming nuclear. I guess I thought, in some small way, I was continuing the legacy of Queen Esther and saving my people, the Jewish people, from a nuclear Holocaust."

He looked at her as if discovering something about himself for the first time. "In the beginning I was still me, but over time, the Cyrus Hassani I had been disappeared. You're the first person outside of Mossad I've ever told the truth to." Cyrus paused, searching Layla's eyes for a reaction, any sign of understanding from her. He found it perplexing, but he experienced a strange relief in unburdening himself to her. He supposed it was in some way comparable to what a person feels when they confess their sins to a priest. Never had he trusted anyone with his secret, and he knew by telling her he'd placed his fate in her hands. "Obviously, there's much more to tell, but what I've told you pretty much sums it up in a nutshell."

"You were very brave, Cyrus." Layla reached for his hand. "You did something truly noble for Israel—for the world." He wasn't like any man she'd ever known. That he'd sacrificed his life and happiness for the sake of others, touched her soul. It didn't take a spy to know that by sharing the truth with her, he'd placed his life in her hands. He did this knowing the risks involved in sharing the truth with her.

Her lips trembled and she tried to fight back tears.

I think I'm already falling for him. So much for keeping my emotions out of it.

The question was, why did he tell her the truth about himself? "Cyrus, thank you for trusting me with the truth of who you are. But why are you confiding all of this in me?"

He pulled his hands away and ran his fingers through his hair. "I'm being burnt, shut down. My job is not finished here, not even close to finished. Nonetheless, I received new orders to E&E, escape and evade. No matter the cost, I must get you out of Iran. Get us both out of Iran, but you most importantly."

"How, and why me? I'm no one important. Why would Israel care so much about me getting out of Iran that they are prepared to blow your cover?"

"I don't know, at least not yet. Right now, we have to focus on getting you out of this house and getting us both to an Israeli safe house. Everything we'll need to get out of Iran will be waiting for us there."

"Can I at least get word to my father to let him know I'm okay?"

He grabbed her shoulders and shook her, his eyes flashing with anger. "Are you crazy? You have to do exactly what I tell you to do. Do you understand me? You absolutely cannot contact your father. They will have us both dead in a matter of minutes."

Okay, scratch the love thing. This guy is royally pissing me off.

Why are you so angry with me?" She pulled out of his grasp. "I didn't ask to be kidnapped or thrown in an Iranian prison or nearly raped." She wiped the tears from her eyes. "Dammit. I don't want to cry."

"I'm sorry for getting angry. I've lived and breathed this mission for the past ten years and now my cover will be blown, it's just a lot to take in. Look, your father is in Israel, all right? I shouldn't have told you that, but I don't want you crying about it. I don't know how or why, but he sure as shit isn't there on vacation."

"What is happening to my life?" She covered her mouth and shut her eyes tight, trying to keep the panic at bay. This was all too much. Her father was in Israel? What more twists and turns would be thrown at her? "Just a few weeks ago, I was an art history major at Harvard. Now, I'm in Iran with my life in danger, and my very existence has put a top Mossad agent's life in peril."

Cyrus pulled her into his embrace. "Layla, it's going to be okay. I can get us through this. Look, we've been in this shower too long. It looks suspicious. You're going to wrap your naked body around mine, and I'm going to carry you to bed. I need it to look as if we had some major sex in the shower. So put your acting hat back on. No more tears. We have to make this look good. And please for God's sake, don't blurt out anything."

She swatted his shoulder. "Fine! I'll be the next Meryl Streep! Get my academy award ready."

CHAPTER 18

Tehran, Iran
Grand Bazaar
December 18th
10:00 a.m.

The Grand Bazaar was located on Arg Square in southern Tehran. Saeed dropped Layla and Cyrus off at the main entrance known as Sabze Meydoon.

Before Saeed drove away, Cyrus said, "I'll call you when I need you. Oh, and my friend, I had a package delivered to you that I would appreciate you taking care of for me. My instructions are inside." He clapped Saeed on the back and waved him off. He took a moment to watch the Range Rover drive away.

A quick telephone call to Jalal had gained permission for the outing. Jalal had fallen for Cyrus's story that a shopping trip and a few trinkets would further cement his relationship with the girl. All women loved shopping. Cyrus informed Jalal that he'd had sex with Layla already and she was putty in his hands. Soon he'd be able to turn her. Jalal chortled about the shopping trip and praised Cyrus for his excellent work.

So far so good.

The largest bazaar in the world, with more than six miles of shops and stalls was teeming with locals and tourists. Cyrus held tightly to Layla's hand as they strolled through the marketplace. His eyes monitored everyone around them, searching for a tail as he pulled her through the crowd. Layla, wearing a dark pink scarf draped around her head and neck, craned her neck this way and that, as she gazed around her.

Stopping on occasion, Cyrus gave authenticity to their visit by pointing out architectural elements, explaining that some of the buildings, walls, and passage-ways were more than four hundred years old.

105

"A footnote in the history of Persia," he explained to her, "a land whose history and civilization dates back thousands of years before the birth of Christ."

He pointed out the domes and the towering vaulted ceilings. Sunlight poured down from the skylights like golden waterfalls shimmering with dancing dust motes. The light glowed like a halo around Layla's head. Her ethereal beauty captivated his senses. He wished he could pull off her scarf and watch the sunlight play in her gorgeous red hair.

For God sakes man, you're not on your honeymoon. Keep your wits about you!

He shook off his romantic notions and pointed out the beauty of the intricate tile and brickwork, artistically laid out in traditional Persian patterns, adapted into Islamic architecture after the Islamic conquest of Persia nearly fourteen hundred years ago.

Cyrus did his best to keep Laila engaged and calm. She was trembling beside him. He'd passed her a note that morning over breakfast explaining to her what the plan would be. She read the "love note" and squealed in delight about the proposed shopping trip, hopping onto his lap and spreading kisses all over his face. Much as he'd enjoyed her performance, he was completely on edge. He had to keep her safe and get them out of Iran before Jalal became suspicious.

Layla was mesmerized by all the sights and sounds around her. Cyrus had explained in the note that they had to make the shopping trip as real as possible. That was no problem—she was enthralled by the busy stalls and bustling shops. Even though their excursion was just for show, Layla couldn't help it. She enjoyed being in Cyrus's company.

Each corridor contained a different world. One was devoted to figs, dates, and nuts, in all varieties, both dried and fresh. In the fabric corridor, thousands of yards of fabrics of every quality and for every purpose, from embroidered needle points for upholstery to fine silks from India and China, were displayed on bolts or rolled around cardboard tubes. The scent of spices perfumed the air. It was exotic and intoxicating, the endless array of orange and yellow saffron, cumin, turmeric, and cinnamon, their pungent fragrances stimulating her senses. The myriad sights and sounds sparked her imagination. As an art history major, Layla was fascinated by the beauty of the architecture and appreciated Cyrus's knowledge. She wished they were there under different circumstances, as real tourists, enjoying a day at the bustling market.

They stopped for coffee prepared in the Turkish style, sweet and syrupy, so heavy, she tasted the grounds on her tongue. Cyrus had ordered a plate of freshly baked baklava—layers of paper-thin pastry filled with walnuts, honey, and cinnamon.

"I spent my childhood visiting these same walkways," he confided. "My mother would bring my sister and me here, and she would buy us baklava. I haven't been here in years. Here, try it?" He broke off a piece and held it to her lips.

"Umm, this is delicious," she exclaimed. Finishing the last bite, she clasped his hand, and before he could pull it away, she sucked the honey off his thumb.

His face reddened. He glanced out the window at the two men who loitered. Fortunately, they were deep in conversation. "This is Iran…you can't touch in public. Men and women never touch in public. Besides which, Jalal most likely had us followed. We're probably being watched."

She raised her brow in defiance. "How was I supposed to know that?" She looked around; her brow furrowed. "I'm clearly a foreigner. Don't they bend the rules a little for people from other countries?"

He brought his mouth close to her ear and whispered, "You need to behave. This is incredibly dangerous. Your acting back at the townhouse was Oscar-worthy, but out here, I'm in charge. I've been given a final mission in Iran, and as God is my witness, I'm going to accomplish it. Finish your coffee. Our next stop is the carpet corridor, which is the most sprawling in the bazaar. It's where our real journey will begin. It's where we'll disappear. When we get inside the shop, keep your eyes down and don't speak. Understood?"

"Understood. And please, stop growling at me and treating me like a feather-brain. I fully appreciate the gravity of our situation. And I fully comprehend how angry you are that you're being forced to abandon your mission here because of me. But let me remind you, that none of this is my fault."

Cyrus downed the rest of his coffee. "I know that Layla but give me a break. I was thrown into this mess unwittingly as well. Now, I have to get us out of it. I need you to do exactly what I tell you to do. At some point, it might be the difference between life and death."

She stared into his eyes. Those fathomless eyes. He was right. She had no hope of getting out of Iran without his help. She stood, adjusting the pink scarf around her hair and neck. "Lead the way. I'm ready."

———— ✦ ————

They continued to stroll through the arcade of shops until they reached the pavilion housing the carpet vendors. These were not little shops, but enormous showrooms where carpets hung from the walls. Rows of tables were stacked with hand-knotted rugs in a myriad of colors and patterns.

A salesman greeted them. Cyrus spoke with him in Farsi and introduced Layla as his fiancée, telling the man they were looking to purchase a carpet for their future home. They walked around the showroom inspecting carpets. Out of the corner of his eye he glanced out the window noting that one of the two men who'd been tailing them, had disappeared. His instincts on high alert, Cyrus returned his attention to the salesman and shook his head at his latest suggestion. Another man approached, introducing himself as the owner, and asked whether they would like to see some of the older, rarer carpets he kept in a private showroom in the back. Cyrus readily agreed and clasped Layla's hand as they followed the owner into a room without windows, filled with beautiful, antique Persian carpets. Without a word, the man handed Cyrus a key and slid a large carpet away from the wall, revealing a door. Nodding at Cyrus, without further ado he left the room.

With the man now gone, Cyrus dropped his backpack, removed a black *chadar* from inside, and handed it to Layla.

"Don't ask any questions. Just put this on and make sure none of your hair shows." He stuffed the pink scarf in his backpack. "As soon as you're ready, I'm going to open this door, and you're going out alone."

Her eyes widened. "You can't dump me in a strange place. You know I can't communicate. What if someone asks me a question? Besides, I thought we were in this together. Why aren't you coming with me?" Her voice rose in panic.

"Listen to me, Layla—you're going to be fine." He cupped her delicate shoulders, giving them a gentle squeeze. "I know you can do this. I have to lure those two fools away who've been following us. Listen carefully. Outside are the delivery docks where the goods ship in and out of the bazaar. Don't be afraid of the workers on the docks or the people on the streets. No one will bother a woman wearing a *chadar*. As far as men are concerned, you're invisible."

He removed sunglasses from the backpack and put them on her. He stood back appraising her with satisfaction. "Much better—those blue turquoise eyes of yours are way too alluring. When you get outside, you need to go left and keep walking. In a few blocks, you'll see an entrance back into the bazaar. Go in and cross out the other side onto the main avenue. He handed her a paper with a simple map drawn on it. "I've mapped out the directions for you. Because you can't read Persian, I've written the Persian street signs out so you can match the characters on them as you go. I've also given you landmarks to look for. When you see a clock tower between two minarets, you will have arrived at the Imam Khomeini Mosque. I promise you; you can't miss it. Wait for me there on the street. I'm going to leave this place in a hurry and lose the two guys who've been tailing us."

"But what if I get lost?" Her normally rosy cheeks had paled, the sprinkling of freckles over her nose standing in bold relief.

He drew her into his arms and kissed her with a hard and demanding kiss. When he pulled away, his eyes held hers. "I know you can do this. You're tough and you're resourceful and too fucking beautiful for your own good."

He smiled, enjoying the heat that filled her cheeks.

"Why did you kiss me like that?"

"Because I wanted to see your cheeks turn the same color as your hair, and I wanted to get your mind off the danger. Most of all," he lifted her sunglasses, "because I love seeing the fire in your eyes when you get angry."

"You better not get killed." She poked him in the chest. "And you better show up at the mosque or I'll be more than angry. I'll be spitting mad!"

"I can't wait." He grinned and replaced her sunglasses, opened the door, and nudged her out. "You've only got about ten minutes to get yourself away from the bazaar before they figure out my diversion is just a diversion, and they realize they've been hoodwinked. Now move."

After closing the door on Layla, Cyrus slid the carpet back into place, hiding the exit door. Without a word to anyone, he walked with a casual pace, leaving the back room and exiting the showroom. He walked in the opposite direction, away from where he'd sent Layla. Only one of the men was minding their post. The other hadn't returned yet.

Come on, asshole, follow me.

He quickened his pace now that he was solo and blended into the crowds, knowing the tail was after him. In the crowded passage, it proved difficult for the man to keep Cyrus in his sights, and with expert ease Cyrus chose his moment to disappear into a crowded shop and exit through a back door.

CHAPTER 19

Tehran, Iran
Grand Bizarre
December 18th
12:30 p.m.

Layla stumbled through the door in a daze, petrified she would get lost and be on her own. She looked back once, but Cyrus had disappeared back inside the carpet warehouse. Her lips still tingling from his passionate kiss and that movie-star look in those smoldering eyes of his, she hurried along the street.

He'd been right about one thing, the men loading the trucks didn't acknowledge her presence. She barely drew a glance. When she found the doors leading back into the bazaar, she sighed with relief. She crossed over and exited onto the street.

Like the bazaar, the street surged with crowds. The best Layla could do was inch her way forward. Street merchants waved their merchandise in her face, imploring her to stop and see their wares. She was unsure where she was going, and people continually jostled and ran into her. Even in the cool air, she felt hot. A trickle of sweat slid between her breasts. The press of humanity unnerved her. One street seller stopped her in her tracks, his face angry that she'd ignored him and his wares. His words, which were incomprehensible to her, seemed to be accusing and aggressive, and keeping her head lowered, she frantically searched her brain for a reply. In a flash of déjà vu, the days spent in Evin Prison came back to her, and she remembered the Farsi word for no. "*Na, na, na…Mersi,*" she repeated, stepping around him and hurrying away.

She pulled the map Cyrus had given her from her pocket, studying the street signs as she walked. She was frightened, but her desire to find the Imam Khomeini Mosque spurred her forward, allowing her no time to think about the danger she was in. She almost shouted with glee when she saw the clock tower flanked by two yellow, mosaic-tiled minarets looming above a pointed, arched entry into the mosque. The mosque, beautiful and imposing, straddled a large square situated near the bazaar. Within the square, women pushed strollers with infants, and tourists shot photos to preserve the memories of a lifetime. She walked up the stairs to get a better view of the street, searching left and right through the traffic, looking for any sign of Cyrus.

What's taking him so long? Why isn't he here?

Every time a voice rose above the norm, her pulse quickened. An overwhelming fear of being handcuffed and returned to Evin Prison had her legs shaking so bad she had to grip the wall for support. So great was her fear, she nearly fainted when two IRGC uniformed soldiers walked past her. Absorbed in conversation, they never even glanced her way. She sighed with relief and returned her attention back to the street just as a motorcycle pulled up to the curb. A man wearing a white helmet and a worker's jumper sat astride the bike revving the engine. She eyed him warily. She couldn't tell if it was Cyrus, but the man began frantically waving at her. Not sure if he was actually signaling her, she looked around, but no one else stood anywhere near. She pointed at herself, and he nodded. She ran down the steps toward him.

"Jump on," Cyrus told her, his familiar voice calming her immediately.

"Why didn't you tell me you were going to be on a motorcycle!" Her hands went to her hips. "And where's my helmet?"

He laughed. "No helmet. You're going to have to trust me. Come on, there's no time to argue."

Swinging onto a motorcycle in a *chadar* was no easy task. Self-consciously, she lifted the black fabric and slid her jean-clad leg over the seat. A vision of how ludicrous she must look made her laugh.

"What's so funny?"

"This. Me. All of this is crazy."

"You think so? If I were you, I'd hold on because we're out of here!"

The motorcycle took off with such a powerful thrust she nearly toppled off the seat. She wrapped her arms around Cyrus's waist in a death grip as he sped away, weaving in and out of traffic.

She screamed in his ear, "You bastard, I nearly fell off."

"I warned you to hold on tight," he yelled back.

She pressed herself tighter into his back.

"Are you cold?"

"Freezing."

"We're going to make a stop, ditch the motorcycle, and switch to a car."

She buried her face in his back, wondering if she'd made a mistake trusting him. How long would they be able to avoid the authorities? Everything about her circumstances had changed. No longer was she just a prisoner of a deadly regime—she was a fugitive prey to be hunted and captured, her life in the hands of one man, an enigma.

What have I gotten myself into?

Cyrus drove the motorcycle through a back road, entering his property through a rear gate. Layla got off, and he stashed the bike in the garage. Also in the garage was a black Morattab Pazhan, an Iranian-produced copycat of the British Land Rover Defender model. The four-wheeled-drive, off-road vehicle used by both civilians and the military had been purchased for him by Mossad to be used in the event of an emergency.

That day having now arrived, the car would be their escape vehicle. It was packed with food and supplies, held a full tank of gas, and stood ready to go. Cyrus removed the license plates and replaced them with another pair hidden underneath the rear floor mats. "There," he said, "if they alert the police to be on the lookout for us, this license plate number won't show up in their database. We don't have much time, so let's go inside. I need to grab a few things before we leave."

"Where are we?" she asked, staring at the house.

"This is my family home." He looked around, stoically. "I don't spend much time here." He closed the garage. "Come inside. We need to find you a heavy jacket."

Layla followed him into the house. They walked through the gloomy rooms with their sheeted furniture.

"It must be painful being here with the memories of your family," she said in a quiet voice.

"I need to hold onto the pain, to remember what's been lost. It's what's kept me focused on my mission all these years."

"It seems like you've sacrificed an awful lot for this mission—maybe even your soul."

Cyrus, stunned by her intuition, was speechless. She was far too observant.

What he hadn't told her. What had completely enraged him, was the other order from Mossad. If he failed on his mission and was unable to get Layla out of Iran, his orders were to kill her rather than allow her capture by the Iranians, which meant the Israelis did not want her father to become a target for blackmail.

If Cyrus was capable of taking Layla's innocent life. If he killed her, there would be no way back for him, and no way forward. Everything he had fought for would have been for nothing. He would become a soulless monster for whom there would be no redemption.

He stared at her as if seeing her for the first time—shaken by the young woman who had completely changed his life in so short a time.

"Why did you kiss me back there. In the room behind the carpet shop?" Her eyes dropped shyly. "It's not like we were in the townhouse with all the cameras."

Cyrus's brows furrowed as he realized his kiss had confused her. Was it as unforgettable to her as it had been to him? What could he say? That when he wasn't worrying about her safety and getting them out of the country, that his mind kept envisioning making love to her? That each time he kissed her he felt reborn? That if the world weren't so fucked up and they'd met under different circumstances, he'd probably be in love with her by now? "I'm sorry," he said instead. "I shouldn't have done it. You have enough to contend with. I apologize. Forgive me."

She nodded and reached for his hand. "I appreciate everything you're doing for me, Cyrus. You're risking your life for me. Thank you," she whispered.

"You're welcome," he whispered back.

She smiled. That beautiful smile that made him truly want to be her Superman. He cleared his throat. "We're going to a Mossad safe house about twenty kilometers from Tehran. It's a city west of here named Karaj that lies at the foot of the Alborz Mountains, near Dizin, a ski resort."

"And then?"

"Then we're to meet with a Mossad contact, a man who's going to make us new forged passports."

"Why do you think I'm so important to Israel and Iran?"

"I don't know. You tell me. Who is your father, and why is Israel willing to sacrifice me and my mission to save you?"

"I told you. He's a nuclear physicist and a professor at MIT. Beyond that, I don't know."

He studied her face to see if her expression revealed more than her words. "Well, I'm pretty sure your father is much more than that."

You may not know it, sweetheart, but you're a pawn in a deadly game.

Luckily, he was a good chess player. "Let's not worry about that right now. We need to get out of here."

CHAPTER 20

North Tehran, Iran
MOIS Headquarters
December 18th
1:00 p.m.

Jalal Rahimi was livid. His jaw tightened as he listened to his agent report the foul up.

"Tourak, are you telling me Cyrus Hassani walked away from the American woman to go to the bathroom, and 'poof,' he vanished? Then in a grossly negligent decision on your part, the American woman, who knows nothing about Tehran, managed to slip your surveillance and she too disappeared?"

"Yes, *Agha*."

"And, even after this bungling of your duties, you have no idea how or why this was accomplished?"

"Yes, *Agha*."

"It seems more likely Cyrus grew tired of being ineptly watched. I can't blame him. He is probably right now having a big laugh over your incompetence."

"Yes, *Agha*."

"Send a team to his house and search it. I want to know anything that seems out of the ordinary. Meanwhile, keep surveillance on the safe house in case Hassani returns with the girl, making you look even more of a fool. It's likely he engineered the escapade to expose the ineptitude and weakness infecting our so-called elite agents. Not to mention, he must want to get her back into bed and was no doubt eager to get away from you two idiots."

After hanging up, Jalal called his secretary. "Amir, get me Moscow Center. I need to speak with Mikhail Pradkov at SVR immediately."

117

Jalal steepled his fingers as he waited for his secretary to put through the call. He considered the implications of Cyrus and the girl's disappearance.

Is it possible my protégé finds himself enamored with this American girl? If you betray me, Cyrus, you will regret it. I think it's time we find out exactly who this little bird is.

The phone rang and he answered. On the line was the director of the Foreign Intel Service of the Russian Federation. SVR was the current incarnation of the notorious Soviet espionage service, the KGB. The SVR's reach was unlimited. It had agents in place in every major city in the world. The Cold War may have been over, but Moscow's espionage network had grown even more extensively.

"Mikhail, how kind of you to take my call. I hope all is well with the great bear of the north?"

A chuckle of amusement answered Jalal's greeting. "The bear is, as always, hungry for more. What can I do for you, Jalal?"

"In truth, my friend, I didn't want to trouble you, but it seems I have a dilemma."

"Our renewed brotherhood has facilitated a close camaraderie between our nations, which permits me to offer you whatever assistance I can. Feel free to speak your mind."

"An American woman, Layla Wallace, is visiting Iran. I would like to know more about her and her family. I'm sure your people in Washington can provide me with a complete dossier on them. I suspect this woman may be of inordinate value to the Americans. Your help would be much appreciated."

"Layla Wallace. I will speak to our embassy and see what they can dig up. I'll get back to you as soon as I have something. The woman is in your possession?"

"At the moment, she is on the run. It is possible the CIA may have reason to assist her. However, I'm certain she will be under our control again very soon."

"The CIA? In that case, it seems I should address this with more urgency."

"It's unlikely she will stay at large for too long. But yes, Mikhail, your utmost consideration is warranted."

"Consider it done."

"Oh, by the way, I heard the good news that you will be supplying us with S-300 surface-to-air missile systems and a fleet of fighter jets, which can only guarantee the Islamic Republic's ability to defend itself, and if needed, take the fight to our enemies."

"Yes, it's a done deal. In April, when the JCPOA was agreed to, all the obstacles for sales to you of military technology vanished. It seems we are in business, my friend."

"I'm sure it will be a long and fruitful relationship. I look forward to your update on Miss Wallace."

"You will be hearing from me."

"*Spasibo.*"

CHAPTER 21

Karaj, Alborz Province, Iran
December 18th
2:00 p.m.

It took just a few minutes for Cyrus to clean out his safe and grab Layla a warm jacket. He locked the door of his childhood home, not expecting to ever see it again. They drove northwest on Route 2 to Karaj in the Morattab Pazhan Land Rover.

Cyrus was silent as he drove, his jaw set with determination as he stared ahead at the highway. He wore his aviator glasses and a turban, while Layla wore the *chadar* that shielded her from the prying eyes in passing cars.

"Are you upset? You're awfully quiet," she asked, breaking the silence.

"Why should I be upset? Everything is going according to plan."

"I'm talking about your having to leave your home and Tehran—you may never see either of them again."

He sighed; it seemed her uncanny ability to read him was growing even sharper. "Don't worry your pretty little head. Whatever I'm feeling won't hamper my ability to complete the mission that's been given to me." He turned to her, his face set with resolve. "I'm going to get you out of Iran."

"I know that. I thought maybe you'd like to talk about it. Sometimes it helps. After all, we're in this together, and I feel terrible. I'm the reason you can never go home."

He felt a stab of guilt. She suffered as much as he did in this winner take all game of hunter and hunted. She deserved his kindness, but he couldn't give it to her. He already had let her get too close. Any sign of weakness from him and she might not obey his orders at a crucial juncture.

He needed her to be unsure, dependent, and reliant on his command. Still, he couldn't be overly harsh either or she might try to fight him. "Look,

121

don't worry about my family home. Any meaning that house held for me, and any attachment I have to the city of my birth, is long gone. I'm glad this charade is finally over. I can move forward and build a new life."

"But you don't want a new life. You said so yourself, that I've blown your cover. That I'm the reason your mission is over."

"It was bound to happen. I've been living a life of subterfuge for a long time. Iran hasn't been a home to me for years. *'You can't go back home to your family, back home to your childhood, back home to romantic love, back home to a young man's dreams of glory and of fame…back home to the old forms and systems of things which once seemed everlasting but which are changing all the time—back home to the escapes of Time and Memory.'* One of your great American authors, Thomas Wolfe. I read his books while I was in Paris at university."

She gaped at him. "How do you do that, recall the lines of something you read long ago?"

"I believe they call it a photographic memory."

"I've never known anyone who had that. Let alone in a language that is not native to them."

He shrugged. "Just one of my many talents. I'm fluent in six languages," he shrugged. "I can also mimic any accent in English I hear."

"You're kidding? What accents can you do?"

"Shoot, Miss Layla. Yer just about the prettiest little thing I ever seen. Why yer even prettier than my horse Delilah, and she's mighty pretty." He flashed her a grin that could rival any cowboy from Texas.

Layla burst out laughing. "Oh, my God. You missed your calling. You should have been an actor."

"Why thank you, Miss Layla." He inclined his head, touching a pretend Stetson.

Her laughter mellowed to a soft smile and she laid her hand on his thigh. "You don't hate me, do you, Cyrus?"

The warmth of her touch shot right to his groin.

God! Even the slightest, insignificant touch is enough to undo me.

Hating her was the furthest thing from his mind. It was so easy to forget his past and their precarious situation. He wanted nothing more than to whisk her away to a resort and spend his time making her laugh and making her come. But he couldn't their lives depended on him keeping a clear head…

He removed her hand from his thigh and placed it on the seat next to him, patting it. "Hey, we're pretend lovers," he joked. "Why would I hate a woman I haven't properly seduced? Hell, I'd be a fool not to leave that door open." He needed to kill his arousal, so he opened the center console and pulled out a pack of cigarettes. Shaking the pack, he gripped a cigarette between his lips.

"What are you doing?"

From the corner of his eye he saw her frown. "It's not marijuana, it's a cigarette. I smoke sometimes when I'm under pressure."

"Not in this car you're not. Not with me in it. It's a terrible habit."

"You're kidding?"

"It's bad for your health."

He snorted. "Look at where we are? On the run from killers who would stop at nothing to slice our throats, and you're worried about a bit of nicotine?"

She pressed her lips together and crossed her arms over her chest.

"Fine." He tossed the cigarette out the window. "Next time I feel like a smoke I'll just think about our 'pretend sex'. That should kill any desire I might be feeling."

"God how you can you be so nice one minute and then such an asshole the next," she huffed. Layla's face flushed beet red and she stared out the window. "You're the last man on earth I would have sex with. And by the way, that was all a show back at the townhouse. You can thank my three years of Mrs. Finnegan's drama training at Douglas Academy for that."

He threw his head back and laughed. Layla Wallace was the most vibrant, unusual woman he'd ever met.

From Tehran, they drove less than an hour west to Karaj, the fourth largest city in Iran. It lay at the foot of the Alborz Mountains, and in winter Karaj was dressed in a blanket of pristine white snow. The safe house lay in a quiet, residential neighborhood not far from Route 2 in the Jahanshahr district.

They stopped at a market, and Cyrus bought enough groceries and supplies for a few days. As she unpacked their bags and stored away their groceries, Cyrus carried an armload of wood in from the backyard and set a roaring fire in the stone fireplace. Layla stood before the fire and warmed her hands. She'd removed the *chadar*, and her hair shone like burnished copper in the dancing firelight.

Cyrus's heart constricted in response to her beauty. How was it this woman, this thorn in his side, was capable of derailing his best efforts to avoid his emotions? They were in the crosshairs of a deadly enemy who would stop at nothing to ensnare them—there was no time for the attraction that reverberated like an electrical current between them, no matter how intense.

"Why don't you make yourself useful and prepare us some dinner? I need to check in with Tel Aviv and find out what comes next."

Without a word, she glared at him before stomping off to the kitchen.

Finally, he admitted. *Now I can focus.* He went into the bedroom that served as an office and pushed a desk away from the wall. Lifting a board hidden beneath the desk, he pulled out a small book he'd been instructed would be waiting for him.

He sat at the desk and pulled the eyeglass case with the satellite receiver glasses from his coat pocket. He put them on and began to write down the recent messages waiting for him on the computer lens. He was about to remove the glasses when a new message flew across his vision. He wrote it down, and then the transmission disappeared from the screen of the glasses.

The technology was perfect, except he had no means of responding to the sender—he could only receive. He removed the glasses, returned them to his pocket, and proceeded to decode the message. He carefully memorized the transcript and walked out of the bedroom, throwing the page on the flames in the fireplace.

Layla was finishing up when Cyrus joined her in the kitchen. The aroma of sautéed chicken and vegetables infused the air. The set table greeted him. Cyrus washed his hands at the sink and sat down. She carried the frying pan and a bowl of steaming rice and set it before him.

"It smells great," he offered, picking up the serving spoon and scooping up some rice along with vegetables and chicken onto a plate and set it at her place setting.

Sitting, she made no comment. Still seething from their earlier exchange, she was determined to avoid a confrontation.

He took a forkful of rice and chicken and ate with relish. "Delicious."

She nodded in acknowledgement and ate, still refusing to converse with him.

"You know, I think this is the first time you've cooked for us."

She glanced up and saw his grin.

"You're a good cook, Layla," he added.

Her heart did a flip flop at his smile. "Thanks." *Don't fall in love with him. Don't fall in love with him.*

"I guess you don't want to know I heard from your father."

"You what?" she squealed. "Can I talk to him."

"No, but he sent you a message."

"What did he say? Is he okay?"

Cyrus crossed his arms and leaned back in his chair.

"Please, Cyrus?" She reached across the table and placed her hand on his forearm. The heat of his skin made her want to trail her hands up his arms and lean in to kiss him. "Please?" she said softly.

He leaned forward, not removing her hand. "Your father wants you to know he will do whatever is required to bring you home. He wants you to do exactly whatever the agent, me, tells you to do. He's waiting for you in Israel, waiting for you to come home to him. He also wanted you to know your mother's spirit is looking after you."

Tears blurred Layla's vision. "Thank you," she whispered.

"You're welcome," he whispered back. He lifted her hand and placed a soft kiss on her palm.

It had become a familiar exchange between them—her whispered *thank you* and his whispered *you're welcome*. Layla searched Cyrus's face for more information. She couldn't understand why any of this was happening, but she accepted what must be the only explanation—her father held some value that she knew nothing about. Something governments would do anything to get their hands on. Now, she not only worried about her own safety but her father's. "What happens next?"

"I'm meeting our contact, the man who's going to forge our passports."

"When?"

"Tonight. But before I go, there's something you have to do for me."

When Layla stepped out of the bathroom, she no longer resembled herself. Her hair was dyed black. When she looked at Cyrus, she began to laugh. He too had undergone a transformation. Where before he'd been a clean-shaven man, a heavily bearded man now stood before her. His Nile-green eyes were now the color of a muddy brown riverbed. "Nice beard. And your eyes. Very sinister."

"Part of my training at Mossad. Every agent masters the art of disguise, using prosthetics, makeup, and facial hair. I think I'm pretty good at it. How do you like the new me?"

"I don't. I like you better without all that extra facial hair. In fact, you've become completely resistible to me."

He ran his hand over the brush of beard encircling his jawline, frowning. "I'm not particularly pleased with it, either." He scrutinized her. "You, however, look sexy as hell. Now, put these contacts in." He handed her a small case containing brown contact lenses.

When she returned from the bathroom, the transformation was complete. "Voilà!" She pirouetted for his approval.

He smiled. "I'd say you look like a very attractive Iranian girl. In fact, too damned attractive. If I took you to bed right now, I'd be sleeping with a brand new woman."

"Don't start. You'd be sleeping with a stranger if you slept with me. It isn't likely you'll be sleeping with either one of us, the old me or the new me," she huffed.

"Okay." He snickered. "Sit in this chair. We're going to shoot a couple of headshots for our new passports."

While Layla had been in the bathroom, Cyrus had set up a camera on a tripod. After taking several digital photos of her, they switched places, and she took photos of him.

"I have to meet our contact. Lock the door after me, and don't open it for anyone. I shouldn't be long."

Layla's insides began to churn, and she wrapped her arms around herself to keep herself from shaking. They'd hardly been apart since he'd rescued her, and the prospect of their separation frightened her. "What if something happens, and you don't come back?"

He tilted his head, smiling. "My brave little tigress, are you admitting you'd miss me? Come here." He opened his arms, and she rushed into them, clinging to the solid breadth of his chest, her face pressed into him. "You're not going to be rid of me that easily," he said. "I promise you I'm not leaving you. I'll be back as soon as I can. You're safe here." He kissed the top of her head. "You have to trust me, Layla, trust I'll never let you down, *eshgham*."

She looked at him, her eyes filled with tears, and nodded. "What does *eshgham* mean?"

"It means dear one."

CHAPTER 22

Tel Aviv, Israel
December 18th
11:00 p.m.

Aleck Wallace arrived safely in Israel. Without having to clear customs, security whisked him away to a safe house near the beach in Ramat HaSharon, a suburb of Tel Aviv. The safe house was a lovely villa with views of the Mediterranean, which he might have enjoyed if his daughter were there to share it with him. Until she was safe in Israel, he would find no joy in any of it. Outside, an impressive team of bodyguards saw to his needs and kept watch over him. The prime minister had advised it would not be long before the FBI and the Iranians found out exactly where he'd disappeared to. It was crucial he remain under wraps until confirmation of his daughter's rescue.

He paced the grounds of the house, fraught with anxiety, his patience wearing thin. When the prime minister called to check on him, he exploded. "Dodi, I will not be kept a prisoner in this house, out of the loop. I want—no, I demand—to know what's going on. I can't sit here twiddling my thumbs, waiting for word from you. You must understand, my friend, as a father, what kind of nightmare I'm living through."

"Calm down, Aleck, I understand completely what you're going through. If you don't mind a blindfold, I'll have my men bring you to Mossad headquarters and bring you up to speed."

"Why a blindfold? What do you think I might do, bring down the Israeli intelligence service?"

The prime minister chuckled. "It's for your own good, Aleck. No one knows the true location of Mossad unless they are an affiliate. That's the way it works. I'm sorry."

"Fine, I understand. Arrange it, Dodi. I'm tired of being kept in the dark."

———— ❋ ————

In the manner the prime minister had stipulated, a blindfolded Aleck, under cover of darkness, arrived at Mossad headquarters. From the elevator, his security handlers led him into a room and removed his blindfold. A glance at his surroundings confirmed that he'd been escorted to an operational staging room. The wall held a massive screen displaying what he assumed to be a satellite or drone feed. A curved table with dozens of computers faced the screen, where men and women worked diligently at their keyboards.

A man entered the room and approached Aleck with an outstretched hand. "Dr. Wallace, my name is Isaac, and I'm the director of the Special Operations Division, Metsada. Welcome to The Office."

"Thank you, Isaac." The two men shook hands. "Please, call me Aleck."

One of the computer experts interrupted their greetings. "Isaac, we have confirmation from the satellite. Cyrus has intercepted the latest batch of messages on the eyeglass receiver. I also have a satellite transmission confirming they have arrived at the safe house in Karaj."

"Put it on the screen, Chaim."

"Yes, sir."

Aleck, Isaac, and the others in the room watched the screen. It was like watching Google Earth, only far better. The satellite's camera focused on the Earth's surface from orbit, and the image of Earth drew closer and closer. First, the continent of Asia grew discernible as the telescope seemingly dropped from the heavens, until the Middle East became visible. Finally, the topography of Iran was recognizable. The target of the satellite's probing eye grew nearer. It found its mark, a specific neighborhood, and like a laser point, it finally focused on one particular house. Smoke rose from a chimney into the winter sky.

With his eyes locked on the screen, Aleck asked, "Isaac, did you send my message to Layla?"

The lines around Isaac's eyes grew more pronounced with his smile. "Yes, your message was delivered and received. I'm sure Cyrus shared it with Layla."

Suddenly there was movement on the screen. A figure emerged from the house and walked away on foot.

"That's Cyrus, sir. He's left to meet with Jibreel."

Knowing that Layla was inside the house was maddening. "Why is he leaving Layla alone?"

Isaac placed his hand on his shoulder. "It's okay, Aleck, she's safe inside. Cyrus is smart to make the initial contact alone. There's no reason for her to go with him. He's a pro. Working alone, he's almost invisible. Everything is proceeding exactly as planned. You could not ask for a better trained or more loyal field agent. He's a born Iranian, a man who has risked everything for Israel."

"He's a traitor to his own country. Can such a man be trusted?"

"He's a Jew, a man who has seen his country become a tyranny and a threat to not only Israel, but to the entire world. A man of such clear moral integrity is a rarity. Aleck, do you know the motto of Mossad?"

"No, I don't believe I do."

"Our motto is: Where there is no guidance, a nation falls, but in an abundance of counselors there is safety. Cyrus is the guide who will bring Layla to safety. A man whose integrity is unquestionable. I might add he's a trained assassin. He will get Layla out of Iran even if it costs him his life."

Aleck was humbled by Isaac's words. He should have known not to doubt Rebecca's people. He scrutinized the screen, wishing he could see the face of the man Layla's life depended on.

As if on cue, exactly as Isaac had intimated, the figure disappeared.

"We've lost him, sir. He's vanished."

Isaac smiled again. "If we can't find him, neither can anyone else."

CHAPTER 23

Tehran, Iran
MOIS Headquarters,
December 18th
11:00 p.m.

The hallways of MOIS headquarters were all but empty as evening spread its wings over the Islamic Republic. In the inner sanctum of Jalal Rahimi's office, a lone light cast its feeble glow over a desk. The man who sat behind the desk had a grim face. He didn't like to be out of control, and he certainly didn't like being made a fool.

His protégé, whom he had treated like a son, had suddenly gone missing with the young American woman entrusted to him. Jalal contemplated all the possibilities. Never once had he doubted the loyalty of Cyrus Hassani. Cyrus belonged to him—he was his most trusted aide. However, what was he to make of today's events? He rubbed his beard with dissatisfaction as he waited for the call from Mikhail Pradkov.

The ringing phone shattered the silence. He picked it up, anxious to unravel the mystery.

"*Dobrey vicha*, Mikhail. Thank you for getting back to me so soon."

"*Asr be kheyr*, Jalal. I've heard from my people in Washington. It's late, so I'll get right down to the matter of your intelligence request. Your American escapee is the daughter of a prominent nuclear physicist, Dr. Aleck Wallace, a professor at MIT. At one time, he was involved with a government nuclear project, but for reasons unknown, it ceased operation.

"It seems Layla Rose Wallace is his only child. The mother died ten years ago. The mother is of interest. Rebecca Rose was born and raised in Israel, where her parents live to this day. Also noteworthy, Aleck Wallace was the roommate at Harvard of the prime minister of Israel. A coincidence warranting deeper analysis. All of it probably amounts to nothing except for the strange disappearance of the professor a few days ago following his daughter's kidnapping in Dubai. Which, Jalal, you conveniently failed to mention. The FBI flubbed up and didn't do their homework. Apparently, what the professor worked on in the past is of national interest and makes him extremely valuable, particularly to adversarial nations such as yours and mine.

"The FBI conducted a surprise visit to his home the other night to place him in protective custody, but he had already flown the coop. By the way, he didn't leave on a commercial flight. How he got out is the fodder of speculation. My guess is the Israelis. It seems his disappearance left the FBI holding their jock straps, and from what my people tell me, there's an all-out push to ascertain his whereabouts. I would surmise the FBI's failure to locate the girl or expedite her release might have forced her father to seek help elsewhere.

"As you can imagine, a call to the prime minister of Israel would elicit an immediate response, given their history and the father's value. If it is the Israelis, they've stumbled upon a godsend. Aleck Wallace could significantly raise their stakes in the nuclear field. The man is a genius, and from what I understand, has continued his work on a new method of enriching uranium that's a game changer.

"A man who has devoted his life to raising his child will do anything to protect that child. All the Israelis have to do is rescue her, and he'll do whatever they ask. I take it you haven't managed to recapture the little bird, or we probably wouldn't be having this conversation.

"I also imagine with a little help she may already be crossing the Zagros Mountains on her way to Turkey. Ah, but who inside Iran would be willing to help her? An interesting question, don't you think?"

Jalal seethed with anger, and Mikhail's condescending remark only fueled his indignation. "I assure you, Mikhail, this bird will never know freedom. I will clip her wings, and I will clip the wings of those who help her. Thank you for your help, Mikhail. Call on me at any time. If I can, I will reciprocate the favor."

"Oh, I assure you, the time will come, my friend."

His conversation with Mikhail left Jalal with a taste of bile in his mouth. It was clear—Cyrus, for reasons unknown, was helping the girl escape Iran and consequently aiding the Israelis, Iran's mortal enemy.

Jalal fingered his beard as he considered his course of action. This was a personal affront—Cyrus's actions not only made him a traitor to his country but also a traitor to Jalal himself. A tidal wave of anger rose in him.

Methodically, he launched a campaign to intercept the two fugitives. First, he had the videos from the safe house where Cyrus had stayed with the American delivered to his office. The minute he reviewed the videos, he knew Cyrus had fallen for the girl. He cursed himself for not watching the footage sooner.

The amount of time the two spent in the bathroom was the tip-off. Furious that he had left this to lesser men, he now took charge, painstakingly mobilizing his assets. His call to the Interior Ministry put the border patrol at Bazargan on high alert. All travelers whose age fit the criterion of Layla and Cyrus were to be detained and questioned. All vehicles were to be searched. No one would be allowed to cross the border into Turkey without clearance from Tehran.

Even without closing the border between Iran and Turkey, Jalal had made it impossible for anyone to leave Iran without official permission. He put out an all-points bulletin on Cyrus's automobile and license plate number, placing the vehicle on a find and detain list, which he had distributed to all police and military patrols. He activated IRGC teams of military units into an all-out manhunt. A thorough man, he cast a purse seine fishing net blocking all likely means of exit from Iran. When he located the traitor and his whore, he would close the net around them, trapping them like fish.

He sat back in his chair, contemplating his revenge.

Once I have you, Cyrus, I will try, judge, and pronounce sentence on you. Then I will kill you myself, slowly and painfully.

As for the girl…

He fingered a photograph of her delivered from Mikhail. Looking out from the picture, the beautiful girl seemed to be smiling at him.

I have something special in mind for you little bird.

CHAPTER 24

Karaj, Alborz Province, Iran
December 19th
1:00 a.m.

Cyrus kept to the shadows of the neighborhood of Jahanshahr. The normally bustling residential area was, not surprisingly, quiet on a cold winter's night. From the Alborz Mountains, a frigid wind was blowing, keeping the local inhabitants safely within their homes.

His instructions were to meet his Mossad contact at 1:30 a.m. in the Fateh Garden. If the streets had seemed deserted, the park was a virtual ghost town, otherworldly. Nothing stirred except the wind whistling through the leafless branches of the deciduous trees lining the walking path.

The ground was blanketed with a layer of frozen snow that crunched beneath Cyrus's boots as he walked. He counted the canopied picnic tables running along the edge of the path, and when he got to ten, he brushed the snow from the bench and sat down.

He took out his pistol and attached the silencer. Taking aim, he shot out the bulb of the lighting fixture that illuminated the pathway. Darkness provided safety from any unforeseen surprises. It wasn't as if anyone could have snuck up on him. There were no obstructions in his field of vision. However, it was better if his eyes were adjusted to the darkness in case of trouble, and better if he was cloaked in darkness if anyone approached.

He pulled the drawstrings on his hood tighter and raised the collar on his coat to keep out the wind.

As he waited for the messenger, he thought of Layla and how she'd turned his world upside down. As much as she infuriated and frustrated him, being near her made him feel alive.

For years he had pretended that his mission was worth the loss of family, friends, and love, but now, because of one stubborn red-head, he'd begun to question everything.

His mind floated back to their conversation before he left.

He'd called her *eshgham*. She'd asked him what it meant, and he told her "dear one." He hadn't told her the true translation or the intimate meaning. "My love."

The thought of harm coming to her tore his heart inside out. He'd do anything to prevent that from happening, even if it cost him his own life. The absurdity of the situation was almost laughable—his great and noble mission to save the world had narrowed down to one driving compulsion—to save one woman, and in doing so save himself.

If it came down to it and The Office insisted he eliminate her—he'd go rogue. There was no way he'd harm a hair on Layla's head. There was no question in his mind there was only one way forward, and that was to get out of Iran with her.

Every muscle in his body tensed at the snap of a twig. A lone figure approached, a man of considerable size, his hands in the pockets of his overcoat.

"Shalom Zand, *oseh ma'asei v'reishit.*"

Hearing the password Tel Aviv had given him—a prayer: "Who does the work of Creation"—Cyrus's body relaxed. He pocketed his gun and stood, offering his hand.

"Shalom. I'm Zand Ardavan. I'm sorry you had to be dragged out on such a cold night." Tel Aviv had insisted they follow protocol. Layla and he must use their new identities, Zand and Noor Ardavan. The less the two men knew about each other the better.

They shook hands, the steam from their breaths intermingling in the frigid air. "I do this as much for me, my friend, as you. Call me Jibreel."

Cyrus smiled at the fitting name. Jibreel was the Arabic name for the archangel Gabriel, meaning messenger of God, God's right hand. Cyrus reached into his pocket and produced a flash drive holding his and Layla's photos. "Here are the digital photos of my wife Noor and me for the passports."

"Excellent." He pulled an envelope from his pocket and handed it to Cyrus. "This was delivered to my mailbox for you. I've been told to have your passports ready by tomorrow."

Cyrus nodded. The sooner the new false passports were ready, the better. "Where should I meet you?"

"At Hot Chocolate. It's a coffee shop in Jahanshahr. Meet me at dusk, five p.m. It should be crowded and noisy, perfect for our purposes."

"Jibreel, I appreciate the risk you're taking for me and my wife. I hope that one day I can thank you properly."

"I look forward to that day. I understand that your wife is pregnant and desires that your child be born outside Iran. Believe me, I understand that desire better than anyone. I'll see you tomorrow."

They shook hands again, and Jibreel walked away down the path in the same direction from where he'd come. Cyrus watched him leave, nervously gripping the envelope. He waited until Jibreel disappeared into the dense fog. A few minutes later, he tucked the envelope in his jacket and rose, moving swiftly through the park, retracing his steps to the safe house.

The house was silent when he returned. He locked the door behind him and found Layla curled on the couch asleep. He watched her for a moment. Sitting on the edge of the sofa, he whispered, "Why don't you go to bed?"

Her eyes blinked open. "Cyrus," she cried, her arms encircling him, her face pressed to his shoulder. "You're back! I was so worried."

Reluctant to let her go, the warmth of her body against his thawed him faster than the heat from the fire in the hearth.

"Of course, I'm back. It's freezing outside. I couldn't get back fast enough." He didn't tell her that he was significantly worried about the weather and afraid it might endanger their escape. The cold snap was expected to go on for days. If anything went wrong, they would be fighting not only the enemy but also the elements.

"So, what happens next?" She pulled away enough to study his face.

"I met our angel, Jibreel. Tomorrow I meet him at five. He'll give me our new passports, and that's it. We'll be out of here either tomorrow night or the next."

"Just like that?"

"Just like that." His eyes dropped to her lips, which were only inches from his. A rush of desire spread through his veins. He wanted to kiss her, to taste her, to reassure himself that his feelings were real.

One kiss. Would it be so terrible if we shared one kiss? I know I shouldn't. It will only confuse her. But who knows what tomorrow will bring? What if tonight is all we have?

The old Bob Seger song suddenly popped into his head…*We've Got Tonight*. He almost laughed out loud. First Eric Clapton and now Bob Seger. If their lives weren't in real danger, this would feel like a Hollywood movie.

Layla was three steps ahead of him. Before he could protest, she pressed her lips to his, her fingers framing his face in a caress. He wanted to crush his lips to hers, to explore the passion that fired through him, obliterating all reason. He ached to know more, to test the limits of his desire for her, but he dared not.

They broke apart, staring at each other, her hands still holding his face. He fought against the tidal wave of need that threatened to engulf him the only way he knew how—with a tongue-in-cheek comment that was sure to raise her ire. "Wow, do all American girls react that way when their men leave the house? Maybe I should disappear more often. Who knew I'd be missed so much? I don't suppose you feel like some pretend-real sex, do you?"

She gaped at him then hauled back to slap him. He grabbed her hand before it landed.

"Didn't your father ever tell you that it isn't nice to go around slapping people?"

"You're an arrogant bastard." She broke free of his grasp. "Why do you make me feel like a schoolgirl with a ridiculous crush?"

He continued to laugh, even though the fire that lit her eyes only served to arouse him more. "Layla, I'm sorry. It's just too predictable. Beautiful girl rescued by a not bad looking older fellow—cross that out—older scoundrel, escapes with him from her murderous pursuers only to find herself drawn to her captor/rescuer. I believe that's called Stockholm syndrome, isn't it?"

"I think you're giving yourself too much credit. Try this on for size. A man who thinks he's God's gift to women is forced to abandon his life as a spy when he's ordered to rescue a kidnapped girl. He's an emotional wreck and a heartless asshole. Preferring to hurt the one person who might save his soul."

Their gazes locked, the tension hanging between them like a living, breathing thing.

He turned away, refusing to allow her to see how on-the-mark her words were. "Go to bed, Layla. Tomorrow will be here soon enough."

"I'm sorry, Cyrus. I spoke out of anger. I…I'm grateful, really I am, for everything you're doing for me, for us."

He turned to her, one eyebrow raised, considering his best response. "Think nothing of it, my dear. It's better to clear the air. It will allow us both to concentrate on the more demanding tasks ahead of us. I'll take the couch. Good night."

"Good night." She turned and fled the room.

The envelope in his coat demanded attention. A few quiet hours without the disruptive presence of his redheaded muse would allow him to prepare for tomorrow.

He opened the envelope and found two keys and a flash drive. He turned them over in his hand and grabbed the satellite eyeglasses. Messages were waiting for him. The Office must have decided there was no reason for him to decode the messages. The transmissions were now being sent in Hebrew.

He sat at the desk and wrote everything down.

Memorize legends of Noor & Zand Ardavan on flash drive, then destroy flash drive.

Two Keys: One for strongbox in the garage behind pegboard holding hanging tools.

Arms & explosives are for your use.

Second key for Nissan Seranza, equipped with satellite tracking system for The Office's eyes.

Leave Morattab in garage.

Use Seranza for escape.

Rendezvous Bazargan-Gurbulak border.

Extraction team will meet you there.

Cyrus plugged the flash drive into the computer and printed everything on it. He read it through once. In the morning, he would load everything from the Morattab into the Seranza and select which armory to take. Mossad had provided for every possibility—they were leaving nothing to chance.

CHAPTER 25

Karaj, Alborz Province, Iran
Safe House
December 19th
9:00 a.m.

The morning was cold and gloomy. A cloud of fog had crept down from the mountains and settled in the valley, obscuring the sun and its potential warmth.

A dark and twisted nightmare of Cyrus being strung up and hanged from a crane had her tossing and turning all night. She awoke shivering, wishing his arms were around her, but too chicken to go to him. Their disconcerting exchange the night before had left her miserable.

She checked her watch. In only a few hours they would leave the relative security of the safe house and embark on a dangerous journey. She trusted Cyrus, but they were going up against the might of Iran, a country not known for its leniency. The risk of capture and imprisonment was extremely high.

When she emerged from the bedroom, the house was empty. In the kitchen, coffee had been prepared, and there were sweet rolls filled with cinnamon and walnuts waiting on the counter. She sat by herself, warming her hands on a steaming mug of coffee as she gazed out the window to the backyard, cloaked in a heavy gray mist.

How was it that she consistently misread him? Why did he run hot one minute and cold the next?

I could have sworn he wanted to kiss me, the way he stared at my mouth.

She sipped her coffee, searching for an explanation. Perhaps it was his way of staying in control? Of keeping his distance from her so that he could get them out of this precarious situation. Flirting could also be his way of controlling her and nothing more.

But he'd turned on her, becoming cutting and sarcastic, almost purposely goading her into anger…

What if he's been deep undercover for so long, he's afraid to try? Afraid he's not good enough? Afraid he can't be a normal, loving man?

Then again, if they did get out of this alive, wouldn't he want to get as far away from her as possible? She's the reason why he had to break his cover, why he was risking his life.

A lone tear slipped down her cheek, which she quickly brushed away. So why was the thought of never seeing him again so painful? Could he be right? Could her own feelings stem from Stockholm syndrome?

So why do I want to punch him in the nose every time he acts like a jerk?

The inside door to the garage flew open, causing Layla to jump and spill her coffee. Cyrus froze, his muscles bulging beneath the weight of the freshly cut wood he held. "Sorry if I scared you." He gave her a sheepish grin, like a boy who just got caught tracking mud through his mom's freshly mopped floor.

She waved away his apology. "It doesn't matter," she grumbled, wiping up the spilled coffee with her napkin.

He walked past her into the living room. Thumping sounds of logs and sparks and crackles reached her ear. Sitting in front of a cozy fire was one of her favorite things to do. If only things were different between them.

When he returned, he stood in front of her. She couldn't help but notice how good he looked. His mussed hair fell forward on his forehead, and his cheeks were ruddy from his exertions in the crisp morning air. His face was clean shaven, no longer sporting the brown contact lenses or beard. Averting her eyes, she tried to ignore the attraction that made her heart do somersaults. Impossible when he was standing right in front of her, his eyes riveted on her.

"Hey." He reached forward and caressed her cheek. "I'm sorry about last night."

She cursed her red hair and fair complexion and the heat that rushed to her cheeks. "No need to apologize. I'm getting used to it."

"It's my fault. I instigated it. Can we call a truce? I can't do this without you. I mean, without your help."

She didn't have the energy or the will to confront him with what she was really feeling—besides, now wasn't the time for interpersonal revelations. "Okay. Truce."

He studied her face. "Don't you want to know what I've been doing all morning?"

"Why do I have a sneaky suspicion you're going to inform me whether I want to know or not?"

"Well, I've packed the Seranza with everything we'll need and a whole lot more. I'm trying to make this as easy for you as I can, but the truth is, nothing about this is going to be easy. You know the saying—hope for the best but prepare for the worst. I think it's our best way to meet what faces us. I want you to know that I'll do whatever it takes to get you home."

"Weren't you the one who told me you can never go home?"

"I was talking about me, not you. Our futures are completely different."

"Are they? It seems to me that we're as tied to each other as two people can be."

"For now, that's true, but later, it will be another story."

"Yes, I suppose it will be. But of course, you know what the ending is, don't you?"

"No one knows the ending of any story until it's written. You and I both know that."

"Touché."

"*En garde.*" His cocky smile accomplished its desired effect. As if rewiring her circuitry, it left her speechless.

"As charming as mixing it up with you is, I actually have something important for you to do."

"What?"

He grabbed her hand and pulled her through the house into the office. He gave her the handwritten pages from the desk. "I need you to memorize everything printed on these pages—our lives may depend on it."

Layla scanned the pages. "I don't understand. Who is Noor?"

"You are, or at least you're going to be. You need to forget who you are and become Noor, the woman described in these pages. It's your legend. Tel Aviv has built a detailed history of your new assumed identity. Birth location, Spain. You're fluent in Spanish, right?"

She nodded.

"Good, me too. They've concocted a family history, schools, and of course, stories of how we met and when we were married. Everything about our identities I downloaded from the flash drive that was in an envelope Jibreel gave me. I printed it out for you. I need you to know your name and history better than you know your real name and history. You have to be letter perfect. Every detail imprinted in your brain until it is as much a part of you as your real identity. A slip-up could cost us everything."

Speechless for a moment, she gaped at him. "We're married?"

His smile was devastatingly sexy. "Yes. If we're stopped, it's the only explanation for our traveling together. Unless I was your brother, of course. That would be a tough one to pull off." He cocked his head, smiling, watching her reaction. "Your name is Noor and I'm Zand Ardavan, and we've been married for two years. From this moment on, until we cross the border out of Iran, you're Noor Ardavan, my beautiful, Spanish-born wife." The cleft in his chin deepened with his grin. "Oh, by the way, you're pregnant."

"Great, an immaculate conception."

"Yeah, that 'pretend sex' is more powerful than we thought."

She rolled her eyes and sat down to memorize the notes.

CHAPTER 26

The Hot Chocolate coffeehouse was bustling, just as Jibreel said it would be, crowded and noisy with customers looking for a hot cup of java and a bit of respite from the plummeting temperatures outside. Cyrus was dressed in character, having assumed the persona of Zand, a bearded architect. He wore an appropriate costume of slacks and sports jacket. He'd arrived early to meet Jibreel.

Sipping an espresso, he sat at a table that faced the street. He wore the satellite eyeglasses so Tel Aviv could monitor the scene in live time through him. He scanned the pages of a newspaper while keeping his eyes trained outside.

At exactly five p.m., he detected the hulking figure of Jibreel approaching from across the street. Cyrus sighed with relief—everything appeared to be proceeding on schedule without a glitch.

Last night in the dark, it had been difficult to see enough of Jibreel to form a clear picture. Now, in the fading light of day, he saw a tall, well-built man with long, straight black hair. He wore dark glasses, a short leather bomber jacket and jeans, and carried his weight gracefully.

Jibreel was about to cross the street when a fleet of police vehicles exploded around the corner, their sirens screaming and lights flashing. The police cars screeched to a stop in front of Jibreel. His reaction was instantaneous—he wasn't about to be captured in possession of fake passports. He took off at a dead run down the street in the opposite direction, toward an alleyway, before law enforcement had exited their vehicles.

Cyrus watched the unfolding drama, helpless. There wasn't a thing he could do. Had he tried to interfere, he would have given away the whole operation and become an additional target. Cyrus knew Tel Aviv was monitoring the situation—there could be no deviation. It was imperative that he follow orders and not abandon Layla and their only chance of reaching freedom. He wanted to help Jibreel, but Jibreel had willingly taken the risk, and he was a professional.

Cyrus kept his eyes peeled on the alleyway as he waited for the horrific scene to play itself out. Jibreel disappeared down the alleyway with the police in hot pursuit. Cyrus had to give him credit. For a large man, he ran with surprising speed and grace.

A few minutes later two police officers emerged from the alleyway with a handcuffed Jibreel between them, his face bleeding as if he'd taken a punch. They were half dragging him, but he looked no worse for it. In fact, if the truth be known, there was a certain bravado in his swagger, like a prize fighter who takes a punch and gets back up before the round ends.

Before Jibreel was hustled into the back of the waiting police car, he managed to look toward the coffee shop, his eyes finding Cyrus. Jibreel's nod toward the alley was all but imperceptible to anyone who might have thought to watch, but for Cyrus, his meaning couldn't have been clearer. Cyrus raised his cup of espresso to his lips and nodded back just before Jibreel's bulky frame disappeared into the police car. In a wail of sirens, the police tore down the street and disappeared.

Cyrus wasn't the only customer at Hot Chocolate to stare. Episodes like this put everyone's nerves on edge. However, no one made any comment. People pretended these kinds of incidents never happened, that the IRGC or police didn't arrest people for no apparent reason and make them disappear. When the irrefutable evidence hit them smack in the eye, most people clammed up, afraid to acknowledge what they'd seen lest they bring negative attention on themselves. It was no wonder that a few minutes later everyone had returned to his or her own conversations and their own affairs.

Cyrus finished his coffee, his eyes still peeled on the entrance to the alleyway. When a decent amount of time had passed, he left the coffee shop and nonchalantly walked across the street, took a brief glimpse around him, and ducked inside the alley, away from prying eyes.

The alley was dirty, with trash spread about, but completely empty of people. It serviced a row of stores on one side and garages on the other. Cyrus tried to find some sign of the struggle that must have taken place, but there was nothing indicating anything out of the ordinary. The short alleyway emptied onto a back street. He walked the alley several times, finding nothing. Fear pricked his neck, fear that Jibreel's arrest had something to do with Layla and him, or that he hadn't evaded capture long enough to ditch the passports. Either way, he and Layla would be in even more danger. Getting out of Iran would become impossible.

Cyrus stopped in the center of the alley, trying to think as Jibreel would have thought. Jibreel didn't want to be caught with those passports. They were a sure ticket to prison for him. That was why he'd run, his purpose to dump the passports somewhere and save his own neck. Cyrus stopped and repeated one word of his thoughts aloud—"Dump."

That's it! He dumped them in a dumpster, of course.

Using only English with Layla had him thinking in the language.

There were several dumpsters in the alley. He ran to the closest and lifted the metal lid. The rancid smell of rotting food accosted his senses, but he ignored the smell, scouring through the contents. Nothing. He ran to the next and lifted the container's lid, searching. Again, nothing. He came away empty handed. Finally, lifting the lid of the last waste container at the end of the alleyway, he cried out in anguish. "Shit, it's empty." He was about to slam it shut when he noticed a goldenrod mailing envelope jammed between a metal brace and the lid.

How had Jibreel managed to get this far down the alley and stick the envelope to the lid without the police seeing him? It seemed impossible. Cyrus ripped the envelope loose and tore it open. "Yes," he whispered. *Very clever, Jibreel. I wish you good luck, my friend. Without the passports, they haven't got a case against you. You saved us all with your quick thinking.*

Cyrus pulled out the two burgundy passports with their front covers bearing the Iranian Coat of Arms and the words "Islamic Republic of Iran." He flipped to the inside back cover and smirked at the words emblazoned in bold lettering: "The holder of this passport is not entitled to travel to occupied Palestine."

We'll see about that.

His racing pulse returned to normal, only to have it launch into orbit again when he read the warning from Tel Aviv race across the eyeglass lens. "Get out of the safe house. Now!"

Jibreel's heart thundered in his ears. Why had MOIS arrested him? Thank God he got rid of the passports. His photography studio was clean. The police wouldn't find anything there. He had to get word to his uncle. His uncle would get him out. He would be angry, but he would never allow his mother to suffer.

In the backseat of the police car, handcuffed and subdued, Jibreel projected a false impression of calm as his thoughts raced to formulate a plan. Hatred simmered in him. A long-nurtured hatred of the Islamic Republic of Iran for its stance on homosexuality fueled his spite. He had spent his whole life suppressing his inborn sexual orientation. Wishing to bring no shame to his prominent military family, he lived a lie. His father, a decorated commander killed in the Iraq war, was revered. His mother's brother, an acting general in the air force, treated him like his own son. At one time Jibreel had served as a photographer for his uncle, until he had fallen in love with someone on his uncle's staff. His uncle found out, arranged a cover up, and dismissed them both with a warning that next time he would allow the tribunals to intervene.

Homosexuality, illegal and punishable by public hanging, was enough to end any love affair. Whatever love the two men held for each other could not withstand the thought of their becoming societal pariahs. Or even worse, the threat of death. It ended, leaving Jibreel devastated. When he recovered, he dedicated himself to a course of action. He would leave Iran and live in the only country in the Middle East where a homosexual could live a life of normalcy, Israel.

He opened a photography studio in Karaj, earning his livelihood photographing tourist ski vacations in Dizin and Shemshak, saving his money for the day when he could leave his homeland.

Not long after his dismissal from the Air Force, shrouded in mystery as it was, a *katsa* approached him. Mossad, active in its outreach to discontented individuals across the Middle East, found a perfect convert, and Jibreel stumbled upon his way out of Iran. The Mossad *katsa* recruited and trained him in the art of falsifying passports and agreed to provide him with a lucrative income. He agreed to take the risk under two conditions: they would deposit his fee in an Israeli bank, and he could immigrate to Israel at the end of his contract.

The passports for Zand and Noor Ardavan were to be his final job for Mossad. No torture or punishment could break his resolve. He would not compromise the young couple that, like himself, sought freedom from an oppressive regime. His uncle must help him.

CHAPTER 27

Route 2 – Karaj to Tabriz
December 19th
7:00 p.m.

Cyrus raced back to the safe house and hustled Layla out. Thank God he'd packed everything ahead of time.

Driving the heavily trafficked Route 2 northwest to Tabriz in the evening would at least offer them cover of night. He gripped the steering wheel so tightly his knuckles were white. The six-hour drive from Karaj to Tabriz would get them to Tabriz around midnight. First thing in the morning, they would drive the three-and-a-half hours to the border at Bazargan. The Bazargan-Gurbulak border crossing was the busiest in Iran, with a long queue of trucks and cars. Cyrus was counting on that controlled chaos to expedite their entry into Turkey.

He was worried. Worried about Jibreel's arrest. Worried that MOIS would torture him and he would reveal his and Layla's fraudulent identities. If so, they would be walking straight into a trap at the border crossing. It was a risk they would have to take.

But most of all, he was worried about Layla. When he'd told her the news of Jibreel's arrest, she had turned white, peppering him with questions and what ifs. He understood her fear. His own nerves were frayed, but there wasn't time to second guess Tel Aviv's mandate. They had to get out now. Their best chance was to get to the border crossing as soon as possible, before Jalal figured out the connection between the arrest of Jibreel in Karaj and Cyrus's escape with Layla.

There were no further transmissions from The Office. For the time being, they were on their own as they drove the main artery to Tabriz. Their expeditious departure had taken its toll. Layla slept with her head resting on the center console. The quiet gave Cyrus time to think.

He had booked a room at the Tabriz El-Goli Pars Hotel situated at the outskirts of the city, a favorite of tourists. A one-night stay for a man and his wife was a normal and routine occurrence. If they tried to cross the border at night when there was less traffic, there might be greater scrutiny. It was better to leave in the morning and cross with a multitude of people.

Layla's sleepy voice interrupted Cyrus's thoughts. "Cyrus, what's the first thing you'll do when we reach Israel?"

Amusement softened the hardened lines of worry that etched his face. "Probably eat a falafel. I fell in love with them when I was training in Israel."

Layla smiled dreamily. "That sounds good. I think I'll join you."

Seeing her smile made his heart ache. "Actually, I think I'll take you out on a date."

"A date?"

"Yes, somewhere really fancy, somewhere you can get all dressed up to the nines and dazzle me with your gentile beauty."

"I look like my mother. My so-called beauty is one hundred percent Jewish."

"To me, you're coloring is about as exotic as a unicorn. But either way, there's no denying that you're beautiful—"

"You're just teasing me, aren't you, about going on a date?"

"I sure as hell am not. You're not going to deny Superman his day in the sun, are you? The least you could do for your hero is let him dream of his reward from you, a romantic night on the town. In fact, if I'm dreaming, we might as well make it an all-nighter." He flashed her a wink. He loved their verbal duels. The way they parried back and forth as if fencing. He waited, expecting her to put him in his place.

"I don't think there's anything I'd deny you," she said in a soft voice.

He looked down, trying to see her eyes in the dim light that radiated from the dashboard. Her reply was not what he'd expected.

It must be the strain of the day's events.

It amazed him that she could, with a few innocent words, tear down his cold, calculating, mercenary pretense. He reminded himself that here in Iran she was dependent on him. Everything would change once she was free to be herself, free to continue the journey she'd been on before she was kidnapped. It was inevitable that her time in Iran, including him, would become a bad memory, better left forgotten.

Even so, he couldn't help himself. His desire to possess her and send her hurtling into ecstasy burned inside him. Continuing their flirtation was irresistible. It fueled him. Their conversations gave him a purpose, easing the worries of their dangerous situation.

"Now there's something to look forward to, a woman who'll deny me nothing," he prodded. A vision of holding her naked in his arms filled his loins with a powerful yearning. He found it difficult to breathe, so intense was his desire. Brushing his fingers across her cheek, he allowed himself the smallest of visceral pleasures, the satisfaction of touching her in some small way.

I wish you weren't so damned adorable, so angelic.

"You know, Cyrus, I'm so used to your teasing by now, that it barely gets a rise out of me. I've figured out it's your way of deflecting your emotions. Instead of showing who you really are, or what you're really feeling, you hide behind provocative humor meant to sidetrack us from discussing our deeper feelings. It's okay, though I just wish for once you could be honest with yourself."

Taken aback by how close to home Layla had struck, he took a minute to regain his composure. It was as if she could read his thoughts. "Layla, even if you're correct, which I'm not saying you are, I've told you that there's nothing normal about our predicament. We're in a fair amount of danger, and that creates an artificial bond that has no bearing on the reality of our lives. Once we're out of this hellhole, in all likelihood you'll never want to lay eyes on me again."

"Keep telling yourself that if it makes you feel better. Just don't try and tell me what I'm feeling isn't real. You can play those mental games on yourself, but I'm not having any of it."

She was killing him. His stubborn red-head with her vulnerable eyes and her emotional truths. These revelations had to stop. They didn't have time to sort through all their personal baggage. It was dangerous. It weakened him. He had to stay sharp and objective. Their future was too precarious and uncertain.

If it means shocking her with cruel realities, then so be it.

"Layla, you and I are as different as night and day. Let's leave it at that, shall we? We're only an hour from Tabriz. Why don't you get a bit more shut-eye? Tomorrow's going to be a trying day."

Layla closed her eyes, leaving Cyrus to his own machinations. He tried to focus on the road, anything other than looking down at the woman he'd become too attached to.

CHAPTER 28

Tehran, Iran
Oghab2 Headquarters
December 20th
7:00 a.m.

General Ahmad Shahsafi, in his air force dress uniform, entered the office of Jalal Rahimi at Oghab2 prepared to do battle.

"General, to what do I owe the honor of your visit? Would you care for a cup of tea?"

"No, thank you. This is not a social call. Allow me to get right down to the reason for my visit."

"As you wish."

"My nephew, Jibreel Behzadi, is being held in Karaj at Gorhardasht Prison on accusations of sodomy and rape. The charges are false and slanderous. A statement given under torture by a former aide of mine is not admissible evidence. I would like this embarrassing episode to disappear."

"I certainly understand your distress, General. Your nephew is a photographer, isn't he?"

"Yes. An innocuous profession, I'm sure you'll agree."

"It is, unless, of course, your nephew supplements his photography business with a criminal sideline."

"What criminal sideline might that be?"

"Passports, General. Fraudulent passports for enemies of the revolution."

"That's ridiculous. What evidence do you have to support such a preposterous claim?"

"It's true that we haven't sufficient proof as of yet, but...*you and I both know that I don't really need it.*"

The general frowned. "What can I do to persuade you that my nephew is innocent?"

"I need to know if he was contacted recently by this man." Jalal handed him a photograph of Cyrus Hassani. "If so, I want to know everything there is to know about that contact. Particularly where Hassani is going and with whom he is working. Who might be helping him in his traitorous endeavors?" He handed the general another photo of Layla. "We would also like to know if he's had any contact with this woman. She is an escaped prisoner."

The general took the photos and studied them. "I will speak to my nephew myself and get back to you. I want your assurance that once my nephew has given you the information you seek, you'll release him, and the matter will be closed."

"You have my word, General. Get me the information on Hassani and the girl, and your nephew is free to go."

When the General left, Jalal picked up his phone. "See that a helicopter is put on emergency standby for me; I want a squad of fighters put on high alert and ready to leave at a moment's notice. You've placed all border control on high alert for the apprehension of Hassani and the girl, yes?"

Jalal listened to his aide confirm his orders.

"Excellent. We should know which direction the wind blows very soon."

CHAPTER 29

One mile from the Bazargan-Gurbulak Turkish border crossing, the traffic came to a stop. An endless line of cars and trucks sat bumper to bumper, their diesel fumes rising in a smoky haze that coated the tongue with a disgusting taste.

"What do you think is going on? Is it always this slow?" Layla asked, concerned.

"I don't think so."

They were jammed between a bus carrying tourists and a truck carrying chickens. They inched up a car length.

"At this rate it will take hours to get through." Cyrus looked around at the snow-covered landscape. As far as the eye could see, farm and ranch acreage stretched out across the bucolic, picturesque landscape before rising into the hills and mountains of Azerbaijan. The trip, monotonous and uneventful, had seemed destined to succeed. Now, Cyrus knew all bets were off.

He glanced in his rearview mirror just as five SUVs with darkened windows rushed up the road shoulder, headed for the border crossing. He frowned. This did not portend well. They might be driving into a trap. He grabbed the satellite glasses from his pocket and put them on, wondering if Tel Aviv had any idea what was happening ahead. A frantic stream of words appeared on the lens with instructions for him to abort their attempt to cross into Turkey.

"Shit!"

"What is it?" The panic rising in Layla's voice temporarily distracted him.

157

"We can't cross into Turkey."

"Why not?"

"Stay here!" It was an order.

Fear crept into her eyes, but he ignored her and jumped out of the car.

"Where are you going?"

"Layla, do as I say and stay here. I'll be right back." He slammed the door and walked down the line of cars and trucks. When he found a semi that he knew would have a CB, he knocked on the door of the cab. The driver looked at him questioningly, and Cyrus waved for him to roll down the window.

"What can I do for you, sir?"

"My wife is pregnant and has to go to the toilet. Have you heard anything from other truckers about what's going on up ahead that's causing this delay? Why we're moving so slow?"

"Yeah, there's some kind of emergency. The Pasdaran are looking for someone. They're searching every car and truck. The truckers are in an uproar, but it looks like we could be here for hours. I'm sorry for your wife's discomfort. It may be some time before you reach a restroom."

"Thanks. Now at least I know what I must do."

Cyrus was walking back to the car when he saw in the distance a military helicopter flying low over the line of vehicles toward him. He dropped his glasses and bent to pick them up, ducking behind a truck wheel just as the helicopter flew above him. After it passed, he rose, his eyes squinting as he followed its path toward the border station.

Back in the car, he grabbed the steering wheel and leaned his head against it, trying to think. Everything was falling apart.

"Cyrus, what is it? Is everything all right?"

Layla's hand on his shoulder reminded him that he needed to keep his cool. "We have to find another way out, but it's okay. I have a plan. Right now, we need to get away from here and get off this highway."

"But where will we go?"

"Azerbaijan. We're going to cross the mountains."

"But it's winter. Aren't they impassable?"

"No, it's doable. We have plenty of supplies and a four-wheel drive. I just need to plot our route and keep us off the main roads. We can't go this way, Layla, they're looking for us. I need you to be strong, okay?"

Tears filled her eyes, and her lips quivered, drawing into a grim line of fear, but she nodded.

He forced a smile, his hand caressing her cheek. "Good. Now let's focus on getting out of here." The truck filled with chickens pulled ahead one car length, and Cyrus took the opportunity to make a U-turn and head back in the direction they had come.

"What are you doing? If they see our car turn around, they'll come after us!"

"No, look behind us." Layla turned around, and sure enough, other vehicles, seeing them go the other way, began to turn around and follow them. "Not everyone wants to wait ten hours to cross into Turkey. Most will give up and try another day."

"Where will we go?"

"Back to Karaj where we'll buy a canoe and chains for the tires."

"A canoe? What do we need a canoe for?"

"It's the only way to get to Varian Village, which is the last place on earth anyone will come looking for us. It's secluded in the mountains on Amir Kabir Lake. In fact, you can't even get there except by boat. I know a house there; the people only use it in the summer. We'll stay one night and tomorrow continue on the Chalus Road to the Caspian Sea, which is about a six-hour drive. From there it's a straight shot along the Caspian coastline to the Azerbaijan border at Astara, maybe six hours farther.

"This route will avoid most of the heavily traveled roads and keep us off the radar of the IRGC. During the summer, the Chalus Road is a tourist haven, but this time of year, the road is treacherous and practically impassable. It's not exactly a direct route, but it will get us out of Iran, hopefully without having to confront any authorities."

Layla said nothing, but her face showed her strain and turmoil.

"Hey, look at the bright side. You're going to travel one of the most beautiful roads in the world and spend the night in one of the most pristine spots on the planet."

"Lucky me."

Cyrus laughed, trying to make light of the situation. "Come on, Layla, where's your sense of adventure?"

"Oh, let me see? The military might of the Islamic Republic of Iran is hunting us, and Superman thinks this might be an opportune moment to go sightseeing in the outback. As if things couldn't get worse, he's making jokes as if there's something comical in our situation. I'm beginning to think that I should change your name from Superman to Madman."

"God, I love your feistiness. I could listen to you dish it out all day long. You'd certainly fit well in Israel where the women are as tough as the men."

"I'm so glad I keep you amused. It would be a shame to waste all this quality time we're spending with each other." She glared at him.

Cyrus unleashed a smile that could melt any woman's heart. "You know, one day we might look back on this time together as an exciting interlude in our lives."

"In order to look back on this time together, we need to survive your so-called interlude. Besides, I hardly expect to look back on any of this with anything remotely resembling fondness."

Cyrus held his smile, letting her have the last word as he kept a vigilant eye in the rearview mirror. He didn't tell Layla what he feared most…that Jalal Rahimi would blame her for his treason and be driven to vengeance. Jalal was a true believer in Sharia, the laws of Islam taken from the words and actions of Mohammad. One of the *Sunnah's* commandments was that a non-Muslim who leads a Muslim away from Islam is to be punished with death. If Jalal justified Cyrus's betrayal of him as a betrayal of Islam, it would not be beyond him to obtain a religious decree sentencing Layla to death, a *fatwa* that he would take as his personal duty to fulfill.

Cyrus feared that he had inadvertently placed Layla in more danger than she could ever imagine. Jalal would find them—of this he was certain. When he did, Cyrus would have to be ready. He knew how his opponent operated. Jalal was incapable of mercy. Only their deaths would satisfy his bloodlust and desire for revenge.

CHAPTER 30

The midnight sky foreshadowed no imminent danger to the two people who silently rowed across the tranquil waters of the Amir Kabir reservoir. The moon shone through the wispy cloud cover, illuminating the lake in an ethereal, silver light. It was freezing, and Layla shivered from both the cold and a gripping fear that had settled in her chest. That fear, as much as the frigid air, made it difficult to breathe.

She was tired beyond reason, both mentally and physically. She sat in the front of the canoe clutching a heavy backpack, while Cyrus paddled toward the tiny village nestled in a forest of pine and alder trees. The glass-like surface of the lake, reflecting the moon and stars rippled, breaking into fractured images each time Cyrus dipped the oar in the frigid water as he guided the canoe silently forward.

The serene beauty of the place would have been lost to her were it not for a vision that intruded upon her thoughts. In her dreamscape, she transformed the dark of night into a blue-sky day with dappled sunlight perfectly reflected in the mirrored surface of the lake. She imagined trailing her fingers in the pristine mountain water, in the heat of summer, as Cyrus rowed them to shore. His deep, green eyes never leaving hers when he made her laugh from yet another silly thing he said. The romantic picture filled her with longing. The reality of what they meant to each other and what the future might hold was the complete opposite of this conjured, waking dream.

She huddled deeper into her jacket and looked down at an AKM assault rifle, a stark reminder that her life was in the hands of the brooding man that rowed her toward shore. The fantasy shattered as she stared at the cold, metal instrument of death, catapulting her from her dream into the present.

Cyrus's attention was focused, his eyes trained on the tiny hamlet where they would spend the night. It gave her an opportunity to observe him. Not even the disguise of beard and contacts could diminish the magnetism that emanated from him. He was a perfect combination of brawn, charm, and intelligence, unlike anyone she had ever known. She was incapable of resisting this man of a thousand faces with his pleasantly accented English and his expertise in all things related to love and war. His strength of purpose and determination made all other men pale in comparison. His faults were rational, even understandable, considering the damage done to him by living a dual life, a life in which he could trust no one.

Self-preservation should have sounded an alarm within her, warning her she was in danger, not only from the Iranians but from Cyrus himself. Instead, she made excuses for who he was and what he'd become. She chose to believe that under the right circumstances he could reverse course and adapt to a normal life, casting away the warrior he'd become. She recalled the idiom—a leopard doesn't change its spots. But she was blinded by a need to play the story out to its conclusion, to find out if her belief in him was warranted.

For all his promises to get them out safely, Layla believed time was running out and that she would never leave Iran. If her instincts were right, there was something she needed from him. He would fight against giving it to her, fight to deny her the satisfaction of her desire, but she had made up her mind, and like him, she was determined to get what she wanted, to win.

Surrounded by darkness Cyrus helped Layla walk up the hill, to the cabin of stone and wood where they would rest for the night. Their progression was slow given the supplies they carried and Layla's exhaustion. At least the full moon lit their path, making it easy to see.

When they reached the cabin, he found the key in its hiding place and opened the door. When he tried to turn on a light, he cursed; there was no electricity. He hadn't considered that the utilities would be turned off for the winter. No electricity meant no heat. The possibility of freezing to death raced through his mind. Layla stood mutely in the entry, her body shaking uncontrollably from the icy chill. Cyrus dropped the backpack and went to her, rubbing her arms. "I know it's cold. Just hold on a few minutes more, and I'll get a fire going."

Her silence worried him. She was shaking so badly that he could hear her teeth chattering. Opening the backpack, he began emptying it. Then he removed the fake beard and contact lenses, placing them in their case. "Remove your contact lenses." He held out his hand as she shakily complied and then he deposited them in another case. Without missing a beat, he lit a fire, providing a small amount of heat. Aware that Layla hadn't moved, her body frozen in place, he pulled her toward the fire and rubbed her hands. They were as cold as blocks of ice. "Any better?"

She stared into his eyes, unable to stop the trembling. "I-I-I c-c-can't f-f-feel a th-th-thing," she whispered. "So-o-o cold."

Cyrus opened the sleeping bag and laid it on the old, worn Persian rug in front of the fireplace. He only had one sleeping bag, but it was large enough for both of them. Besides, he figured he'd be holding her through the night in order to keep her warm.

"This is going to seem crazy, but we need to get all these layers of clothing off and get you into the sleeping bag." As he spoke, he removed her coat and began to peel away her clothes. When she was left with only long underwear, he took her hands and helped her into the sleeping bag. Then he removed his own clothing and got in the bag with her. He rubbed her arms, hands, and back, trying to get the blood flowing to her extremities. In the firelight, her skin was, pale and translucent, her lips tinged with blue. "I'm going to hold you against me until you warm up." He wrapped his body around her.

"Cyrus?"

The whisper of his name on her lips sent heat pulsating to his loins. *Hell of a time to get a hard-on*, he thought.

"What is it, *aziz-am*?"

"I need to tell you something, just in case I never get another chance," she whispered.

"What are you talking about?"

"Shh, please let me tell you this without interrupting me."

Respecting her request, he searched her eyes, waiting for the words that would bring her peace. At this moment, whatever she wanted he would give her.

Her eyes were wide and questioning. "I don't believe we're ever getting out of Iran."

He began to protest, and again she shushed him, placing her finger to his lips.

"I promised my mother on her deathbed that I would save myself for someone I truly loved. If we don't get out of Iran, I may never know that feeling. I know you don't love me." She dropped her eyes in embarrassment. "I don't want to die never having been loved... I want you to make love to me." She looked back up at him her eyes were glittering with unshed tears. "I want you because of who you are and the way you make me feel—I would want you even if I had met you in another time, or another place, or under different circumstances. I want you—only you."

For a moment, all he could hear was his blood pounding like thunder in his ears. Never in his life had he expected to feel like this. From the first moment he'd seen her, he'd fought what he considered his dangerous attraction to her and now, in a plea that no healthy male in his right mind would turn down, she offered him a chance of redemption, of which he felt unworthy. She offered him the Holy Grail—herself. Vacillating between joy and sorrow, he felt like a condemned prisoner receiving his last meal, wanting to savor every morsel and knowing that he may never taste its perfection again. All of his carefully constructed barriers came tumbling down around him as he stared into the beautiful turquoise eyes of the woman who unknowingly held his heart in her hands.

I know it would be wrong, but dear God, how I want her.

"Even if I agreed, I don't have any way of protecting you, no condom. What if you get pregnant?" Even as he said it, he knew it was a pathetic excuse. Her giddy laughter made him smile at his foolishness.

"I'm worried about surviving two more days, and you're worried about a baby being born nine months from now?" From the determination in her eyes, he knew he would be hard-put to dissuade her. "I promise you, if we survive and I'm pregnant, I'll never bother you. It won't be your problem."

"That's not what I meant, Layla. I...I'm just trying to lay out the possible consequences."

She trembled, shivering against him, and he pulled her closer, willing his warmth into her.

"Forget the consequences, Cyrus. You and me—we're all that matters. Everything else is ugly. Only this, what we're feeling here and now, is beautiful."

Was she speaking from her heart, or was this some kind of aberration concocted out of fear? All he knew was that it was impossible for him to control his desire. His arousal pressed against his jockey shorts. He savored the pain, his eyes devouring her full, inviting lips. He wanted her more than anything he'd ever wanted in his life.

Shuddering, she bit her lower lip. His cock twitched and jumped. Even if he still tried to convince himself otherwise, one part of his body knew exactly what he wanted. His ability to resist her was long gone.

Damn it. I'm tired of doing what's right. I want to erase every memory of that unworthy Saudi boy, to show her what it means to love and be loved by a man. A man that appreciates all that she is.

His voice, deep and husky, thick with lust, broke the silence. "I'll be gentle, *sheereen-am*. At least I'll try." His eyes burned with intensity.

"I don't want you to be gentle. I want everything you want," she whispered, "and more."

"Then, I will be like a summer storm swirling through your garden. I will take you and make you mine."

He kissed her gently. "Put your arms up over your head."

With each item of clothing he removed, he pressed himself against her, sharing his heat with her. His lips softly kissed every inch of newly exposed skin, raising goosebumps. She arched into him, moaning softly from the way he savored her. Lacing his thumbs in the waistband of her long underwear, he lowered them, running his hands over her rear, squeezing the pliable flesh until she moaned again. He inhaled the scent of her excitement, intoxicated. "You're so beautiful, *eshgham*. So desirable. I've never wanted any woman as much as I want you. All I want to do is lose myself in this feeling of loving you."

He took her breast in his hand, fondling its perfection. He kissed her, explored her mouth with his tongue, hungry to taste all of her. She kissed him back with a flowering passion that ignited him, his cock growing ever harder against her stomach. He pulled back for a moment from her sweetness, his breath coming unevenly, the words tumbling from him. "Layla, I pray you don't wake up and regret this. I want this to be beautiful for you. I want you to feel loved. I'm not sure of what I'm feeling, whether this is love, but if it isn't, then it's better than love."

She giggled. "Was that a confession of love, or am I hearing things?"

He chuckled, his warm breath in her ear. "For once your teasing is on target, angel. A man like me doesn't expect to be loved or to love, but with you I don't seem to have a choice. There are forces at work that I have no control over."

She sighed, running her hands over the dark stubble on his face. "I'm not asking you for forever, Cyrus. I'm asking you to be mine tonight."

"I am yours—I've been yours from the first moment I saw you. We won't make any promises beyond that. But if there was ever a woman placed on this earth that was meant to be mine—it's you, baby."

"Oh, Cyrus, thank you for making me feel loved and desired."

With that he trailed kisses along her cheek, to her neck and the gentle slope of her shoulders. "I'll be gentle my love. I'll take my time. I won't stop until you're pleasured."

"Anything—just don't stop loving me now," she said in a breathless whisper.

No one had told her it would be like this. The way he kissed her, touched her, delighted in her—it wasn't what she'd ever expected. Being out of control, a vessel for his pleasure, excited her. He wrapped his lips around her nipple, hungrily sucking her breast into his mouth until she gasped, knowing she could come just from his lips, his tongue, even his words.

"Oh, Cyrus, don't stop," she begged.

His hand parted her legs, and he teased her clitoris, which swelled and hardened against the rough texture of his fingers.

"You're not cold anymore, *aziz-am*, are you? I feel liquid heat burning between your legs, and I can't wait to plunge deep inside you," he growled.

She arched against his fingers, which only touched her with enough pressure to make her crave more. "You're playing with a woman who's coming undone, and you know it."

"How close are you, angel? Are you wet enough to receive all of me?"

"I don't know. I just know, I want you inside me."

He slipped his shorts off and lifted himself to his elbow, hovering above her. "The wetter you are, the less it will hurt. I don't want to hurt you—I want to love you. I want you so much, *sheereen-am*. Give me your hand and touch my desire for you."

He took her hand, sliding it over his enormous hardness, the pleasure causing them both to suck in their breaths.

"You're so big, so hard."

"See what you do to me? I don't think I've ever been so aroused in my life." He closed his eyes.

She felt the large vein pulse against her palm as she ran her hand up and down his length. The anticipation of feeling his hard cock inside her turned her insides to liquid. When she moaned, a drop of pre-cum released, coating her hand. She slid the warm semen up and down his shaft.

She lifted her head, her lips begging for his kiss. His Nile-green eyes were dark and dilated. He drank in her mouth and with his fingers he parted and probed her tender folds with a soft caress.

"Now, Cyrus, please, I want you now," she breathed, imploring him to love her.

He bit her lip, teasing her, and spread her legs. Then he eased his finger into her, not touching her hymen. "My love, you are my first and my last virgin. *Ātashé del-am*, you are the fire of my heart. You are beautiful. Irresistible. Perfect." With each word he kissed her deeply.

Cyrus poised above her. His cock in hand, he ran it over her clitoris, watching her face. Her hips rose, pressing against the head of his cock. Another drop of semen escaped. He rubbed it over her clit until she moaned. Then he pushed, entering her slowly until he touched the membrane that stood as a barrier against his complete possession of her. He grasped her face between his hands, her eyes aglow from the fire, gazed back at him. Her beauty took his breath away. "You are mine. Now and forever," he whispered.

"I'm yours, Cyrus."

Those words extinguished his last bit of control. He thrust deep within her, joining their bodies, making her his forever.

Layla cried out in the moment of his conquest, and then a radiance spread across her face. She closed her eyes and breathlessly urged him on. He growled with his mounting passion, the feeling of possessing her completely. She was so tight, her pussy locked around his hardness, clenching his cock, gripping it as if it were hers alone. It took everything he had not to come in the face of such pleasure. He paused, hip to hip with her, allowing her to feel the large shaft that filled her. "You're so tight, baby. Does it feel good?"

Layla sighed, "Yes…Yes my love."

The music of her sighs heightened his need, and he began to deepen his thrusts.

Surely, I've died and gone to heaven.

Her thighs tightened around him. He gloried in her body's response to his.

167

"You are mine, *sheereen-am*, all mine."

Her gasping breaths told him she was near. He thrust harder and faster, possessing her, driving her higher and higher until she screamed his name, bathing him in her glorious pleasure. She shattered beneath him, trembling.

Burying his lips in her neck, he slowed, wanting to prolong this moment forever. Savoring every sensation, he rose to his elbows so he could watch her face as he pulled out from her before plunging again into her tightness and heat. His breath was ragged when he asked, "Are you okay, baby? Do you think you can come again?"

She sucked in a breath. "You feel so good inside me. I never dreamed it would be like this."

He couldn't control the sudden push of his loins against her that her words elicited.

"Oh, yes," she breathed, "I can definitely come again."

Smiling, he kissed her, his tongue seductively arousing her as he continued to thrust into her in a slow, measured rhythm.

"That's good," he murmured against her lips. "I want this to be the most beautiful thing you've ever experienced."

He pulled completely out of her, and she cried out, "No, Cyrus, please, don't stop."

He grinned. He had to see her shatter beneath him one more time. He alternated his thrusts between deep and shallow, rubbing against her clit. He felt her reignite, and then unable to stop the intense explosion that had been building, he stroked long and deep, losing himself in the pumping until he heard her cry "Cyrus," and felt her body shudder uncontrollably beneath him again.

The cry of his name on her lips undid him. Stiffening, he buried himself deep within her, his groans joining hers as he released, his life force gushing from him into her. He never wanted it to end...

A guilty thought crossed his mind. *I know it's wrong, but I hope my seed makes you pregnant.*

She lay blissfully vanquished beneath him as he rocked gently inside her, kissing her, their bodies drenched in contentment. Flames of light played across her delicate features as he gazed into her eyes.

He rested on his elbows above her. There was no need to speak. It was a testament to his need for her that his cock remained semi-hard, nestled inside her. He didn't want to leave the wet warmth of her and break the bond of their union, but they needed to sleep a few hours before the sun rose and it was time for them to be on the move. Regretfully, he pulled out from her, enjoying the small sigh of protest that escaped her lips.

He moved quickly, dressing them both, and threw another log on the fire. Returning to the sleeping bag he kissed her and wrapped his body around hers to keep her warm. "Sleep, *eshgham*."

Sighing, spent with exhaustion, she nestled against his warmth.

He was drifting off into sleep when she whispered, "I love you, Cyrus."

CHAPTER 31

Tel Aviv, Israel
Mossad Headquarters,
December 21st
4:30 a.m.

Aleck arrived at Mossad headquarters to find everyone in the nerve center scrambling to save the operation. Sleep had eluded him, plagued as he was with worry over the peril his daughter faced. The failed border crossing into Turkey meant she was no closer to freedom or safety than at the moment of her kidnapping. In fact, with a manhunt now unleashed, she was in more danger than ever. Aleck couldn't contain the anger that seethed through his veins.

"Isaac, where are they?"

Isaac's hand on his shoulder was an empty assurance. "They're at a village in Karaj."

"Back where they started?"

"No, it's a tiny, summer resort on a lake, hardly a speck on the map. Somewhere Cyrus must know is safe. I'm sure Layla was in no condition to continue. He needed to find a refuge for the night."

"Now what? Where are they going to go from there? Certainly, they can't attempt another crossing into Turkey? Do you have a contingency plan?"

"We're working on it now." He turned and ordered, "Bring up the map of Iran." Instantly, a map appeared on the big screen. Isaac pointed with a laser pen. "Bring it closer."

The image focused on a winding road through the Alborz Mountains. Isaac moved the red beam of the laser, highlighting a spot bordering a small, blue mass of water.

"This is the village of Varian where they currently are. With a population of just under three hundred and accessible only by boat, it has its safety advantages."

"It's in the middle of nowhere. Nowhere near a border."

"It's only two-and-a-half hours from the Caspian Sea."

"How are you going to rescue them from the Caspian Sea?"

"We're not. It's a six hour drive up the coast to the border of Azerbaijan."

"You're losing me, Isaac."

"Aleck, we have a long history of enterprise with Azerbaijan and an understanding with the Azer government. We lease and control a secret military airbase near the Caspian Sea, northwest of Baku. Sitalcay Military Airbase is a former Soviet base, and we have fortified it with helicopters, jets, and an elite commando team. The base is operational, and we maintain follow-on and search-and-rescue teams there. If we have to, we have the ability to swoop in and extricate Layla and Cyrus from Iran."

"But wouldn't that provoke a confrontation with Iran, a dangerous international incident?"

"Possibly yes, possibly no. Iran's leadership is much too smart to engage in a military show of action, before their nuclear ambitions becoming operational. As of this moment, they have no nuclear bomb. Of course, this Iran deal with the US brings them ever closer to the day when they become a viable nuclear threat."

"You don't know that, Isaac. Perhaps this new deal between Iran and the US is the beginning of a dialogue between all the parties that can lead to peace. Iran could change and take its place among the nations, bringing prosperity to its people."

"Unfortunately, Aleck, we do know, and there's no chance for peaceful resolution. Cyrus's position within Oghab2, Iran's nuclear watchdog, gave him complete access to their nuclear ambitions. He's been our greatest source of knowledge on their progress. Aleck, they have begun laser-excitation U-238 processing."

Aleck paled. In a nanosecond, he realized the sacrifice the Israeli government had made in its efforts to rescue Layla. Without their greatest spy asset, their eyes went blind and their ears went silent. It became clear to him how important his own expertise could be in countering the clear and present danger of a nuclearized Iran. The project he had shelved, but continued secretly to work on over the years, might be the only way to defend against the radical Islamist regime. The prime minister knew this, and for this reason was willing to use the full might of Mossad and the Israeli military to rescue his daughter.

Aleck chided himself, feeling guilt for having even thought for one minute that Israel's only reason for helping him was because of his nuclear know how. He was being unfair. Israel had a long history of risking everything to save Jews in danger around the world. However, the coincidence of his unique expertise and the government's desire to stay ahead of the game and protect this tiny jewel of a country from those that lived to destroy it was obvious.

"I'm sorry, Isaac, for my impatient rant."

"You have nothing to be sorry for. We're all on the same page. We owe it not only to Cyrus but also Layla. Cooler heads must prevail, and we will."

"So, what do we—"

"Excuse me, sir, but we have a problem." The computer expert nodded at the screen.

Isaac and Aleck riveted their attention on the screen. A boat was crossing the water toward Varian. The technician brought the eye of the satellite closer. Two armed men in camouflage became discernible.

"Send out a warning to Cyrus, now!"

CHAPTER 32

Karaj County, Alborz Province, Iran
Amir Kabir Reservoir
December 20th
5:30 a.m.

Even in the face of the danger that threatened them, Cyrus had never felt more alive or happier. He awoke at dawn, watching Layla sleep in his arms, her breath against his neck as sweet as last night's kisses. Responding to the ache in his groin, he felt tempted to make love to her again. To take her hard and swift, filling her with the force of his desire. He longed to hear his name on her lips again in the moment of her orgasm.

Cyrus contained his yearning—Layla needed to get as much sleep as possible before this day began that would determine their future. Kissing her forehead, he reluctantly left her sleeping. He quickly got dressed and headed to the small store that operated out of a resident's home. He wanted to get coffee and breakfast and return to the cabin before she awoke.

He walked down the hill whistling. The air, brisk and scented with pine, brought a bounce to his step. The snow drifts around him shimmered as the sun rose in the sky, making its morning greeting. The world that had been dark and dismal for his entire adult life now appeared filled with magic.

He entered the shop, which was actually just a detached guesthouse converted into a tiny store for necessities and provisions. He was surprised to find quite a few people waiting in line and milling about. Feeling no sense of urgency, he took his place at the end of the line, turning his back to the door.

Layla awoke yawning and stretched within the cozy cocoon of the sleeping bag. She broke into a smile, warmth engulfing her as she remembered the passionate, life-changing events of last night. The soreness between her legs was proof that she was no longer a virgin. She closed her eyes, remembering every intimate detail and everything Cyrus said to her. She wished she could write it all down and press it like a rose between the pages of a book, saving it forever.

There was a fresh log on the fire in the hearth, and she turned fully to savor its warmth. When she heard the front door open, she called, "So, what have you been up to this morning?" She glanced over her shoulder expecting to see Cyrus and froze.

Before her stood two men pointing Kalashnikovs at her. One of the men barked orders at her in Farsi. He motioned with the Kalashnikov's barrel for her to get out of the sleeping bag. He said something to the other man, who disappeared farther into the house, his AK-47 aimed to shoot as he went to inspect the rooms. The soldier watched as she slid from the bag. A grin lit his face when he saw that all she wore were silk long johns. His eyes traveled up and down her body appreciatively. The look in his eyes spiked her heartbeat, pumping adrenaline through her veins. Without the warmth of the sleeping bag, she trembled uncontrollably, causing her nipples to poke out beneath the silk. His eyes locked on her breasts and she crossed her arms over her chest in a protective gesture.

The other man returned and said something and shook his head, which Layla took to mean that no one was in the house. Seeing her standing there shivering, he openly ogled her and said something that brought laughter to the other man.

Oh, dear God, where are you Cyrus?

She closed her eyes and prayed that Cyrus was smart enough not to barge in like a superhero and be shot or captured. When she opened her eyes, the bigger of the two men had put his gun down and was walking toward her with a leering smile on his face. He undid his belt and zipped down his fly, pulling out his cock. She screamed and tried to run past him, but he grabbed her about the waist and pulled her against him.

He stank of sweat and tobacco, and she felt dry heaves coming on. He grabbed her breast, squeezing it hard, and she cried out in pain. He held her in a vice-like grip, her fists trapped at her sides. She screamed for him to stop and tried to knee him in the groin, and missed, but she continued to fight him, kicking and thrashing. She freed one arm and dug her nails down his face.

He roared with rage and slapped her so hard she saw stars.

"Do not fight me, American whore," he spat in English. "It is over. Your boyfriend has deserted you, and he is a dead man anyway. All you have is Massoud and me. We are here to return you to prison, but not before we give you two large presents. When we are finished, you will not fight so much."

Massoud roared with laughter. "Leiss, my friend! Maybe you should let me soften her for you."

"Stop the wise-cracks and help me subdue this she-devil," Leiss grunted.

Massoud came up behind her and pressed his cock into her back as he grabbed her arms. Leiss pulled a handkerchief from his pocket, and tied it tightly over her mouth, gagging her.

Her muffled screams were barely audible as they dragged her to the couch and threw her down. Leiss removed a pair of handcuffs from his pocket and dangled them in front of her. "No more fighting, little bird." He smirked. "Now we take turns fucking America. Maybe you like it so much that we do it more than once."

Massoud chortled as his hands twisted her nipples so hard tears came to her eyes. Nausea and dizziness almost made her faint. She breathed through her nose, trying to keep from throwing up, scared she could choke on her own vomit because of the gag.

"I'm going to *kiram too koset.*" Leiss's hands groped between her legs. "I think in *Engilisi* it means fuck your pussy." He laughed, moving toward her.

Cyrus walked up the hill toward the cabin, smiling, knowing that his life had changed forever. Once they got to Israel, he was determined to find a way to hold on to her. If it meant no Mossad, then so be it. He wasn't prepared to give up what might be his only chance of happiness. He didn't know whether a man who had lived his life as a spy, whose life was a complete lie, could function as a normal person, but for Layla he was willing to try.

Steam rose from the coffee cups, and the aroma from the freshly baked sweet rolls he carried in a bag spurred his hunger and he quickened his pace. He'd forgotten to check the glasses to see if there were any messages. He would do it when he got back to the cabin. They would eat and then be on their way. If his computations were correct, they should be at the

Azerbaijan-Iran border by sunset. The Office would be able to get their coordinates and their destination and be ready to help them.

In his haste to get back to Layla, he stumbled, nearly dropping the coffees. Pausing, he heard a muffled cry, and his senses went to high alert. His gaze scanned the front of the house, looking for anything that might indicate a problem. Seeing nothing, he crept closer and quietly put the coffees and the bag of rolls down.

Moving silently to a window, he peered in to investigate. The shiny metal handcuffs dangling before a cowering Layla affected him like a red cape dancing in front of a bull.

Rage engulfed him.

His first impulse nearly propelled him to charge through the door and kill the bastards. He took a deep breath, using sheer will to calm himself as he removed his coat so his movements wouldn't be impaired. He had to use caution. There were two armed adversaries. Years of training took over. The jealous lover became the proficient killer, cold and calculating. Rolling his pant leg up, he pulled his Glauca B1, with its seven-and-a-half-inch steel blade, from its leg harness. He knew the layout of the house and tiptoed around to the kitchen entrance. He slipped inside, not making a sound, leaving the door and screen open. Two men argued in the other room. Grabbing the screen, he swung it shut and it closed with a bang.

One of the men was cursing in Farsi, but the noise caused both men to go silent.

"Go see what the hell is going on in the kitchen. Be careful—if it's the traitor, shoot him—but not to kill. *Agha* wants that pleasure for himself."

Cyrus heard a vicious slap and Layla's muffled cry of pain. His blood pumped hot with fury.

You're going to pay for that, motherfucker.

He hid behind the door and waited; the knife poised ready to strike. The kitchen door was kicked open, and a man entered with his assault rifle raised, finger on the trigger, ready to shoot. Before he had time to blink or register Cyrus's presence, Cyrus covered his mouth with one hand and with his other slashed the blade across his throat, cutting his windpipe and his two carotid arteries.

The Iranian's eyes grew wide as blood gushed from his neck, draining from him. His only protest was a dying gurgle. Cyrus sheathed the knife and grabbed the Ak-47 from the soldier's death grip. Quietly, he lowered the body to the floor.

Cyrus peeked around the door into the living room. Layla was lying on her stomach on the couch, her hands in cuffs behind her back. The bastard had pulled her bottoms off and was masturbating as he spread her legs. "Hurry up, buddy," he yelled out. You should see the sweet, red-haired pussy on this whore."

When there was no answer, he turned toward the kitchen, a frown creasing his heavy brows. A split-second later, his eyes widened as the flash of a blade whirled across the room, slicing into his forehead with a loud crunch of shattering bone. The force of the impact nearly split his head in half, killing him instantly. The dead man toppled over onto Layla, who screamed into the handkerchief gag.

"You're safe Layla," Cyrus said. "I'll be right back." Cyrus pulled the body away and refrained from turning her over or removing the handcuffs until he had disposed of the dead man in the kitchen with the other body. He didn't want her to see the gruesome carnage. After depositing the bloody carcass on the kitchen floor, he took the key from the dead man's pocket. Running back into the living room, he removed the gag from Layla's mouth and unlocked the handcuffs. He held her in his arms as she sobbed hysterically, her face pressed into his shoulder.

"Shh, it's okay, *aziz-am*. You're safe. I promise, you're safe."

Her words, garbled in his shirt, were barely discernible as she choked on her tears. "I was so afraid they would kill you—that you'd walk into a trap. T-they were monsters. They were going to rape me and kill you."

"I know. Thank God I stopped him before he...Shit, I can't even think about it. All I wanted to do was kill him when I saw what he was doing to you. Here, let me see your face, where the bastard hit you."

She raised her face to him, and he planted kisses over her puffy red cheek.

"It's not bad. You'll be fine. I'm sorry I wasn't here with you."

She sighed beneath his gentle kisses.

"That's it, my angel, let your tears fall. I'll always be there to catch them." He kissed her long and deep, losing himself in the sweetness of her mouth. Regretfully, he broke their embrace. He rested his forehead against hers. "We have to get out of here, Layla. We need to get on the road before these two are discovered missing. Do you understand?"

She nodded. "I'm okay. Cyrus, if you'd been here with me, they would have killed you and then raped me. It's a miracle we survived."

"You're a brave girl."

"I was so frightened."

"I know, my love." He rocked her in his arms. "It's all going to be okay."

Cyrus disposed of the bodies as best he could, dragging them outside and burying them in a snowy grave while Layla packed up and dressed. They shared their breakfast, cold coffee and sweet rolls retrieved from where Cyrus had abandoned them before the deadly confrontation.

Layla peppered him with questions about how he planned to get them out of Iran. He explained that at Astara, a city on the Caspian Sea, Iran and Azerbaijan shared a border crossing that was relatively quiet and sparsely manned. "We'll simply walk from Astara, Iran, to Astara, Azerbaijan. Israel has an airbase nearby and will be waiting for us."

"How will they know? They were expecting us to cross in Turkey."

He pulled the satellite eyeglasses from his pocket and handed them to her. "Because of these."

"What are they?"

"Put them on."

Hebrew words appeared on one of the lenses. "I don't understand."

"Mossad is tracking us through their satellite system. They know where we are at all times. What you see are missives sent from Mossad headquarters. Unfortunately, I can't communicate back with them, but they'll know exactly where we're headed and put it all together. We're not alone, Layla."

"Then why didn't they warn us about the danger of those two monsters?"

A curtain of guilt fell over his features. Painfully he admitted, "They did. I just didn't see it in time. I was so jubilant about us—our night together—I didn't even think about the glasses. I'm sorry—it was my fault that we were caught unawares. I'll never forgive myself for letting them get to you."

She placed her hand on his. "It's okay, you saved me—and you're not dead. That's all that matters."

He raised her palm to his lips and kissed it. "By this evening you'll be free."

"We'll be free," she corrected.

He nodded, saying no more. He hated keeping secrets from her, but she had enough to contend with. There seemed to be no good reason to tell her that he knew why Jalal Rahimi had sent the two assassins. What he overheard from the two men convinced him that Jalal considered this a personal vendetta. His intention was clear, he intended for Cyrus to watch Layla being raped, and then kill Cyrus and use Layla to blackmail her father.

The fact that the two soldiers had found them meant that Jalal was closing in. He also knew that Jalal would stop at nothing to get his revenge.

The only thing he and Layla had in their favor was that Jalal would have to accomplish this on a small scale, using only a few trusted men. The complete covert operation had become dangerously unacceptable and damaging. Neither the Supreme Leader nor the Security Council would ever approve of his actions. This would end in a battle between him and Jalal. His former boss would only find satisfaction by personally delivering Cyrus's last breath.

The closer Cyrus could get them to the Azerbaijan border, the better would be their chances of survival. He knew that Jalal would insist on fighting him man to man—a fight to the death. If he destroyed Jalal, there was a chance that he and Layla could somehow make it to the border. It would be a race against time, a long shot, but it was their only chance.

CHAPTER 33

Tehran, Iran
MOIS Headquarters
December 21st
12:00 p.m.

Jalal had kept his promise, releasing General Ahmad Shahsafi's nephew Jibreel after he provided a brief description of a man who had come to him for fake passports. The nephew claimed to have rejected the request, turning the man away. During his uncle's interrogation, the best Jibreel could recollect was that the man was a bearded, brown-eyed architect, someone who did not fit the description of Cyrus. The nephew said the man claimed to have a Spanish wife who was pregnant and wished to return to her family. Jibreel had seen a photo of the woman, and he described a pretty woman, dark-haired and dark-eyed. Neither of his descriptions matched up to Layla and Cyrus, but hair dye, a beard, and contacts could have easily changed their coloration and physiognomy. Jalal suspected that Jibreel was lying, but now was not the time to stir things up with a high-ranking general. What he did gain was invaluable—now he knew his prey had altered their appearances.

Jalal leaned back in his chair, closing his eyes. He had spent the night at the border station, personally inspecting every person that crossed into Turkey, unwilling to trust others to see through Cyrus's and Layla's disguises. The night had passed without incident; no one fitting their description had shown him or herself at the Bazargan-Gurbulak border. It was a colossal waste of time and energy. Somehow, the traitor and his whore had slipped through his net, eluding capture.

He returned from the border crossing empty handed. Jalal felt certain they would not attempt another crossing at the Turkish border. He had effectively sealed it. He concentrated his efforts on all the roads that led to Azerbaijan, the next most likely escape route. He had sent two of his most trusted henchmen to search a twisting, scenic route, the Chalus Road, which cut through the Alborz Mountains before descending to the Mazandaran Province and the Caspian Sea. Hours had passed without word from his men, and he had a growing suspicion that something was wrong. A second team was on its way to investigate the fate of the first team. One of those men was Mohammad, the guard Cyrus had prevented from raping Layla at Evin Prison. Mohammad's hatred of Cyrus was a fire that consumed him—he would gladly die exacting his revenge. Jalal's menacing smile broadened as he contemplated Mohammad's satisfaction when raping Layla after bringing Cyrus to his knees. For Mohammad it would be better than the seventy-two virgins that awaited every martyr in heaven for being a *Shahid*. It would be a punishment, praise be to Allah, befitting Cyrus's crimes.

Jalal was reasonably sure he had prepared for every possibility, but it was like a game of chess, trying to figure out what Cyrus's next move would be. His former aide was a brilliant tactician and a formidable enemy. Jalal felt the anger rise like lava from a volcanic eruption as he again pondered the duplicitous actions of the man he had treated like a son. The more he analyzed and examined Cyrus and his history, the more he began to suspect that perhaps Cyrus's conversion had not been impulsive, not due to his bewitchment by the American Jewess.

Is it possible that my right-hand man is not only a traitor but also a spy? Was the dreaded Mossad operating within Oghab2? The assassinations of nuclear physicists and personnel, the computer malware Stuxnet that destroyed the centrifuges at Natanz... Were they all linked to Cyrus?

The thought was paralyzing but possible considering Cyrus's access to Iran's entire nuclear complex and all its secrets. If revealed, it would be the greatest scandal, the greatest failure Iran had experienced since the Islamic revolution, and all of it would lead back to Jalal. It would be enough to destroy everything he had worked his entire life for. If the ugly truth that the enemy had been working right under his nose became known— that Cyrus had been feeding information to Israel—or even worse, the Americans, his enemies would surely seek to destroy him. The accusations of gross negligence and abetting the enemy would certainly cost him his career, if not his life.

I must stop Cyrus. I must kill him.

Jalal sat rigidly upright, reinvigorated by his anger. He examined the map on his desk. He had to be sure. He couldn't afford for Cyrus and the American girl to escape. His finger traced the circumference of Iran. He studied each border crossing as he weighed their advantages and disadvantages. The Milak-Zaranj crossing was a sure death. No foreigner could expect to cross from Iran to Afghanistan and live to tell the tale. He crossed Afghanistan off the list. He considered Iraq, but the war had made entering that country equally dangerous. The Kurds were a possibility, but they had their own problems fighting ISIS and the Turks. He crossed it off the list. Pakistan was out of the question. Cyrus was too smart to risk the girl's life in a country where kidnapping and the female slave trade were rampant. Even with Cyrus's military training and fighting ability, he was no match for the tribal militants that ruled the border area. A beautiful girl like Layla Wallace would be a target. He'd never risk it. That left Armenia, Turkmenistan, and Azerbaijan.

"Azerbaijan," he whispered. The fact that Israel had an airbase in Azerbaijan made it the perfect place for the fugitives to seek refuge. He pounded his fist on the desk.

It has to be Azerbaijan. It's the only place, besides Turkey, where the Israelis could extricate them with minimal damage.

Nothing irked him more than the damned relationship between Azerbaijan and Israel. Israel had provided the know how to modernize the Azerbaijan armed forces. The relationship between the two countries had expanded from the selling of artillery, aviation, anti-tank, and anti-infantry weaponry to trade and investments in telecommunications and a multitude of other industries.

The cozying up between what should be mortal enemies is an affront to Allah himself.

Jalal angrily cursed.

The ringing of the telephone interrupted Jalal's thoughts. He answered and listened, the scowl on his face becoming uglier with each passing second. He screamed at the caller, "Stay where you are. I will pick you up with the helicopter. We will intercept them in Mazandaran before they ever reach the border." He slammed the phone down, trembling with anger.

The deaths of Leiss and Massoud, their bodies found in a shallow snow grave, were undoubtedly Cyrus's doing.

The fools! I warned them to take no chances. An unfortunate price to pay for confirmation of the whore and whoremaster's whereabouts.

His eyes shone with satisfaction as he thought about what he would do to Cyrus once he captured him. And capture him he would.

This time I will take care of you myself. You will never reach the Azerbaijan border.

CHAPTER 34

Tel Aviv, Israel
Mossad Headquarters
December 21st
12:00 p.m.

Beneath the orderly din of controlled chaos, Aleck apprehensively observed Mossad headquarters abuzz with activity. The countdown to operation Adam and Eve was underway, with all assets focused on extricating Cyrus and Layla from Iran; or as the members of the team had begun to joke, casting them out from the Garden of Eden.

Aleck was beyond worried about Layla and could not share in their humor. He kept his thoughts to himself. These men and women were working around the clock to save his daughter. They dealt with life and death every day. Their work was precarious and highly stressful—who was he to judge how they kept their sanity.

Given the limited options, Isaac had surmised that Cyrus's intention was to make a run for the Azerbaijan border. From the satellite, they were able to see Cyrus drag the two attacker's bodies out of the house and watched Layla and Cyrus flee in the canoe across the reservoir and drive away in the Seranza. Like a heart monitor, the satellite glasses sent minute-by-minute updates on their location. Cyrus pushed the Seranza, distancing them from Varian, at times skidding over the icy road, driving like a man possessed.

On another screen from the satellite, they had seen the follow-up MOIS team arrive in Varian and discover the bodies. By that time, Layla and Cyrus were already speeding north on Route 22 along the coast of the Caspian Sea. However, they were far from freedom. Isaac, watching from Mossad headquarters, warned Aleck that things were going to get dicey. Oghab2 by now had figured out their plan for escape and had a good idea of their location. From the satellite, they could see added military muscle arriving in Astara, sealing the border. Someone was in a desperate race to circumvent the fugitives' escape.

They were on to Cyrus and rapidly closing the doors of exit, leaving him and Layla no way out. With a border crossing impossible, they aborted that option and statisticians and military experts frantically devised a new plan, a much more dangerous option. The only way to rescue the two was by invading Iranian airspace and risking the possibility of an Israel-Iran confrontation.

Operation Adam and Eve could put the nation of Israel in peril. The consequences of which were certain to lead to international condemnation and possibly war. For this reason, the prime minister had convened an emergency meeting of his cabinet to get their approval and blessings for the operation. The prime minister made an impassioned speech to his cabinet and won their nearly unanimous support. The normally cautious advisors were united in their fears of a nuclearized Iran. The decision came quickly—Israel would risk the United Nations' charge of an "act of aggression" and proceed.

The operation was given a green light. Sitalcay Military Airbase in Azerbaijan received high alert status from headquarters; their instructions were to prepare for a military maneuver that would include flying dark into enemy territory. The elite force would include a sniper team and a rescue and emergency medical team in the likelihood of injuries. Isaac and Aleck watched a UH-60 Black Hawk helicopter being loaded with equipment necessary for the black-ops foray.

"Aleck, the helicopter is equipped with low-observable technology, allowing it to fly invisibly under Iranian radar. We modified it with low-vibratory technology, which gives it the ability to fly quiet and unobserved. The IAF named the copter the *Yanshuf*, the owl, because it flies silent and is undetectable."

"I wish I could say it makes me feel better, but I'm scared to death for them."

Isaac patted Aleck on the back. "We're the best in the world at this, Aleck, but I suppose a prayer to God wouldn't be a bad idea."

"Sir, we have a Panha helicopter flying low over Route 22 at a speed that indicates they are searching for something."

"Now would be a good time for that prayer, Aleck. It looks like they've found them."

Aleck's face turned white, his knuckles gripping the arms of the chair in which he sat. His daughter and Cyrus were so close to rescue, but an armed helicopter could mean that everything was about to go to hell. Aleck, an atheist, found himself praying to God.

Isaac addressed everyone in the room. "We're going to have to do this sooner than later, ladies and gentlemen."

Turning toward the screen, his voice assumed a take-charge, military-commander edge. "Send a message to Cyrus. Apprise him of the incoming helicopter. Tell him to head for the pick-up destination at the wildlife refuge.

"Jacob, it's time to get that bird in the air. Adam and Eve are waiting."

"Yes, sir."

Aleck watched as Isaac gave orders to his team. The operation was monitored on the giant screen that broadcast simultaneous images of Cyrus and Layla's vehicle, moving at a clipped pace, and the Black Hawk lifting off from the airbase runway.

Aleck watched barely breathing, his eyes riveted on the screen that displayed an Iranian helicopter closing in on his daughter and Cyrus.

"How fast can the Black Hawk go?" Aleck couldn't contain himself from asking.

"About one hundred eighty miles per hour. Twenty minutes is our estimated time of arrival."

Aleck stared at the two screens, the one that tracked the car his daughter was in and the one following the navigational path of the Black Hawk. It was obvious to him that the Black Hawk would never get there in time to stop the Iranians from engaging with the fleeing operative and his daughter. He could only hope that this spy, mole, whatever he was, was as good as they said. Would the man truly sacrifice himself for Layla if need be?

As he watched the screen he began to pray in earnest to the God of Abraham and his deceased wife, Rebecca. His forehead beaded with sweat as the grim possibility of losing Layla filled him with fear.

CHAPTER 35

Cyrus drove wearing the satellite glasses. When the directive came to exit the highway, he swerved and made a hasty turn as he raced to elude the incoming helicopter that was tailing them. Ahead he could see the signs for a wildlife refuge that would be the point of extraction. The operation, cleared by the prime minister and his cabinet, was in motion. Every fiber of Cyrus's being was focused in a desperate race to save Layla's life.

In a head-on burst of speed, he pushed the gas pedal to the floor. Driving with reckless abandon, he shouted, "Brace yourself!"

He crashed the car through the gates of the wildlife refuge, clanging them off their hinges. Sparks flew off the vehicle as metal scraped metal. Cyrus pushed the Seranza for all it was worth and headed toward the trees that stood on the perimeter of the parking lot. They would need cover until the rescue helicopter arrived. When they exited the highway, he had spotted the Panha helicopter tailing them. Engagement with the enemy was now inevitable.

Jalal was coming. He could feel it in his bones.

"Layla, grab the duffle bag in the backseat. When I stop the car, jump out and run for those trees ahead. I'll be right behind you, okay?"

She was pale, unable to speak, her face contorted with fright, but she nodded. Cyrus snatched a glance at her. "Baby, you can do this. We're almost home."

She gave him a wobbly smile and he hit the brakes and turned the wheel. The Seranza did a one-eighty, tires screeching, dirt flying, and came to a stop with the passenger side facing away from the helicopter that was landing. They both jumped out of the car as bullets whizzed by them and ran toward the trees.

Cyrus dragged Layla behind a tree trunk. "Don't move from here, no matter what happens. Keep your head down."

"Where are you going?" Panic filled her voice.

He shouted, "I want to draw the fire away from you. Damn it, just do as I say for once without an argument." He crouched and ran, leaving her, his heart pounding and adrenaline fueling his actions. Dead leaves, scattered by bullets, rained all around him. He scrambled behind a tree and caught his breath.

By the directions from which the fire was coming, he calculated there were three enemy combatants. He focused on how to eliminate them. The real threat, Jalal, would be waiting in the helicopter, watching how things played out. A fight to the death between him and his mentor was coming. He needed to make sure he was the last man standing.

Cyrus hid behind a large tree trunk, waiting for a break in the bombardment. When the momentary pause came, he slipped around the tree and fired off a burst of ammo from his Uzi. Hearing a cry, he saw a man hit the ground.

One down, two to go.

Another round of shots hit the tree. Bullets hit the bark, and wood splinters fell to the ground. The sound was deafening, but his ears strained to hear the approach of another helicopter.

Come on, Mossad. I don't know how long I can keep these guys at bay.

He was worried that Layla would choose this moment to exercise her independence and put herself in danger.

Whatever you do, Layla, please don't move—and stay down, baby.

Then he heard the one thing he dreaded, Layla's scream. "*Cyrus!*"

A prickly sweat broke out on his skin, instantly turning cold. He was about thirty feet away from her. Running would expose him to a barrage of bullets. Chances are he would die trying to get to her, but he had no choice. He pulled his knife from its sheath. Summoning every ounce of courage, he ran, the finger of one hand pressed to the trigger of the Uzi, blindly spraying bullets as he went.

A voice yelled out in pain, wounded or dying.

Two down.

He stopped short of where he had left Layla and crouched down. His eyes having adjusted to the darkness, he had no trouble seeing the burly figure who had Layla pinned to a tree trunk, his fingers pressed around her neck as he squeezed her breasts. Layla fought like a tigress, but with all air cut off from her windpipe, her efforts were useless. She was perhaps a minute away from unconsciousness. Cyrus went ballistic with rage. He pointed the Uzi at the man and fought to control the anger in his voice.

"Mohammad, let her go!"

The growling man swung around, holding Layla in front of him as a shield. The surprise of Cyrus's appearance had thrown him off his purpose. His fingers relaxed on Layla's neck. She gasped for breath, coughing as air filled her lungs.

"You die tonight, traitor. Jalal promised me this whore as a reward for killing you. Last time you stopped my pleasure, taking what was mine. I've been plotting my revenge from that stinking cell you sent me to, waiting for the day when I could destroy you. That day has come, infidel. Now you'll have to watch me fuck the redheaded witch until she begs for death. Maybe you'll learn a thing or two about how to fuck when you see my cock banging her until she cries out for mercy." He rubbed the barrel of his AK-47 against Layla's inside thigh suggestively.

"Touch her again, Mohammad, and I'll kill you."

Mohammad roared with laughter, tightening his grip around Layla's neck. "You think I care what you say, Cyrus? You and your arrogant superiority. You rose through the ranks on the coattails of your betters, while men like me did your bidding. Instead of being grateful, you looked down on us like dirt. Now you'll see who has the power when I—" His words were cut short when Layla screamed like a banshee, grabbing Mohammad's balls in a vise grip, her nails digging through the khaki fabric, squeezing with all her might.

Mohammad yelled in anguish, throwing her to the ground. He lifted his AK-47 with the butt pointing at her head, readying to smash her. Before he brought it down on her head, a loud thud sent him stumbling backward. His eyes rounded with horror as he looked down at his chest, the hilt of a knife protruding. He fell to his knees, desperately grabbing at the knife that pierced his heart, as if he could stop what had been done. A moment later, he fell forward, dead.

Cyrus ran to the body, extracted his bloodied knife, and wiped it on his pants before sheathing it. Layla sprawled in the dirt, panted like an animal, shaking as if in the throes of demonic possession. Cyrus gathered her in his arms, pressing his lips to her temple. "You're amazing, my love, but we're not out of the woods yet." He pulled her to her feet, wishing he could wipe away the horrific images of terror and death that she now carried within her. He held her against his chest, willing his strength into her. "We need to move, *aziz-am*, deeper into the forest."

Cyrus froze when he heard the voice in Farsi say, "Such a touching display. I am truly moved, *my son*. A man who never demonstrated any heart or compassion suddenly finds such tender regard for another. Turn around slowly, traitor."

Cyrus turned, placing his body in front of Layla. "Jalal. I always knew it would come to this."

Jalal's smile revealed a row of gleaming white teeth. "At least she is beautiful, I'll give you that. Perhaps when I'm finished killing you, I will keep her as my *sariyyah*, praise be to *Allah*. She will make a lovely concubine. Her father should be quite willing to trade his secrets for such a daughter, don't you think?"

"I will never let that happen." The timbre in Cyrus's words carried a controlled threat.

"Ah, well, perhaps this moving display of new-found love is not without source. Perhaps it fits well with you being a spy for the Mossad?"

"What I did was in the best interests of the world."

"Such lovely platitudes. Save them for your host in hell, *masha'Allah*, where you will burn for all eternity. Actually, I should be grateful to the redheaded witch. Because of her, you have been exposed and can no longer harm our nuclear arms program." He motioned with the barrel of the AK-47. "Shall we go?"

Cyrus squeezed Layla's hand. Jalal pressed the muzzle of the rifle into Cyrus's back, prodding him forward. When they cleared the woods, Cyrus looked up into the pitch-black sky, searching for the rescue helicopter. He needed to stall.

"Jalal, you've always professed such confidence in your martial art skills. You might consider this a perfect opportunity to prove them. You against me, Kung Fu To'a versus the Krav Maga of the IDF, a fight to the death. You're not afraid, are you? Or is your skill only good in the practice arena?"

"Do you think I'm fool enough to fall for your goading? Why should I risk myself when I have you exactly where I want you? A few minutes from now you'll be dead, and I will have killed a traitor and delivered a woman into custody who will serve as a blackmail tool, delivering us a powerful weapon against the Israelis."

"Why? Because you know the Supreme Council is going to blame you when it's revealed that I've been working for the Israelis for years. That your ineptitude endangered the entire nation."

"Who's going to tell them? As far as they're concerned, you turned traitor for a woman."

"Wrong. I've written a letter of confession, which is being delivered to the director of MOIS. You're finished."

"I don't believe you. Why would you care what happens after your escape?"

"Purely vengeance, Jalal. The most basic of human instincts."

"What kind of revenge could you harbor for a man who has always treated you like his own son? It is I who was a father to you, who took you in, barely a man, and guided your rise to the pinnacle of power. This is who you seek to destroy?"

"You are not my father, Jalal. Your support for me has always been for your own protection. I was there to cover your ass, to do your bidding, and clean up any loose ends."

Cyrus paused. "You're right, though. You deserve to know why I feel the need for revenge. It's a story that unfolded a long time ago. Thirty years ago, to be exact. You were a young man, hungry to make a name for yourself. An opportunity presented itself, one you couldn't resist. A woman was arrested, Adeleh Shirazi Hassani. She was an activist for women's rights, a voice against the madness that was propelling our nation back to the dark ages. When she was given into your custody, you sought to break her, to force her to confess to plotting against the regime. It was to be your moment of glory, the beginning of your climb to greatness. But the woman was strong. She defied you, refusing to betray herself or anyone else. Her beliefs held true. She would not grovel to the likes of you." Cyrus paused, his eyes cold and unwavering in their contempt.

Jalal's pace slowed, the memories playing vividly across his face.

"When torture failed, you raped her, repeatedly. A few months later, upon her release, she returned to her family. She learned she was pregnant, but it was too late in the pregnancy to do anything about it. She convinced her husband that the child that grew in her was a gift, a sign from God that from evil, goodness could be born. That woman was my mother, and the child born of your sin my sister." Cyrus let the truth sink in.

"When you took me under your wing, you never suspected I was her son. The incident was long forgotten by you, and the name Hassani common enough in Iran. You didn't remember, or chose not to remember, but I knew the truth, and I have never forgotten. You ask why I care? Perhaps you should ask why I waited so long to take my revenge."

Jalal stopped in the middle of the parking lot, his past sins returning like a ghost from a grave. "I have a daughter? But I thought—dead in a boating accident?"

"No, alive. Safe and well in Israel. Fortunate, isn't it, that the only child you ever fathered will never know you, or know that you're her father? Thank God, she is her mother's child in every way."

Layla's hand covered her mouth, muffling a cry.

Fixing his attention on her, Jalal pointed the AK-47 at Layla. "This will end here, Cyrus, you and me in a fight to the death." He withdrew a pair of handcuffs from his pocket. "But first I'll make sure the American doesn't do something to unbalance the scales. I saw what she did to Mohammad, and I'm not about to become her next victim. On the ground, Cyrus, while I handcuff her." Cyrus raised his hands in submission and knelt with his hands behind his head.

Before Layla could protest, Jalal handcuffed her hands and pushed her to the ground. "Sit, infidel, and watch your lover die." He threw the rifle and watched it skid across the snow.

Cyrus jumped to his feet and the two men circled, sizing each other up. Behind his fixed smile, Jalal's eyes gleamed black like flint. Cyrus drove away all thoughts of what fate might await Layla should he not prevail. Through the years of sparring with Jalal he'd never once beaten him, but what mattered was this fight, the real fight that would determine everything. He only had to beat him once.

Jalal made the first move. He flew through the air, his boot landing on Cyrus's chest. Cyrus reeled backward, nearly losing his balance as Jalal landed solidly on the ground, swinging his leg in a comeback, roundhouse kick. The initial kick winded Cyrus, but the second kick missed its mark.

Cyrus regained his breath and punched, his knuckles connecting with Jalal's lower-rib pressure point. A gasping breath of pain stunned Jalal for an instant, enough time to allow Cyrus a follow-up knuckle punch to Jalal's chin. Cyrus didn't deliver the impact he had hoped for. His body weight wasn't fully behind the thrust, and Jalal remained standing.

With a balletic leap belying his advanced years, Jalal somersaulted over Cyrus, and before Cyrus could turn around and defend himself, Jalal hit him with a knuckle punch to the trapezius muscles, sending a sharp, shooting pain up and down his back and neck. Cyrus, with no time to recover and turn, kicked backward and landed his foot on Jalal's groin, eliciting a grunt of pain, followed by an ugly curse. Jalal's face contorted in anger. He responded with a series of punches, using fists and elbows.

The fighting became dirtier and more frenzied as each man attacked with one move after another. There was no recovery time, only balls-to-the-wall power as each tried to gain an advantage. Hatred fueled their fists. Their bodies absorbed the explosive blows like punching bags.

Cyrus blocked a one-knuckle punch to his abdomen and followed through with a finger jab in the soft tissue above the collarbone. Jalal moaned, hesitating enough for Cyrus to grab his biceps, knee him in the groin, and push him to the ground. He wrapped his hands around Jalal's neck, preparing to snap it.

Cyrus felt the sweet rush of glory that comes with winning. Then a shock of pain caused his hands to lose strength. He hadn't seen the knife that Jalal plunged into his abdomen. The dirty move delivered a shock of pain worse than any he'd ever experienced. Jalal pried Cyrus's fingers from his neck and rolled him sideways into the dirt. Jumping up, he watched Cyrus's blood seep from him. "I believe you're dying, my son. You didn't really think this could end any other way?" His grin was cold. "Fairness in fighting is for fools, not warriors."

Layla, who screamed when the knife entered Cyrus, crawled on her hands and knees to him. Her face covered in dirt and tears, she begged, "Cyrus, don't leave me. Oh, God, please don't leave me."

Cyrus tried to smile, his life ebbing from him. He whispered, "I let you down, *eshgham*. I never saw the knife. I'm so sorry."

"No, you never let me down." Her lips kissed his forehead. "I love you, Cyrus. I need to tell you that. Hold on, please, hold on."

He tried to speak, but it came out a whisper. "I love you too, Layla."

"Get up, bitch! All these confessions of love are making me sick." Jalal grabbed Layla by the hair and dragged her to her feet. "It's time for these games to end. Say goodbye to your lover." He pulled her toward the waiting Panha helicopter.

"No, stop," she cried. "I can't leave him." Tears streamed down her cheeks as she turned her head, her eyes never leaving Cyrus. She fought like a tigress trying to break free from a snare.

"He will die alone, just as he deserves, but you, my dear, have a different fate awaiting you."

Cyrus was too weak to call out, but he raised his head, watching Jalal drag Layla away.

Please God save her. Please God save her. Please God save her...

He prayed as he had never prayed before. Chanting it over and over again in his mind.

Layla fought against Jalal's grip, trying to break free.

Cyrus's failure to protect her shredded his soul. He was fading. If he didn't get help soon, he knew he'd die.

Forgive me, Layla for not keeping you safe. My love...

The unmistakable sound of spinning rotors echoed above him.

Am I dreaming?

Using the last of his strength, he raised his head in time to see the Iranian Panha helicopter disappear in a fiery explosion, hit by a rocket from a shoulder-launched assault rocket.

To Cyrus's relief, Jalal was thrown off balance by the explosion and the falling pieces of burning metal. He relaxed his grip on Layla just enough for her to break free. She ran in his direction. Jalal's face contorted in anger, and seeing the Kalashnikov lying a few feet away, he ran to pick it up. He turned, raising the barrel, aiming at Layla, when a searchlight beam hit him in the face, blinding him. Raising one hand to his forehead, he tried to block the beam.

An amplified voice came from the Black Hawk, "*Drop your weapon!*"

Jalal yelled, "Fuck you!" ignoring the warning. He raised the Kalashnikov and fired blindly in Layla's direction. Layla, running for her life, threw herself over Cyrus protectively.

"I love you, Layla, forgive me," he whispered. He knew she couldn't hear him over the roar of the helicopter and the bullets flying.

Jalal got off only a few rounds before the sniper's bullet took him right between the eyes. The Kalashnikov continued to fire in random directions until he fell backward in the dirt, dead.

Cyrus held on to consciousness only long enough to see him fall.

He smiled.

Go to Hell, bastard...

Then everything faded to black.

The Black Hawk landed, and a team of medics with a gurney rushed to where Cyrus lay wounded, Layla's body shielding him. She refused to move.

Screaming hysterically. The leader of the rescue operation talked her down and reassured her that Cyrus would receive the best of care, but she needed to give the doctors some room. With his arm around her shoulders, he led her back to the Black Hawk and got her aboard.

"Where's Cyrus? You can't leave him here." Shock and hysteria were erasing her ability to think clearly.

"We never leave anyone. I promise you they're bringing him now." He motioned to a medic. "Check her for injuries, and then give her something that will calm her."

Removing her coat, a medic checked her. "Just cuts and bruises. She's fine." He rolled up her sleeve and gave her a shot containing a sedative. He strapped her in and covered her with a blanket.

Layla's drug-dazed eyes followed the gurney carrying Cyrus as he was loaded to the back of the Black Hawk.

The commanding officer radioed his pilot. "It's a go, cargo secured. We have to get out of here before we have the entire Iranian armed forces breathing down our necks. Now! Get us the hell out of the Garden of Eden." Lt. Col. Jacobson spoke into his transmitter, "Operation Adam and Eve completed. I repeat, Adam and Eve are safe. We are leaving the Garden of Eden."

They secured Cyrus at the back of the helicopter where an emergency team worked frantically to stabilize him with an IV and plasma. A minute later, they took off, flying at full speed back to the airbase in Azerbaijan.

Twenty-five minutes later the Black Hawk touched down at Sitalcay Airbase. Medics rushed Cyrus off the helicopter into the base hospital. Layla watched Cyrus disappear as a female officer led her away.

"Don't worry. He'll receive the best of care. Why don't we get you cleaned up? They'll keep us informed as to how he's doing. Come, you must be in need of a shower and some food after such a harrowing experience."

Layla nodded. It was all she was capable of. Her heart, mind, and soul were with Cyrus.

CHAPTER 36

Tel Aviv, Israel
Mossad Headquarters
December 21st
5:30 p.m.

A tense quiet pervaded the situation room, all eyes glued to the screen, watching the Black Hawk take off. No one knew what Iran's reaction would be, whether in retaliation for invading their sovereign airspace their military would engage the Black Hawk as it fled back to Azerbaijan. Everyone had heard Lt. Col. Joshua Jacobson transmit the success of operation Adam and Eve and give the order to return to base. Intelligence out of Iran and from satellite observations indicated there was no noticeable increase in Iranian activity that would indicate a problem, but there was always the chance that something could go wrong.

For twenty-five minutes, Aleck watched the screen at Mossad headquarters, waiting anxiously for the Black Hawk to touch down. When the Black Hawk landed at Sitalcay Airbase, he released an audible sigh of relief. Isaac patted Aleck on the back. "She's safe, Aleck."

"Thank you, Isaac." His voice trembled as he forced back his tears. When the doors on the Black Hawk opened and Aleck saw a gurney holding a body handed out to waiting medical staff, he paled. "Dear God, she's been hurt."

Isaac grabbed the transmitter. "Status and condition of Adam and Eve, now!"

Lt. Col. Jacobson, unit commander of the rescue team, came on the line. "Sir, Eve sustained minor cuts and bruises and is doing fine. She's understandably shaken up after seeing Adam stabbed—they've been through a lot together. Adam sustained a significant injury, a knife wound to the abdomen. According to Eve, he and the deputy director of Oghab2, Jalal

201

Rahimi, fought a one-on-one battle that ended with the Iranian stabbing him. His cuts, hematomas, and bruises confirm her account. We arrived just in time and were able to stabilize him. He's in surgery now. Jalal Rahimi was neutralized during the rescue when he refused to stand down."

"Thank you, Colonel, excellent work. I'll be expecting an update on Adam's condition and a full report."

"Yes, sir."

Isaac clicked off and turned to address everyone in the room. "My friends, *toda raba* for your contributions to a successful mission. Operation Adam and Eve is in the history books."

The room broke into applause. Aleck sank into a chair and covered his face with his hands, overcome with emotion, his relief palpable.

Isaac picked up a call on his cell phone. "Thank you, sir." He squeezed Aleck's shoulder, getting his attention, and handed him the phone. "It's Dodi. He wants to talk to you."

"Aleck, my friend, are you celebrating?"

"I'm overwhelmed with gratitude, Dodi. You saved my daughter's life…" Aleck couldn't continue.

"Tomorrow we will fly Layla to Israel, and we can all welcome the daughter of Rebecca Rose to her second homeland. I imagine, Aleck, you're anxious to leave this nightmare behind and get on with your life. The beach house in Ramat HaSharon is yours for as long as you choose. It should provide you and Layla with a comfortable cocoon in which to reunite and contemplate the future. When you're sufficiently recovered, I'd like to show you the facilities and laboratory that we've prepared for you at the Technion. I promise you, it's impressive."

"Dodi, is there no end to your giving?" Aleck managed to jest.

"Aleck, I have great hopes that your brilliance will provide for the security and safety of all Israelis."

"It will be an honor to fulfill that trust."

CHAPTER 37

Tehran, Iran
MOIS Headquarters
December 21st
9:00 p.m.

The director of the Ministry of Intelligence and Security remained at his desk long into the evening. Before him lay a letter written by the assistant of Oghab2's deputy director, Cyrus Hassani. The letter told a troubling story. It was a disturbing tale of actions perpetrated by Jalal Rahimi thirty years earlier. Those actions had set off repercussions, which were playing out now. The letter exposed Rahimi as a man dedicated to increasing his personal power, even at the expense of his nation. Motivated by greed, lust, and revenge, Jalal had placed the Islamic Republic of Iran in a precarious situation.

The director of MOIS considered all the ramifications of his possible actions. He had already begun moving the newly operating nuclear laser-excitation facility from Fordow to a new secret location. Although compromised, Iran's nuclear aspirations would go forward. Nothing could persuade them otherwise.

The Joint Comprehensive Plan of Action between Iran, the US, and P5+1 was signed, with sanctions being lifted. This was not the time to upset the apple cart. Why take on the Israelis now and create an international incident that could escalate into war? The Islamic Republic was busy enough dealing with ISIS, Syria, Saudi Arabia, Lebanon and Hezbollah, Iraq, Yemen, Palestinian Hamas, and extending its reach over the entire Middle East.

As he waited for the phone call that would update him on the events occurring at a wildlife refuge near the Caspian Sea, the director concluded the best action under the circumstances was no action. The Israelis would rescue the kidnapped American hostage and her lover by invading Iranian airspace, and Iran would look the other way. He would kill two birds with one stone. Rahimi would be finished and the woman rescued without Iran having to admit guilt for her kidnapping. When it was over, no one would be the wiser, the entire incident quietly swept under the table. All in all, a satisfying conclusion to what might have been a disaster.

As for the traitor, Cyrus Hassani, he would be dealt with at some future time. Of course, there would be a punishment—such traitorous behavior could not be ignored. The Israelis and their Mossad agent would have to pay and pay dearly.

CHAPTER 38

Ramat HaSharon, Israel
One month later
January 21st

Layla dipped her fingers in the swimming pool—ripples radiated outward, shattering the mirrored reflection of sun and sky. The monotony of time without purpose depressed her. The doctors said she was suffering from post-traumatic stress disorder, but she knew better. She was suffering from the loss of Cyrus. She missed his arms, his kisses, the way he teased her, the look of desire that never left his eyes when he looked at her.

No other man compared.

A month had passed since her rescue from Iran—a month spent trying to find Cyrus. At first, the excuses had seemed plausible. They told her he was undergoing treatment at a secret IDF medical facility; complications arising from his injury necessitated additional surgery and procedures. As the days unfolded, that excuse became less and less believable. More than anything, she wanted to be there for him, to help him recover from his injuries, to let him know that what they shared wasn't an aberration that would disappear when exposed to the light of day. What she felt for him wasn't fleeting or ephemeral. It was as real as the emptiness in her heart without him. She was determined to find out why she wasn't allowed to see him.

Her father insisted that she should return to Harvard and finish her degree, but the thought of seeing Zamir again made her sick. She'd sent him a scathing e-mail that she never wanted to hear from him again. Then she blocked his number and email.

The more her father insisted, the more resolute she became. She was not going back to Harvard. To placate her father, she enrolled for classes the following semester at Tel Aviv University to complete her doctorate in art history. Cyrus was in Israel, and until the day came when he stood before her and told her to go, there was no possibility of her leaving. He would have to look her in the eyes and tell her he didn't love her.

The week before at a Shabbat dinner at the prime minister's house, she had cornered Dodi and begged him to help her see Cyrus. His answer had startled her. "Layla, I'm very sorry, but Cyrus doesn't want to see you."

"But why? It's not possible. I can't believe he would say such a thing."

"He's a very proud man. He has additional surgery ahead and a long recovery. He's thinking of you, Layla, of your future happiness. He knows he's damaged goods. Not just the physical injuries. This is a man who has lived in the shadow world, a world where emotion cannot exist. For too many years to count, he's lived on the edge, making cold-blooded decisions. People died because of decisions he made. I'm sure he's wondering if he has anything left of himself worth giving to you."

"I can help him learn to live again."

"I'm sure you could, but you are very young, Layla. Cyrus is older, perhaps wiser than you. He knows he may not be able to change to fit your expectations. Remember, what you felt in Iran may not survive here in Israel or anywhere else. You fell in love with your captor, and then your captor became your rescuer. All of it was a fairy tale, a false situation where the rules of engagement were manipulated."

"No, not all of it." She was fighting not to cry.

"You and Cyrus are as different as dark and light. What brought you together was an anomaly with no foundation in the reality of your lives. He has rendered a great service to our nation, and his recovery is foremost in our minds. You owe him the time to heal and figure out what he wants to do with the rest of his life. The time may come when he'll want to see you. When it does, I personally will make it happen."

I don't understand why he's doing this to me, to us. For heaven's sake, has he forgotten what we shared, what we felt, what we said to each other?

She punched her fist into the water, frustration splashing around her.

I will find you, Cyrus.

Tears filled her eyes. She felt helpless, but not defeated.

I'll make you remember what it feels like to love. No one, not my father, not Dodi, nor any shrink, can convince me that what we felt for each other wasn't love—isn't love.

CHAPTER 39

Tel Aviv, Israel
Four months later
April 21st

Springtime came to Tel Aviv, delivering warm weather and sunshine. It was a short bus ride from their Ramat HaSharon home to her grandparents' home. Once a week, she visited them in their first-floor garden apartment. It was the highlight of her week, hearing stories about her mother's childhood and her grandparents' survival of the Holocaust. The stories came alive with her grandma's retelling, stories about her family that would have been lost to her had she not stayed in Israel.

The bus was crowded, and Layla stood, holding onto a strap. Beads of perspiration dotted her brow and a wave of nausea came over her. She willed herself to keep from fainting as she got off the bus and walked the two blocks to her grandparents' apartment. Her grandmother opened the door, took one look at Layla, and exclaimed with concern.

"Layla, you look terrible. Come in and let me get you some lemonade."

"I'm sorry, *Bubbie*, I'm just so tired lately." Her grandmother led her to the sofa, sat her down, and placed her hand on Layla's forehead.

"Darling, you're burning up. What wrong with that father of yours? Doesn't he see that you're ill? Always so wrapped up in his work, the man is blind to the world around him."

"*Bubbie*, Dad is Dad. I wouldn't want him any other way. What he does is important; he doesn't need to be bothered with my aches and pains. I'm a grown woman, quite capable of taking care of myself."

"Some care. You're as thin as a chicken."

Layla laughed. "*Bubbie*, you're priceless. Do you have any more compliments for me?"

Her grandmother's anger softened. "Your red hair looks beautiful now that the black is almost gone. It reminds me of my Rebecca. You remind me of my Rebecca. Now, if that isn't a compliment, I don't know what is." A smile cheered her wrinkled face.

"Thanks. Now how about that lemonade?"

"Oh, forgive me, darling. If my head wasn't attached, I'd lose it."

While her grandmother went to the kitchen, Layla sat up and inhaled deeply, trying to get her bearings. Another wave of nausea overcame her and this time she couldn't fight it back. Running to the bathroom, she hung over the toilet and threw up. The last thing she remembered was slipping to the floor and the world spinning.

She woke in a hospital room with a catheter in her arm, hooked up to monitors that beeped intermittently.

"Hi, baby, how do you feel?" Her father sat by the bed and reached for her hand. "Your grandparents and I have been so worried."

"Fine, I think. Where are they?"

"I sent them home; they've been here all day with you. They were tired. They can visit you tomorrow." His eyes were filled with concern. "You gave us quite a scare."

"Dad, what happened? The only thing I remember is throwing up."

"You passed out in the bathroom at your grandparents' house. *Bubbie* called an ambulance. The doctors are running a bunch of tests. They said you're dehydrated and too thin. They want to keep you at least another day; fill you with liquids and get some nutrition into you."

A doctor entered, carrying a chart. "Hi, Layla, I'm Dr. Joel Steiner, the hospital physician in charge of your case." He observed her. "You're looking much better." He glanced at Layla's father and then gazed back at her. "I wonder if I could have a word with you in private." His brow furrowed.

"I'm her father, Dr. Steiner. I'm sure whatever you have to say to Layla can be said with me in the room. Is there anything wrong?"

The doctor looked at Layla with dismay. "No, Layla is a healthy young woman, but I'd rather discuss this with her alone."

"It's okay, Dad. Why don't you call Grandma and Grandpa and let them know I'm fine? I'll fill you in later with whatever Dr. Steiner has to say."

Aleck scowled at the doctor as he left the room, muttering under his breath.

Dr. Steiner didn't pull any punches when he asked, "Layla, does your family know you're pregnant?"

The color drained from her face. "But...*but* that's almost impossible," she whispered.

Dr. Steiner raised his eyebrows quizzically. "Almost impossible? Is that like saying 'a little pregnant'? From a medical standpoint, you either are or you're not." He smiled. "I hope you're not suggesting an immaculate conception?"

"We...I've only made love once."

"Ah, I see your dilemma. Well, the only thing I can say is that it is possible to get pregnant even after one time. I might also add that you are too far into the pregnancy to terminate it. However, there's always adoption."

Layla gasped in horror. "I would never get rid of my baby."

"Good, then we're in agreement. However, to date you've not been a very good mother with your lack of self-care. I think you'll agree that has to change."

Layla placed her hands on her stomach. "I had no idea I was pregnant. I haven't been myself lately. I never dreamed it could be because of that, but now it all makes sense. I'll do whatever I need to do to keep my baby healthy and safe."

"Then we're on the same page, and we can plan your future care. Do you want to contact the father? I presume he'll want to be informed?"

"No, the father will not be part of this pregnancy." Her eyes dropped in embarrassment. "I have no intention of telling him." She looked up again. "I-I would never burden him with this."

"I see. Okay, we're going to keep you one more day just to finish up some tests and make certain you're well hydrated. I can recommend some excellent obstetricians."

"Thanks, Dr. Steiner, I'd appreciate that. Would you please ask my father to come back? I want to share my good news with him. He's never been a grandfather before."

CHAPTER 40

Tel Aviv, Israel
Beit Halochem—House of the Warrior
Seven months later
October 21st

Cyrus lay on a lounge chair in the sunshine, shirtless—ten months had passed since Jalal had stabbed him. He'd undergone multiple surgeries and overcome a severe case of sepsis from an infection that had nearly killed him. It had been a much rougher road to recovery than he'd anticipated. The scar across his abdomen was visible proof of the ordeal he had endured.

Tomorrow was his release day from the recovery center he'd called home for far too long. Mossad had arranged an apartment in Tel Aviv he could use until he was ready to throw down more permanent roots. He had a new job with Mossad in a new capacity, to work in a department that was dedicated to all aspects of Israel's adversary, the Islamic State of Iran. They were offering him a chance to build a new future for himself and continue the work he'd devoted himself to prior to Layla's appearance in his life. The government of Israel and Mossad had kept their promise to him by not throwing him away when his usefulness to them might have come under question. It heartened him to know that he would still be able to continue what had become his life's work.

Layla.

The mere thought of her name was enough to tighten the muscles in his gut. He looked down at the scar across his abdomen that appeared angry and red in contrast to the darkening tan of the rest of his body. When he thought of her—which he tried not to do—it was like remembering a tornado that had ripped through the countryside, leaving only a barren landscape in its wake. She had taken his heart and soul, leaving only the cold practicality of his mind. It was a loss he knew he must learn to accept.

He stuffed a wad of gum in his mouth. He'd given up smoking, and the gum provided an antidote to the rising tide of emotion that images of Layla awakened. He remembered her anger when he lit a cigarette in the car during their wild escape. How he'd loved her spirit.

He knew she had tried to see him, even going so far as to enlist the help of the prime minister, but he'd refused. He just couldn't bear it. Couldn't face her.

There had been plenty of time in the weeks following their rescue to clarify what had occurred between them. Impossible circumstances had created a bond between them that otherwise might not have occurred. He convinced himself that distance and time away from each other were in their best interests.

I suppose she's gone back to Harvard by now.

He tried to remember if she'd said anything about finishing her thesis in June. The only thing he selfishly prayed for was that she didn't resume her relationship with the Saudi boyfriend. He couldn't bear to think of any man, let alone that jerk, touching her.

You'd better get used to it, asshole, the idea of another man loving her. It's a year. Someone's filling your shoes by now. She's too perfect, too irresistible, too much a woman to be lonely for long. You may have been the first, but you sure as hell won't be the last.

He allowed his imagination to dwell on what it would be like if he *ever* saw her again.

Maybe we'll meet for coffee, a couple of old friends sharing a laugh over all we went through in Iran and the ridiculous notion of love that we conjured up. Maybe we can even stay friends, sharing an occasional phone call or a holiday card. The spy and the student, it'll make a great story for her to tell her kids someday.

His chest constricted with pain that had nothing to do with his healing body. Angry with himself for even thinking they could ever be friends. She was like a drug running through his veins, an incurable addiction.

Friendship was out of the question.

He shook his head in frustration. Next week he'd be in Tel Aviv beginning his new job with Mossad.

It will be good to get back to a semblance of life and purpose. Who knows? Maybe there is a second chapter for me so long as I stay clear of blue-eyed redheads.

CHAPTER 41

Tel Aviv, Israel
Two months later
December 21st
10:00 a.m.

Layla left her apartment on Basel Street to walk the few blocks to a café called Loveat, an organic restaurant on Jabotinsky and Dizengoff Street. It was her routine every Sunday to leave Cerise, who was three months old, with Ziva, a fifteen-year-old who lived in the building. Ziva was a good girl and a conscientious babysitter and Cerise adored her.

Her help gave Layla a little break to walk the streets of old Tel Aviv, stroll to the beach, and shop at the farmer's market. When she returned, the baby would be taking a nap, which allowed her time to prepare dinner for her father and grandparents, who came every week on Sunday to see the auburn-haired baby who had brought so much joy to their lives.

After the birth of Cerise, she had convinced her father that she had to get her own apartment and begin a new life. She loved living in a vibrant neighborhood in the heart of the old city, within walking distance to shopping and restaurants and a short bus ride to Tel Aviv University where she was finishing her doctorate.

I have everything I need—a supportive family and my baby. Someday I'll meet someone who wants to share this life with me, and I'll never look back. Do you hear me, Cyrus? Cerise doesn't need you, and neither do I.

It was a mantra she repeated daily. One more way to reassure herself that she was over him.

She wore a long, floral skirt, something she'd picked up in a thrift shop. Layla fancied herself a free spirit, a throwback to another time. Taking a last look in the mirror, she adjusted the large, floppy, turquoise woven hat and brushed her hair. For some reason, she felt an expectancy of good things coming her way. It was a new feeling, and one she had every intention of embracing.

The sun shone brightly on the Holy Land, and a cool sea breeze blowing in from the Mediterranean salted the air. Layla pulled a rolling hand cart for her purchases. Now and then she stopped to look in a shop window. Seeing her reflection, she smiled, turning from side to side, pleased that she had returned to her former figure before her pregnancy. The only part of her anatomy that had changed were her breasts, which were considerably larger. She no longer breast-fed Cerise, but her breasts had retained their fullness. She giggled to herself.

Not so terrible, as Bubbie would say.

At Loveat, a popular café, a line wound outside the door. The outdoor tables were all taken, which was fine with her. It was nice just to stand in line and people watch. She raised her face to the sky, closing her eyes, allowing the sunshine to warm her.

She must have been daydreaming because she obviously hadn't heard her name being called.

"Layla? Is that you?" The deep, accented voice speaking English startled her. She had grown so used to hearing and speaking Hebrew.

She turned and felt the world shift beneath her feet. Her heart hammered in her chest. A year had passed, yet for a moment time stood still.

Cyrus stood like a statue, as if cemented in place.

Layla moved with no awareness of her physical being, as if watching herself in a play, acting out a role on stage.

When she reached him, he bent to kiss her, but she pulled away, and his lips merely grazed her cheek.

Hurt flickered in his eyes, but she didn't care. "How are you, Cyrus? It's been a long time." With a mighty effort, she conveyed no emotion.

"I'm well. A year, I think. Oh, forgive me, Layla, I'd like you to meet Dafna Peretz."

Layla hadn't noticed the pretty dark-haired woman at Cyrus's table. She forced a smile as she shook hands with her. "Very nice to meet you."

Amusement danced in Dafna's dark eyes. "My pleasure, I'm sure."

Cyrus hadn't taken his eyes from her. "What are you doing in Israel? Visiting your father?"

"No, I live here. I have an apartment not far from here."

"But I thought you went back to Harvard."

A rush of anger erupted from her, as if it had been on the tip of her tongue, just waiting for this moment to reveal itself. "You thought? When did you think, Cyrus? Did you think about me all the many times I tried to find you? Did you think about me when I embarrassed myself, begging Dodi to intervene and help me see you? I'm surprised to hear you say that you ever thought of me at all! You cut me from your life as swiftly as Jalal's knife stabbed you." Layla's cheeks burned with shame at her impetuous, hotheaded outburst.

Cyrus looked as if she had just slapped him, his green eyes darkening.

Suddenly he burst into laughter. "I see some things never change. You're still the feisty redhead who says aloud whatever she's thinking without a filter."

"And you're still the arrogant charmer, who thinks he's every woman's dream. As for saying what I think, let me correct you. The difference between us is that I say what I mean and mean what I say, unlike some people I know. Right now, I'm thinking I have to leave. I don't think I can bear another minute of this bullshit conversation. You see, I actually have feelings. Unlike. You." She poked his chest with her finger. "Sorry, but I forgot what a cold, unemotional prick you are." She turned to leave then looked back at the pretty brunette. "Nice to meet you, Dafna. Enjoy your breakfast, or whatever it is you two are doing."

Layla stormed away, forgetting about coffee, or anything else for that matter. She was seething, shaking from head to toe. She ran down the street, her cart bouncing behind her, with little or no awareness of what direction she took. By the time she paused to catch her breath, she had reached the boardwalk at the beach. Finding a bench, she plopped down and stared out at the sea. Tears filled her eyes, her fury replaced with despair.

I thought I was over him. Instead it feels like a day hasn't gone by since we last touched—kissed. Her hands covered her face. *Please, God, don't ever let me see him again. It hurts too much.*

She breathed in a huge gulp of sea air, fortifying her resolve, and stood. She would not allow their confrontation to set her back to square one. She had to get her shopping done and prepare dinner.

One foot in front of the other. You can do this. You have a wonderful life. A darling baby girl you adore and a family who loves you. He's moved on—you need to do the same.

CHAPTER 42

Tel Aviv, Israel
December 21st
1:00 p.m.

Driving Cyrus from her thoughts, Layla managed to get the shopping done. When she got home, Cerise had just gone down for her nap. She paid Ziva and began prepping for Sunday dinner. Then, realizing she had about three hours before the baby woke, she took what for her was a rare indulgence—a bath. She lay in the tub, immersed in steamy, hot water. A rosy glow imbued her skin, and a feeling of complete contentment saturated her senses. In this hypnotic state it was possible to rationally examine what she'd felt when she'd seen him.

Why did he have to look so fricking sexy? Who was that woman? His girlfriend? The thought of him falling for someone else was devastating. *I wonder if she was jealous. I know I would be if I were her. Boy, I'd love to have been a fly on the wall to hear him explain to her that raft of shit I threw at him. Serves him right, the egotistical bastard. God, I hate you!*

She sank beneath the water, trying to drown out her turbulent thoughts of him. When she broke the surface, taking a breath, she heard the doorbell.

"Shit!" She climbed out of the tub and grabbed a towel. *Who the hell could that be? No one's due here until six.* "Hold on, I'm coming," she called, putting on a silk robe and wrapping her hair in a towel. When she looked through the peephole, her heart nearly leaped from her chest.

"Just a minute, please." Her eyes swept the room. Ziva had put all of Cerise's toys away. There was nothing in the room that shouted "baby." She popped her head into Cerise's room and saw her sleeping soundly, her arms above her head, fingers curled. She quietly closed the door to the baby's room.

Steeling herself, she opened the front door a few inches. "What are you doing here? How did you find me? Never mind, don't answer that, I forgot you're a spy. Snooping is your stock and trade."

Cyrus ran his fingers through his long, dark hair. He was visibly uncomfortable. "Can I come in? I... need to talk to you. Please, Layla," he implored

Shit, I'm in trouble. Not only do I have to hide my feelings from him, but there's no way he can know about the baby.

"Look Cyrus, I apologize for the things I said. Why don't we just leave it at that, and you can be on your way."

"Layla, I'm not leaving here without talking to you. I think I deserve... sorry...Please give me a few minutes so I can explain."

All of Cyrus's carefully constructed walls of protection and his well thought out arguments crumbled the instant he saw Layla again. Just breathing the same air as Layla made his heart pound painfully in his chest. Seeing her eradicated all of his best intentions.

She seems different, older, more self-possessed. And that body! Fucking gorgeous. I'm lucky she couldn't see my cock standing at attention, right there for all the world to see on Dizengoff Street. Dafna noticed it immediately—the effect Layla has on me. She gave me a piece of her mind. I guess that's what shrinks do. She told me my stubborn refusal to acknowledge and deal with the emotional side of my life was going to be my downfall. "If I were you," she said, "I'd get down on my knees and ask for that girl's forgiveness. Crawl if you have to."

So, here I am, standing at your door, my hands sweaty and my heart pounding. I'm acting like a fucking teenager. I never expected the little minx to have this much power over me. I never pictured myself down on my knees, begging for another chance.

"Please, Layla. Can I come in? I...I need to talk to you."

The door opened a few more inches, and Layla stood back, letting him in.

God help me, I got her out of the shower. She smells like lemons...and that silk robe—her breasts—I need to think with my head, not my cock. Breathe, asshole, or you're going to tackle her to the floor.

He looked around, observing her home; playing for time. This was her space, exactly as he would have imagined it. The warm, yellow walls and delft-blue sofa, vases of fresh flowers scenting the air. As Cyrus looked around the room, he noticed on the mantelpiece a collection of

Persian mosaic tiles with their distinctive yellow, turquoise, blue and white pattern of flowers and swirling geometric artwork. Beneath the coffee table was a worn Persian Tree of Life carpet that reminded him of their visit to the Grand Bazaar in Tehran. There was something incredibly hopeful about these objects that could only be linked to him. They had been through so much together, most of it veiled with the fear of being hunted and captured, but even the terror of that time hadn't prevented her from surrounding herself with objects that were significant to him and to her.

"Your home is so much like you. Open, uncluttered, and filled with light."

Layla's head tilted quizzically. "Cyrus, I don't understand. What is it you want? After what I said to you, I figured you'd hate me for the rest of your life."

"Hate you? I could never hate you no matter what you said. Words were never how we expressed our true feelings for each other. It was by our actions that we conveyed our truths." His eyes were piercing as they searched hers.

"Well, your actions were pretty clear after Iran. You were just like every other asshole. Not much different than Zamir, really."

It was a blow that cut him to the quick. Being compared to the jerk who had abandoned her in Iran was the ultimate insult.

He moved toward her, the first taste of anger propelling him into action, but she held her hands up. "Please, Cyrus, don't come any closer. Right now, your words are far more important to me than your actions."

He froze. "You aren't going to make this easy for me, are you?" He wanted more than anything to cut through her anger.

"Why should I? Does Dafna know you're here?" She folded her arms across her chest, creating a barrier between them.

He couldn't keep his gaze from drifting to her breasts, pushed up above her arms. Her nipples, pressed against the silk, were peaked and firm. His mouth dried, and his pants became uncomfortably tight with his arousal.

She's jealous. She has no idea who Dafna is.

It thrilled him to know that she was capable of such a powerful emotional reaction when it came to him. It made him want to crow like a rooster. "Dafna is my therapist, not my lover," he clarified.

"Yeah, of course she is. Only you could manage to find a hot babe for a counselor. Does she service your mind *and* your body, like a twofer? Or perhaps just an extra perk now and then? A little head work on the couch?"

He smiled. *God, you're beautiful when you're jealous. Those turquoise eyes. I don't think I'll ever grow tired of looking into them.* "Nice double entendre. Stop it, Layla, resentment and envy don't suit you."

Her eyes flashed a warning. She moved toward him, her finger poking in his chest as she read him the riot act. "Don't you for one minute accuse me of envy. What do I care if you fuck her, or any other woman?"

"Now, that brings to mind a quote by Shakespeare—'*The lady doth protest too much, methinks.*'"

Her mouth opened to protest, but she stopped herself just in time and collected herself. "I don't remember inviting you here today. I believe you came of your own volition. Who you go to bed with is none of my business, just as who I go to bed with is none of yours."

The thought of her with another man was enough to drive him crazy. He drove the image out of his mind. "Actually, I'm beginning to believe that's just what you need, a really good fuck to release some of that incredible frustration you seem to be teeming with. As I recall, I warned you once before that you need to be tamed—"

She rolled her eyes and her hands went to her hips. He remembered every time she'd rolled her eyes at him when they were in Iran. And it suddenly hit him like a sucker punch.

I love her.

He'd always loved her. From the first moment he'd laid eyes on her. He never stopped loving her. For as long as he lived, he would always love her.

"I'm sorry, *azziz-am.*" He closed his eyes. "This is not how I wanted our conversation to go. I wanted to walk away from you, to cut you out of my heart, but when I saw you today, it hit me like a train. You're so deep inside me, I can't let go."

"Why…" she whispered. "Why would you want to throw away what we…?" She was so hurt, so angry she could barely speak. She couldn't understand why he would throw away love. She blew out a breath. "Cyrus, don't you believe that what we shared in Iran was real? That it was more than a result of being thrown together under difficult circumstances? Can't you see that you and I could have made something beautiful, something that would have lasted?"

"I don't know." He shook his head. "You're so young, so innocent, and I'm so damaged. I didn't want to ruin your life. I don't want to…" A halo of pain surrounded him. She could feel it, see it. She raised her hands, placing them on either side of his face, forcing him to look directly into her eyes. He was coming apart, but everything he said felt honest and real to her. She wanted to make it better, to make them better. She wanted them to heal. "What do you see when you look at me?"

"I see everything that's beautiful in this world. Everything I never dreamed I could have."

"Do you love me, Cyrus?" If he lied to her, she'd know.

"I've never loved anyone before. I only know I can't live without you."

"Hold that thought," she whispered, "and kiss me, you stubborn man."

CHAPTER 43

Tel Aviv, Israel
December 21st
2:00 p.m.

Cyrus brushed his lips against hers and felt her body melt into him. He heard the roar of wind sweeping through the trees and waves crashing upon the shore. A low, guttural moan of passion escaped from him as he allowed his yearning to win.

Is it possible to drown in a kiss?

His hands caressed the curves of her body. Electricity passed from her through his fingers, igniting him.

All I want is to make love to you, baby, to feel in the here and now the passion that's haunted my dreams. God, I want to tell you I love you, but I'm afraid.

"Layla, do you know that it was a year ago today that we first made love?" He held her face between his hands and kissed her lips. "Every day since then has felt like an eternity. So many times, I've dreamt of holding you like this again, of kissing you." He wanted to tell her he was lost without her, but he couldn't. He was incapable of anything beyond his desire to possess her.

One year. One year. I want so much to tell you about our child, Cyrus, but I'm afraid…

She would tell him. But not now. Not this moment. Right now, she just wanted to love him. God how she wanted this man. The dark, brooding spy with the tormented green eyes made her feel things no one else could. With a sixth sense, she also knew she had to reel him in slowly, or he'd run, as he'd run before. The demons within him were still too strong.

She kissed him and kept on kissing him. Her naked body beneath her silk robe was hot, begging for his hands, starving for his mouth. She was a woman now and not the girl he'd first loved. Instinctively she knew what she must do. She felt his muscles hardening against her, the staff of manhood pulsing between his legs, enlarging with his desire. She rubbed herself into his cock, eliciting a moan from him. The last time she had begged him to make love to her, he had been unable to resist.

Even if it all falls apart, I don't care. He came here for me because his want was greater than his excuses.

She dropped her hand from the nape of his neck and ran it over the hard organ that was straining through his pants. She wanted him to fill every inch inside her. For a year she'd tried to forget what sex with him was like. For the most part, it was a failure. During the day, she could rationalize away what she'd felt, but at night she tossed and turned with dreams of him.

"Fuck." His breath was a gasp. "If you touch me like that, I don't know what might happen."

"I know what needs to happen. I need you to stop talking, thinking, making excuses. I need you to make love to me. Make me remember what your cock feels like inside me," she prodded, palming him harder. "I need you to remember…to learn…to love," she whispered.

Cyrus slipped his hand beneath her robe and covered her breast, lightly squeezing, his thumb rubbing the nub of her nipple until it became hard and erect. He loved her breasts, the way they filled his hands. "I don't understand it, but your breasts are bigger than I remember them, fuller and rounder. I could have sworn I had memorized every inch of your body."

The rush from his touch turned her voice to smoke. "I hope you're not complaining. I'm a woman now."

"Yes, you are." He bent his head down to the breast that filled his hand, lifting it. He wrapped his lips over it, sucking her nipple until her head fell back in submission, her body arching backward. The white silk robe slipped from her shoulders, and he raised his head from the lushness of her breast, his hand untying the bow. He watched as the robe fell to the floor, pooling at her feet. "You are a woman, *eshgham*, a beautiful woman. I've dreamed of sucking your breasts, and I've come a hundred times in my dreams just thinking about the silky red hair of your pussy." He dropped to his knees in worship, planting his lips on her. "So beautiful." He inhaled. "I love the scent of you, the sweet taste of you." He sucked her clit, delicately running his tongue over it, coaxing and loving the way it mushroomed hard and erect.

He was rewarded with a sensual moan, her knees buckling beneath her. She threaded her fingers through his hair, pressing him in closer. He growled with satisfaction at her response. "Do I please you, my darling? As much as all your many lovers?" he teased.

"Are you calling me a liar?" she whispered breathlessly. Why else would I be on birth control?"

Her provocation worked, and a feeling of rage overcame him. It felt like a punch in the groin. "If I ever see you with another man, I'll kill him. No other man is ever going to take what is mine."

"Yours?" Her brows raised.

"Yes, mine." He stood, taking her lips in another kiss, this time the kiss of a warrior who claims what is his. The blood surged through his veins, quickening his pulse and filling his cock until he felt certain every ounce of blood in his body was pooling in his member. Bent and thick, his cock craved to be buried to the hilt between her legs.

He picked her up, his lips still kissing her, and made for a door in the hallway, which he assumed was her bedroom. He had opened it only a few inches when she grabbed his face in her hands. "No, that's not my bedroom. My bedroom's down the hall." Without a glance into the room, he closed the door and moved swiftly down the hallway to her room. He needed to hear her scream his name as he fucked her.

And, oh, the ways I'm going to fuck you, baby.

Gently he laid her on the bed, his eyes devouring every inch of her. He was no longer the unsure man that had entered her apartment. He moved confidently, gracefully, with self-possession, removing his clothes until he stood naked in front of her. His phallus, erect, arose powerfully from his groin. He was captivated by her shallow breaths, her chest rising and falling in expectation of what he would do to her.

It occurred to him that there might be no other lovers, that she may not have had sex since that night in Varian, the night he had taken her virginity. She wanted him, he was sure of that, but behind her desire, something was hidden. He felt it. Was it fear? Had he done this to her?

I'll just have to tear down that wall. It'll take time, I know, but somehow, Layla, I'm going to win back your trust. In the meantime, I'm going to do things to that gorgeous body of yours, things you've never dreamed of.

———————◦§◦———————

Layla could not tear her eyes from Cyrus's naked body.

Oh my God, I'd forgotten how gorgeous he is.

Her gaze absorbed his masculine beauty, the ways his muscles rippled when he moved. When she saw the scar across his abdomen, tears came to her eyes. "It must have been horrible, what you went through."

"It wasn't great, but that's all behind me. We'll talk about that some other time."

"Promise?"

"Promise."

Her eyes drank up the sculptured proportions until they came to rest on his fully erect cock, which brought a cocky grin to his full lips, not to mention an unmistakable rise of his hard-on.

Great, Layla, not exactly subtle in your admiration of his attributes. But— it worked—he got bigger. He's also behaving like the man you fell in love with, cocksure, and teasing.

"Do you like what you see, *azziz-am*?" He straddled her. Are you thinking about how good it's going to feel when I love you?" He ran his hands up her thighs. "You are mine, angel."

Layla blushed, unable to control her racing thoughts. He was reading her mind. She tried to regain control of her emotions and the situation. Everything seemed to be spiraling out of her control. "I'm not sure I can think when you say things like that." Her words barely rose above a whisper."

"Spread your legs, baby, I want to see all of your beauty arrayed before me."

Without thinking, she obeyed, her legs opening. He lowered his head, his tongue grazing the pink pebble of her clit. He traced his tongue around and around until her hips rose, and he pressed harder, inhaling the delicious scent of her body made ready for sex. When she began to shake in climax, he wrapped his lips around her clit, sucking, stimulating her to greater heights of bliss.

Kissing his way up her body, his cock throbbed against her thigh. "Layla, tell me that you want this," he rasped. "I need to know you want this as much as I do."

Her fingers caressed the shadow of beard on his jaw. A dark lock of hair had fallen across his forehead. Gently, she moved it away. "There's been no other man since you, Cyrus. You're the only man I've ever loved." Her vision was blurred by her tears. "Please make love to me."

His hands slipped beneath her, lifting her toward him, as he slowly entered her. The perfection from their union made them both gasp.

He groaned, thrusting harder and deeper inside her. "Baby, does it feel good?"

"Oh, my love, yes! Don't stop, loving me." He rhythmically plunged as the glow of pleasure ignited through her body.

CHAPTER 44

Tel Aviv, Israel
December 21st
2:45 p.m.

His whole body rejoiced. The muscles of her vagina clenched around his cock, driving him wild. He couldn't get enough—it was the most exquisite feeling he had ever known.

Watching her face flush pink, hearing the breathy moans escaping from her beautiful lips each time he entered and pulled from her, he wanted it never to end.

When her legs wrapped around him, drawing him farther inside, he couldn't stop the ache and the need to release. As if on cue, she cried out, "Cyrus, oh yes. Come with me."

She shattered around him as he burst into her. It felt as if he emptied into her forever. His lips found her neck, sucking. His body continued to shudder long after he came. He continued to thrust, unable to stop himself. "Hmm, you are the most delicious woman I've ever known," he mumbled into her neck.

A smile curved across her lips. "That good, huh?" She giggled.

"Better than good. If you give me a few minutes," he teased, "we can do it again." He kissed her long and slow. It seemed from another world entirely that he heard a mewl, what sounded at first like a cat. When he heard it again, he raised his head. "Did you hear that?"

"Hear what?"

"It sounded like a cat."

"I don't have a cat." She wriggled free of his embrace and jumped out of bed. "Um, I think it's time you should go. She gathered up his clothes and tossed them on his lap. "Here get dressed."

"What?" He frowned, getting out of bed. "We just had mind-blowing sex and now you want me to leave?"

"Look my dad and my grandparents are going to be here in a couple of hours." She glanced at the door. "I-It's too much for me to explain everything all at once. T-too much."

Something on the floor caught his eye. He bent to pick it up. "What's this?" He held up a pink pacifier.

The look in Layla's eyes told him everything he needed to know... Suddenly the world tilted on its axis.

His words only a short while ago came back to haunt him...*Layla, do you know that it was a year ago today that we first made love?*

He felt dizzy, unbalanced. He was standing in the sea, huge waves hurtling at him, sucking him into an abyss that threatened to drown him.

His thoughts raced as he fought to calculate the days and months that had elapsed since their rescue in Iran. He turned and flung open the bedroom door.

"Cyrus wait, I have to explain," Layla cried out.

He strode to the closed door down the hall. The door he'd mistaken for Layla's bedroom. The door she told him was the wrong door. He reached for the handle and turned it slowly, his heart beating so loudly it pounded in his ears like waves crashing on the shore...

The room was bathed in a soft, golden light, revealing walls painted with trees, their leafy branches providing a canopy, a safe haven for the crib that stood against the wall. Cyrus held his breath, his hands trembling as he slowly approached.

Resting his hands delicately on the rail he gazed down at the perfect little angel with the red tufts of curly hair, lying on her side, the only sound from her tiny lips sucking on two fingers.

Tears rolled down Cyrus's cheeks. He sank to his knees, his face pressed against the rails as he cried silently, watching his infant daughter peacefully sleep.

Layla approached and laid her hand on his shoulder. She whispered, her voice thick with emotion, "I'm sorry Cyrus—everything changed so suddenly. We ran into each other and had that terrible fight and then you came here. I-I had to be sure, certain, before I introduced you to your daughter."

His voice broke. "I don't even know her name."

"Cerise, her name is Cerise."

He whispered, "Cerise," as if it were a prayer. He looked up at Layla. "She's mine?"

Her hands flew to her hips. "Of course, she's yours."

"Why didn't you come to me? Why did you go through everything alone? I would have been there, beside you every step of the way."

"I tried to see you before—before I learned I was pregnant. But you didn't want to see me. Remember? And then after I found out, I...I would never force you to be a father. I didn't want you to feel obligated. You had to come to us, to find your own way."

"Oh, Layla, we've been at such cross purposes."

Layla sank to the carpet beside him. She leaned her head on his shoulder. He turned to her—his face wet with tears. "I've let you down so completely— can you forgive me? I-I thought you would be better off without me. I was so wrong...Will you still have me?"

She smiled, and gently wiped his tears away. "You silly Superman," she whispered. "I love you—even though you're so hard-headed that you thought you weren't good enough for me. Don't ever think that again."

"I won't"

"Promise?"

"Promise."

They sat quietly for a while, watching their daughter sleep.

"Your daughter, she's beautiful, isn't she?" Layla gazed lovingly at their baby.

"She's beyond beautiful, and so are you Cyrus cupped Layla's face in his hands, kissing her with every ounce of passion he possessed. I love you both so much. You're my life."

The baby stirred, capturing his attention. Tentatively, he reached beyond the slats of the crib, touching the tiny fingers that curled around his. His heart, bursting with love, skipped a beat when Cerise's eyes fluttered open. She stared into his eyes, her small feet dancing on air, kicking at the blanket that covered her. She smiled at him, cooing.

Whatever doubts plagued him vanished when he stared into the Nile-green eyes of his daughter. She captured his heart and held it in her tiny hands.

"She has your beautiful eyes," Layla said.

"She has your beautiful hair," Cyrus said wrapping his arms around the woman of his soul.

"The woman who had given him his life back. He touched his forehead to hers. "Thank you," he whispered.

"You're welcome," she whispered back.

VENGEANCE: TIP OF THE SPEAR SERIES BOOK 2

SNEAK PEEK

Midtown Manhattan, New York
September 11th
7:00 p.m.

Some firsts are unpredictable.

Some expected.

And some are down-right zingers.

But Layla Rose Hassani's firsts were nothing short of cliff-hangers.

Kidnapped in Dubai, thrown into an Iranian prison, attacked and brutalized, betrayed and abandoned—all "firsts" that even four years later still gave Layla nightmares. But one "first" changed her life forever.

The first time Layla met Cyrus Hassani.

He swooped in and rescued her from an Iranian prison, saved her more times than she could count, and almost died while getting her out of Iran. Layla fell in love with Cyrus during that perilous escape. He was the most irresistible man in the world—and her very own Superman.

Cyrus was the first man she'd made love with—and without a doubt—he was the only man Layla would ever love. The gift for all she'd endured in Iran was four years of a happy marriage and the blessing of their precocious four-year-old daughter Cerise.

But even with so much love and happiness, Layla's fears rippled beneath the calm surface of her life. Cyrus's past as a deep cover agent in Iran working for Israel's Mossad, along with her own past as a survivor of that

EPILOGUE

Layla took a cab to the Jaffa port and walked to Otzarin, the restaurant where Cyrus had texted her to meet him. It was early, and the sun was still high enough above the horizon to assure that she would watch it set into the sea with Cyrus. The cotton-puff, scattered clouds guaranteed the sunset to be spectacular, the clouds soaking up the light and color like bread dipped in gravy.

She marveled at how strange life was. She was going on her first date with Cyrus. Cyrus was the love of her life and the father of her child and he'd never seen her dressed up or looking her best. The entire time they had been together in Iran she was bruised, battered, crying, hysterical, no makeup, wearing sweats. A giggle bubbled up.

Half the time I was yelling at him.

She followed his directions through the old city, meandering through a maze of walking paths called the Zodiac Alleys, searching for the one alley named Pisces where she'd find Otzarin. Art galleries and shops lined the pedestrian streets where tourists and locals explored the treasure trove that was Jaffa. Otzarin occupied a space that was once a guest house for Christians making pilgrimage to the Holy land. A sea breeze blew from the Mediterranean and blended with the fragrance of jasmine and honeysuckle.

Layla closed her eyes and breathed it all in. The past week had been a whirlwind of planning, and talking late into the night, and her family getting to know Cyrus. So, it was a lovely surprise when Cyrus asked her out on a date—for New Year's Eve no less.

The hostess led Layla outside to a terrace where Cyrus waited. She'd never seen him dressed up, and her heart did a black flip when he stood to greet her. His dark hair was brushed back from his forehead, and he wore a white, open-collared shirt with a blue sport coat over dress jeans. His Adam's apple bobbed as he swallowed. The look in his eyes was one of awe mixed with desire. She couldn't believe that after losing him, she'd found him again. Nothing had changed, he was still the man of her dreams. Taking a deep breath, she tried to slow her heartbeat.

"I don't think I've ever seen anything in this world as beautiful as you, *azziz-am*," he said. "The first time I saw that sprinkling of freckles across your nose, I was hooked. You took my breath away then, but now I can't believe my eyes. You're a goddess." He kissed her on both cheeks and poured her a glass of champagne from the bottle in the ice bucket near their small, intimate table. When he handed her the glass, his eyes bore into hers. "To us, my darling."

Their glasses clinked. "*L'Chaim*, to us!" She sipped the champagne, Veuve Clicquot, her favorite. "Please don't tell me it's my freckles that lured you in." It was embarrassing how she couldn't take her eyes off him. Even after two weeks of spending every night with him. She had a feeling it would always be this way and she didn't mind it one bit. She glanced around her. "This place is magical."

He chuckled. "It is, isn't it? I picked it especially for you. I knew you'd love it." He searched her eyes. "Oh, by the way, I'm curious. Since I confessed what it was about you that first attracted me, what was it that attracted you to me?"

"A better question would be, what was there that I wasn't attracted to?" She dropped her eyes, at her candor.

Great, you just admitted that he's the hottest guy you've ever known.

He chuckled, clearly enjoying her discomfort, but then, he had from the beginning.

"Well, now you know the truth, how embarrassing."

"What, you don't think it feels good to have the woman you're nuts about think you're hot? Come on, let's watch the sunset." He took her hand, weaving between small groups of patrons to the edge of the terrace. The view was breathtaking, the turquoise-blue Mediterranean fanned out to the horizon.

Cyrus pointed. "That's the bell tower at St. Peter's Monastery, built on top of a thirteenth-century Crusader castle. Over there at the seaport is the Jaffa lighthouse, built by the Ottomans. It's humbling to think that this place has been a home to people since 7500 BCE and was conquered by

King David and his son, King Solomon. It's said that the cedars of Lebanon that were brought in to build the first temple came through this port. Not to mention that during his conquest of the Levant and Syria, Alexander the Great's troops sheltered in Jaffa. So much ancient history right here beneath our feet. It's humbling. Kind of makes us all insignificant in the bigger picture of history."

She tried her best to keep her eyes on the sea instead of ogling him as he spoke. The depth of his knowledge mesmerized her. He was like a walking encyclopedia.

"This part of Israel feels exotic. It really feels like you've traveled back in time. It's one of the things I love best about Israel, living in a vibrant society amid the ruins of antiquity." She turned and found his penetrating gaze fixed on her.

She nudged his rib. "Stop staring. You're making me self-conscious."

He leaned down—his breath hot in her ear. "The only thing that you should be thinking self-consciously about, beautiful lady, is what kinds of things I'm going to do with that sexy body of yours tonight." His tongue darted in her ear, sending shivers down her spine. "Every time I touch you, I can't control what I'm feeling. The desire that overwhelms me." He chuckled. "I guess it's pretty obvious that I'm putty in your hands."

"You can't imagine how happy that makes me feel. At least I know I have a little power over you. Especially since it's me that feels like putty."

He put his arm around her waist and drew her close. "You have a lot of power over me, Layla. You've had it since I first saw you."

She leaned her head on his shoulder, enjoying the warmth of his love.

He kissed the top of her head. "I was such a fool, Layla, forgive me. I was in such a dark place after that night. Physically and emotionally. I didn't think I deserved to be with you. I wasted so much time."

"You better believe you did, Mister." She smiled and laid her hand on his cheek. "When you're ready, you can tell me what you went through."

"Not tonight. Tonight, is only about you and me."

They watched in silence as the sun sank, painting the clouds in a rainbow of purple, pink, yellow, and reds. For a moment, she wondered if perhaps Alexander the Great hadn't stood and watched the sun set just like this amid a rainbow-colored sky in the old city of Jaffa. She felt certain he hadn't stood here with his heart bursting with love.

Candlelight and wine, moonlight, and the voice of a French chanteuse were the backdrop for their dinner of skewered lamb and couscous. They held hands and gazed into each other's eyes, not wanting to break the perfection of their magical evening.

Over desert and coffee, she remembered the letter that arrived that morning. "Cyrus, I've been offered an internship at the Tel Aviv Museum of Modern Art. It's an amazing opportunity, a step toward my dream of being an art curator. I'm so glad I decided to stay here and not return to America."

"Not half as glad as I am." He grinned.

"So, are you really happy at your new job? How is Superman handling being behind a desk instead of out there saving damsels in distress?"

He chuckled. "It looks like my spying days are over. All I have to worry about is getting lazy and out of shape as I push papers around my desk."

Her eyes gave him the once over appreciatively. "Oh, I doubt those muscles are going to atrophy anytime soon. You must have all the female sleuths at the office bending over backward and forward trying to get you to sample their wares."

"You know, nothing turns me on more than when your blue eyes glitter with jealousy. Except…" his lips pressed against her ear as he whispered, "when you're lying beneath me."

"Hmm…well I hope they know you're taken."

Cyrus's expression grew serious. "I think we should put an end to all questions about other women once and for all."

She laughed. "And how would we do that?"

He painted his hands across the sky as if he were a circus barker introducing an act. "The one and only, sexiest curator on Earth, Layla Wallace… Hassani."

"What did you say?"

"You heard me."

"Are you officially asking me to marry you on our first date?" She grinned.

Cyrus threw his head back and laughed. "We have done things a little out of order haven't we but that's going to change" He dropped to his knee and took her hand. "I don't want to live my life without you or Cerise. I can't live my life without you both. I want to wake every morning wrapped around you, your hair in my face, the scent and taste of your skin on my lips. There isn't anything I wouldn't do for you, *jāné del-am*. You are the fire in my heart."

He reached in his pocket, pulled out a velvet case, and handed it to her. "Open it, Layla. You're the only woman for me, the only woman I'll ever love."

Her hand trembled as she lifted the lid and looked inside. She gasped in surprise. "Oh, Cyrus, it's beautiful." Her eyes brimmed with tears.

His face lit with pleasure. "Here, try it on. It was my mother's. You'll have to get it resized or reset. Whatever you want, so long as you wear it forever."

"You're giving me your mother's ring?" she whispered.

"She wants you to have it."

"Oh, Cyrus I can't wait to meet her and your sister…But how could your mother part with the ring your father gave her?"

"Trust me, she feels as if her prayers have been answered." His lips twitched. "You gave her a granddaughter."

"I can't wait for them to meet Cerise. It's going to be wonderful."

He laughed. "I know it will baby, but you haven't answered my proposal, yet…Or are you having second thoughts?"

"Second thoughts? Let me tell you the truth, Superman." Her heart was so full of love for this man. She placed her hands on his face and gazed into his eyes. "I think I have loved you forever," she whispered. "My soul was only waiting to meet your soul. It was probably the worst day of my life and the best day when you rushed into that jail cell and saved me. You were never my captor Cyrus. Never. You have saved me more times than I can count. I don't know what forces brought us together, but I love you Cyrus Hassani. I will love you forever. Yes, I will marry you."

His eyes shimmered with tears as he bent his face close to hers and kissed her. "Now, let me tell you the truth, *azziz-am*…It was you who saved me. Thank you," he whispered.

"You're welcome," she whispered back.

brutal kidnapping, meant they had to be cautious. The very danger that had brought her and Cyrus together could tear into their lives once more and rip them apart.

Newsflash: Beware the jinx.

She considered spitting on her hands like her grandmother, Dina, often did. If the superstitious gesture would ensure her good fortune, then damn she was onboard.

But would it alleviate her secret fear?

How long before I spin out of control and end up in a ditch with an expired AAA card?

Her prayer?

You can have your cake and eat it too. A successful marriage and career are yours for the asking.

But no matter how many things went right, she still feared losing Cyrus and their daughter Cerise.

She was fortunate indeed, that the past four years had been full of love, laughter, and learning. That foundation of strength had enabled Layla to add another first to her list. Her first internationally curated art exhibition.

Layla turned in a slow circle, gazing around the sprawling gallery of the Museum of Modern Art in New York, bedecked with bold, brilliantly colored paintings on loan from the Tel Aviv Museum of Art.

She smiled at Zachary Biggs, the diminutive dynamo, otherwise known as MOMA's special exhibit's director. "I can't thank you enough for believing in me. You've given me a fabulous first…a 'pinch me' moment I'll never forget."

"You earned it Layla." Zachary's blue eyes twinkled from behind his red, round-framed glasses almost as big as his head. "You've shown what a pro you are. This is a creation you can be proud of."

"Thank you," she said as they began to walk through the exhibit. "Without you, I couldn't have done it."

"I doubt that." Zachary stopped to admire Picasso's *Torso of a Woman.* "I agree with the notion that the curator of an art exhibition is like a movie director and the installation process itself is akin to making a movie. If so, this show is your directorial debut. I knew the first time we met you were a talent."

Layla's cheeks flushed at the older man's praise. "I'm honored by your faith in me, Zachary."

"Mounting successful shows at MOMA is my job," Zachary said, waving his hands with a conductor's flourish. "Nurturing talent is my passion. So, what's next for the rising star curator of the Tel Aviv Museum?"

Layla studied the cubist-style painting with Zachary. "Do you recall that in 1953 a seventy-two-year-old Picasso painted this final portrait of Francoise Gilot, his lover of seven years? This was the last of eight paintings and marked the end of their tumultuous love affair. Gilot left Vallauris, their home, shortly thereafter with their two children and settled in Paris."

Zachary nodded. "Picasso was a genius but not exactly a model partner and father."

Layla's thoughts drifted to her own genius who was back home in Israel taking care of their work of art, Cerise. Her Superman could definitely be controlling, but it was only because he worried about their safety. "I do stress about the demands of career and the toll it takes on a family. I've loved being back in the States. Putting on this show is one of the best things I've ever done, but right now, all I can think about is returning home to Cyrus and Cerise. Three weeks away is a long time. I'm glad, I'm flying back tomorrow."

"It's a shame they couldn't join you in New York for the opening. It would have been a lovely interlude."

"Yes, but unfortunately, Cyrus wasn't able to take time away from work." *That's an understatement.* Her Superman husband was currently at the top of Iran's hit list. When he saved Layla and got her out of Iran, he also broke his deep cover—and as far as the IRI was concerned—committed treason. The once rising star of Iranian intelligence now had a target on his back— kill without question. Thank goodness when he first joined Mossad as a university student in Paris, he'd gotten his Jewish mother and sister out of the country. When the regime overthrew the Shah in 1979, Cyrus's parents had undergone terrible suffering. His mother had been arrested, raped, and tortured for civil activism. Pregnant with her rapist's child, she was finally released from prison and returned home to her husband Aram and her son Cyrus, who was only six years old.

Cyrus's father, who loved his wife deeply, helped her heal and showered love upon the baby girl who was born eight-months later. But the repressive regime continued to batter his parents. His father—a successful architect— lost his practice and the family's wealth. Suffering a heart attack, he retreated to their home, a changed man, and eventually committed suicide.

Cyrus discovered the body.

Heart-broken but determined, Cyrus went away to Paris to study nuclear physics at the University of Paris. When a Mossad agent approached him about joining the ranks, Cyrus readily accepted. The country of his father's childhood had changed, and so had Cyrus.

Tears sprang to Layla's eyes whenever she thought about what her husband and his family had endured.

It would be a long time before he would be able to travel outside of Israel.

Underneath the enormous red glasses, Zachary's face resembled a Sharpei dog. Folds, wrinkles, and jowls headed south. "I was worried the protestors on the streets were going to kill the show."

"I was concerned about that too," Layla agreed.

"Sometimes the first amendment is a pesky thing." Folds, jowls, and wrinkles rearranged themselves into a smile. "Fortunately, it doesn't take a genius to see those so-called BDS and anti-Israel protesters are anti-Semitic and racist."

Zac was right about the protestors. Their motives were questionable. Layla glanced at her watch. "Sorry Zac, I'm late for my dinner appointment. I'm afraid I have to run."

He held out his hand. "It's been a pleasure working with you Layla."

She hugged him. "Thank you, Zachary. Working with you has been a dream come true."

They walked to a bank of elevators. "Is your security detail waiting downstairs?" Zachary asked as he pushed the down button.

"No, I released them for the night." She shook her head. "Those poor guys did a double shift because the other team were called away on short notice for some VIP. I felt awful for them and told them the gallery would arrange my escort. But to be honest, the restaurant is only a few doors down, and the consul general will make sure I get safely back to my hotel."

"Are you sure? I'd be happy to have a guard walk you over."

"No, I'll be fine."

The elevator dinged. Layla got in. "Come see us in Israel."

"Will do. Safe journey, Layla."

The elevator arrived on the first floor, and she hurried through the nearly deserted lobby. Her heels clicked on the honed, green-slate floor, echoing in the large foyer. She appreciated Zachary's concern for her safety and thanked her lucky stars Cyrus didn't know she was walking the streets of Manhattan without security. The frenzied pace of the last few weeks had provided little opportunity for her to reclaim that free spirit she'd enjoyed before marrying a top spy.

She saw no reason why she couldn't walk the four minutes to the restaurant. Tomorrow her watchdogs would see her safely delivered, from the hotel door to the departure gate, for her flight back to Israel.

Fingers crossed—Cyrus will never find out about my little act of rebellion.

She bit back a giggle, feeling like a teenager skipping school, as the museum security guard stood ready to unlock the door for her. She smiled and waited as he did the honors. Nodding good evening, she stepped out onto West 53rd Street.

A warm September evening greeted her, and she was glad she'd decided on the cream linen pantsuit and left her trench coat back at the hotel. Having been closeted all day in the museum, she took a deep breath. She glanced up at the banners hanging from streetlights and read, "Masterpieces of Israel."

What a rush. It's like seeing your name in neon lights.

She headed southeast on West 53rd toward 5th Avenue, a confident bounce to her step.

Midtown, Sunday night traffic was light. Five minutes later she passed under the signature white awning and red lettered signage of the famed French restaurant, Ma Maison. Inside, the scent of flowers transported her to the French countryside. Beyond the reception area, she caught a glimpse of the floral arrangements in towering displays of color on rows of tables that cut through the dining room.

The maître-d' greeted her. "Good evening, Madame."

"Good evening. I'm meeting Avi Zaken for dinner."

"Of course, follow me, please. The consul general is waiting."

Layla followed the man as he deftly navigated the room. The soft, golden glow of chandelier light caressed the faces of the elegantly attired diners. Laughter and conversation blended with the dulcet voice of a French chanteuse singing "La Vie En Rose."

A white-haired gentleman wearing a pin-stripe Saville Row suit got up from the corner table with a warm smile on his face. "Layla, dear." He kissed both of her cheeks. "Congratulations on your triumph. Your father and Cyrus must be bursting with pride. I can tell you everyone back home is exceedingly proud of your accomplishment."

"Thank you, Avi," Layla said, beaming.

He waited while the maître d' seated her in the upholstered, curved, red banquette. Avi took his seat, tanned face, glowing with admiration.

"I'm delighted we could find the time for a meal together. My dinner dates are usually politicians or diplomats—this is a welcome change." He winked. "I much prefer sharing a meal with the most beautiful woman in New York."

"Avi, charming as ever, I see."

"No, my dear, just an honest, overworked government employee. Tell me, have you enjoyed being home in the US?"

"I have, but it's been such a whirlwind trip. I've hardly had a moment to myself. I've loved being back in the US, but the truth is I can't wait to get back to Cyrus and Cerise. Three weeks is too long to be separated from them."

"Ah, the love of a mother and a young marriage, just as it should be. What a beautiful couple you two make."

Their white-jacketed waiter interrupted, pouring Layla a flute of champagne.

Avi nodded his thanks to the server and raised his glass. "To you, my dear, and your family. *L'chaim.*"

"*L'chaim.*" Layla sipped, the bubbles tickling her nose. She took a moment and looked around the room.

"Avi, this restaurant is fantastic. What a treat to dine in such a beautiful place. Thank you for this invitation. It's the perfect end to a perfect trip."

"One of my favorites in New York, the last bastion of classic French cuisine and elegant dining. I don't get here often, but we're celebrating are we not? Wait until you taste the food. The Dover sole is unforgettable."

"Cyrus is going to freak when I tell him. My husband is a wonder in the kitchen. Cerise and I are lucky. I'm afraid my cooking talents are far from gourmet." She lifted her brows and smiled self-deprecatingly. "I wish Cyrus could be here with us tonight. The ambiance and cuisine would be his ticket to heaven."

"It's a shame he couldn't accompany you…" Avi's voice plummeted to a whisper. "I'm afraid, even after five years, it's too dangerous for him to leave Israel."

"Do you think the Iranians will ever forget about him? I want so much for us to travel throughout North America and Europe."

"My dear, be happy you were able to dissuade him, and he permitted you to come here at all. I heard from the prime minister he put up a big stink, demanding increased security for you. I'm afraid it's unlikely the Iranians have forgotten an operative who betrayed their secrets. He's an unsung hero in Israel, but those in the know are grateful for his service. I think it's best he remains just where he is. A rising star at Mossad, doing whatever it takes to neutralize Iran's nuclear threat."

"Speaking of my husband's need to neutralize threats, please don't tell him I blew off my security and walked to the restaurant without my watchdogs."

Avi's face was a study in control. "That security team is clearly not Mossad. I should be chastising you, my dear, but since you arrived in one piece and are as dazzling as a ten-carat diamond to these old eyes, I'll withhold my lecture and agree to keep your secret. However, I do intend to reprimand those lazy good-for-nothings for letting you out of their sight."

Layla burst into laughter. "Please, Avi, don't be too harsh on them. In all fairness, I insisted they take the evening off. As far as your ancient stature, we all know you're as spry and adept as ever. They don't call you the silver-tongued diplomat for nothing."

"That, my dear, is a media sobriquet, an exaggeration."

"I'd say it's more of a well-earned designation. One thing is for sure—when I tell Cyrus about tonight, he's going to be jealous not only of the Dover sole but also of the man who wined and dined me."

Avi raised his hands in mock fear. "Then we'd best not tell him. I've no intention or need to incur the wrath of such a skilled adversary. I may be single and divorced, but I'm harmless. Please tell him dinner with me excited you as much as dining with your father. Speaking of your father, how is Dr. Wallace?"

"Busy as ever between the laboratory and his doctoral candidates."

"Our country is grateful to have him on our side."

"It's hard to believe Israel is now our home. Dad's adjusted better than I thought he would. After my mother's death, I didn't think I'd ever see him happy again. Of course, Cerise has a lot to do with that. She keeps him laughing."

"Grandchildren are the greatest of blessings. And there's the added pleasure of being able to hand them back to their parents when you've had your fill."

Layla chuckled. "I'm lucky that Cerise has her Grandpa Aleck and her great-grandparents, Dina and Morris."

Avi raised his glass again. "To your continued good fortune, my dear."

Layla clinked her champagne flute to his. "You too, Avi, to your good health, and may you continue to represent Israel so ably."

"Thank you, my dear. But I must say, your husband is the lucky one. If he decides to seek another career, he'd have a bright future in politics with his admirable abilities *and* his secret weapon."

"Secret weapon?"

"*You*, my dear! With you by his side, Cyrus could go far."

She shook her head. "Politics? I've never given it a thought, and neither has Cyrus." It occurred to her Avi's suggestion might hold merit...especially if it meant her husband's welfare. If Cyrus were an elected official, he would become a public figure. That might deter the Iranians from acting on any death threat against Cyrus, since any attempts on his life would have major international implications. "Perhaps you've hit on something. I can't imagine anyone being able to resist my husband's charm." She sipped her champagne, hiding a smile as she pictured her blunt and forthright husband pandering to world leaders.

After dinner, while Avi settled the bill, Layla excused herself to go to the ladies' room. Washing her hands, she glanced in the mirror and noticed a young woman pushing a wheelchair into the elegant restroom. The large woman sitting in the wheelchair was bent forward, her face hidden in the folds of a scarf.

Layla smiled at the young woman who pushed the chair. "Don't worry, take your time."

In accented English, the woman thanked her as she tried to help the invalid rise. She struggled to lift the unsteady woman.

"Here, let me help you." Layla kneeled to help and gasped as she felt a sharp prick in her leg. "Ouch!" She looked down and saw the glint of a hypodermic needle. Before she could even open her mouth to scream, her entire body spasmed.

Oh, God. What's happening to me?

Her legs gave out beneath her. She sank to the floor, her ability to control her muscles was gone.

I'm paralyzed!

She tried with every ounce of strength in her being to wrap her lips around one word: *HELP!*

But all that came out of her mouth was a gurgling sound.

The two women worked as a team as they hauled Layla up and dumped her into the chair. The woman who'd pretended to be incapacitated crouched in front of her, unwound the scarf from her head and grinned. Layla's eyes bulged with terror as she desperately willed herself to scream...

Hit! Kick! Claw his eyes out!

The man smirked and reached underneath the wheelchair. When he rose, he held a briefcase. After entering a code, the briefcase snapped open.

Carefully he activated a switch, and the contents lit up and began to hum. He gave a satisfied nod to his accomplice and locked the case. Then he pulled a roll of duct tape from beneath the chair.

Rigid with terror, Layla watched him tape the briefcase behind a Demilune cabinet situated against the wall.

Layla's body may have been frozen, but her mind whirled into high gear as she realized they meant to blow up the restaurant and kill everyone there, including Avi.

I have to stop it!

In a frantic effort to resist she tried to move her fingers and hands, but no part of her body responded. She groaned in anger as they effortlessly wrapped her in the scarf and blanket.

How could she have been so stupid to blow off her security? To risk everything without a thought to the danger? Her husband was a target, which made her a target.

I'm going to die, and I brought it on myself.

All she could do was watch as the terrorist removed the long black cover he'd been wearing. Underneath, he wore slacks, a shirt, and a tie. He grabbed a sports jacket from beneath the wheelchair and slipped it on.

With the transformation complete he nodded to his accomplice. She peeked out the door and waved him out. A minute later, the woman wheeled Layla out.

Layla's bright hair was covered in the scarf and blanket. Anyone seeing her would believe she was an elderly invalid. She tried to scream a warning as they rolled past Avi, but her body was no longer hers. Avi was scrolling through his smart phone and didn't even look up. Every fiber of her being willed herself to scream but the only sounds that emanated from her throat were muted hisses. Between the buzz of the chatting patrons and the music humming around the restaurant, no one could hear her pathetic cries for help.

My God! I will never see Cyrus or Cerise again. I will never see my family again...

An elemental agony gripped her soul, but she was unable to shed tears because of the drug flowing through her veins.

At the entrance to the restaurant, the man with the shoulder-length dark hair waited, holding the door open. Her terror-filled cries echoed only in her mind. She managed a slight tremble and the wheelchair infinitesimally shook, which only registered in the maître d's eyes as pity. He quickly looked away and bid them a polite goodnight.

Outside, a black SUV idled at the curb. The doors swung open, and a man with curly dark hair jumped out. The two men lifted Layla out of the wheelchair, strapping her into the back seat of the vehicle. The woman who'd pushed the wheelchair slid in beside her. The driver hopped back into the front, while the long-haired man who'd pretended to be the invalid left the wheelchair on the sidewalk and took the front passenger seat. The driver zoomed off, much to Layla's despair.

Her heart pounded; fear strangled her. She struggled to regain control of her body—she needed to fight the drug that immobilized her. If she had any hope of being rescued, she needed to stay vigilant. Even the smallest detail might mean the difference between life and death. She did her best to keep as alert as possible, paying attention to every detail.

The vehicle raced away and left Ma Maison behind with a screech of rubber on pavement. The long-haired man in the front seat turned. He pulled a cell phone out of his pocket and punched the keypad. His finger hovered a moment and he glanced at his accomplices. They nodded their approval and he pressed one more number. A few seconds later, a series of deafening explosions reached Layla's ears, followed by the blare of fire alarms, police sirens, and screams of terror.

Through the dark tinted windows, Layla caught glimpses of the shocked faces of people on the street as they turned to watch the firestorm that had erupted. It was chaos—people running as fast as possible away from the blast.

Layla closed her eyes for a moment as the horror sank in.

Oh God! It's September 11th!

Her kidnappers had chosen the anniversary of the worst terrorist attack on US soil to execute their vile deed.

Inside the car, the kidnappers hooted in glee, their excited conversation sounded congratulatory. It was madness.

Hundreds of people are dead and dying, and they're doing a happy dance.

She recognized the language. *Farsi. They're Iranian.* A fear of a different kind crept up her spine.

Kidnapped, I'm kidnapped. These monsters just blew up the restaurant and murdered innocent people, and I'm the cause.

Guilt tore through her.

Oh, God! Avi and all those poor people.

Could she have done something to prevent this? If only she'd brought her guards. They would have accompanied her to the washroom. Could they have stopped the terrorists? But the terrorists had no doubt prepared for any eventuality, including her security detail. They probably would have efficiently subdued them with the same drug they'd injected into her. They would have been dragged into a bathroom stall and ended up as part of the body count. Ironically, her desire for some time to herself on that brief walk had saved two lives.

She swallowed the lump in her scratchy throat. It felt like someone had dragged rusty nails down her gullet. Even the debilitative drug couldn't prevent the tears now blurring her vision…

My sweet Cerise, Mama loves you. Forgive me, my angel. Forgive me.

She shook with the heartrending sobs that only a mother could feel knowing her daughter would grow up without her.

She'll have the same kind of childhood I did. Without the love and care of a mother to guide her.

At least Cerise would have Cyrus to protect her.

Cyrus!

Her very soul fractured in agony.

My darling Cyrus. My Superman. We had four beautiful years together. Please don't slip back into that darkness. For Cerise's sake and for mine.

I love you. I love you both until the end of time…

No!

A voice screamed inside her head.

For God sakes! Fight! Fight for Cerise and Cyrus. Fight for yourself.

You survived torture, near rape, and brutality before. You can survive this.

With every fiber of her being she fought to move. Shocked, she was able to lift her arm.

The drug must be wearing off.

Glancing at the door beside her she realized it was unlocked.

Could she do it? Could she fling open the door and roll out? She'd only ever seen it done in the movies.

The traffic was light now, she might just manage it without getting hit by an oncoming car.

Her arms and legs began to tingle as the feeling returned. Adrenaline pumped through her veins, giving her added momentum.

I'll only have one shot at this.

Her breath caught as the car slowed down and the right blinker flicked on.

Do it now!

Letting out a roar of rage, she elbowed the woman beside her, and reached for the door handle to fling herself out.

For a second she thought she would make it, but her movements were too jerky and awkward. In the next moment the locks immediately shot down and the car sped up. The driver flicked on the radio and blasted rock music.

Layla groaned in frustration. The woman spat out curse words at her in Farsi. The bitch pulled another hypodermic needle from her bag.

"No!!!"

Layla's screams were drowned out by the loud music as she fought off the woman with the needle.

The man in the front turned around and backhanded Layla in the face. Dazed, she fell back against the seat. She moaned as the familiar prick of the needle punctured her skin.

The effect was immediate.

Her body slumped over.

And a black curtain came down over her eyes.

Like what you've read so far? You can get *VENGEANCE*
(Tip of the Spears Series Book 2) on Amazon. Or
visit belleamiauthor.com to find out more.

ABOUT THE AUTHOR

Belle Ami writes breathtaking international thrillers and compelling romantic suspense with a touch of sensual heat. A self-confessed news junky, Belle loves to create cutting-edge stories weaving world issues, espionage, fast-paced action, and of course, redemptive love.

Belle is the author of the international thriller series TIP OF THE SPEAR which includes the highly acclaimed *Escape*, *Vengeance*, and *Ransom*. She is currently planning more books in this exciting and emotionally riveting series.

Belle is also the author of the bestselling OUT OF TIME thriller series which includes the #1 Amazon bestseller—The Girl Who Knew da Vinci and #1 Amazon bestseller—The Girl Who Loved Caravaggio and the upcoming The Girl Who Adored Rembrandt.

Belle is also the author of the romantic suspense series *THE ONLY ONE*, which includes, *The One*, *The One and More*, and *One More Time is Not Enough*.

Recently, she was honored to be included in the RWA-LARA Christmas Anthology *Holiday Ever After*, featuring her short story, *The Christmas Encounter*.

A former Kathryn McBride scholar of Bryn Mawr College in Pennsylvania, Belle is also thrilled to be a *recipient of the RONE, RAVEN, and Readers' Favorite Awards.*

Belle's passions include hiking, boxing, skiing, cooking, travel, and of course, writing. She lives in Southern California with her husband, two children, a horse named Cindy Crawford, and her brilliant Chihuahua, Giorgio Armani.

Belle loves to hear from readers—you can contact her at: belle@belleamiauthor.com

Connect with Belle Ami online:
belleamiauthor.com
BookBub
Amazon
Twitter: @BelleAmi5
Facebook
Instagram
Newsletter Signup (belleamiauthor.com)

www.ingramcontent.com/pod-product-compliance
Lightning Source LLC
Chambersburg PA
CBHW020053180626
46812CB00006B/2312